MATTHEW G. REES grew up in a Welsh family in the border country between England and Wales known as the Marches. His early career was in journalism. Later he entered teaching, working for a period in Moscow. Diverse other employment has included time as a night-shift cab driver. His fiction has been published by *The Short Story*, *Belle Ombre*, *The Lonely Crowd*, *Three Impostors*, *Oddville Press* and elsewhere. A fantasy comedy play, *Dragonfly*, has been performed professionally. He has a PhD in Creative Writing from the University of Swansea.

Keyhole

Stories
by
Matthew G. Rees

A Work of Fiction

Three Impostors
3 Woodville Road,
Newport,
South Wales,
NP20 4JB

www.threeimpostors.co.uk

First published in 2019

Text and photographs © Matthew G. Rees
Cover design by Andy Dark
Layout by Tomos Osmond

Printed and bound by Y Lolfa,
Talybont, Ceredigion, SY24 5HE

ISBN 978-1-78461-704-2

Stories

... the unknown world is, in truth, about us everywhere, everywhere near to our feet; the thinnest veil separates us from it, the door in the wall of the next street communicates with it.

'The London Adventure', Arthur Machen

... I saw a star shining over our valley, a keyholeful of light, telling me I was home.

'The Water Music and Other Stories', Glyn Jones

Keyhole

Brontë Vaughan had a condition that meant she had to be kept from the light. In order that her shuttered world was not entirely without illumination her mother presented her with a kingfisher which a retainer had found ailing in its nest. Its health restored in Brontë's care, the small and brilliant bird darted magically in those catacomb-like rooms of The Fosse to which Brontë was confined.

In time her mother, a woman of great beauty grieved by her conviction that in the act of bringing her into this world she had cursed her child, gave Brontë another and another of the birds. These mated and reproduced so that their number, swarming through the dark chambers of the old house, came to defy calculation. The birds swirled in shoals around young Brontë's white hair and head. They clustered on mantels, perched on clock cases, their droppings striating curtains that were seldom if ever opened and flecking large, hanging tapestries that showed harts running in deep forests behind whose thick and faded fabric the walls of The Fosse stood powdery and damp.

Unlike Brontë, the kingfishers were not locked away entirely, for her mother pursued a procedure whereby at least every other day they were released to the light. Opening the doors of adjoining rooms and then closing them behind her in a sequence that kept Brontë from the sun, her mother would usher the kingfishers, carouselling around her in a sapphire-and-amber whirl, from one room to the

3

next until she and they reached the conservatory of citrus trees that ran along the manor's southerly side. There she would throw open its French windows enabling the birds to issue forth in a wondrous fusillade over the reeded moat that teemed with small fish and was populated with water beetles, springtails and other bugs, and danced over by the most lovely and delicate damsel flies in bright bodices of blues and yellows and reds.

In her dim bower Brontë followed this, or thought that she did, by means of a brass telescope. At first standing, and later, when older, kneeling, this she held to the keyhole of the door of the drawing-room where she was principally sequestered: the door's lock being in alignment, so it seemed, with the keyholes of all of the other doors that led to an apparent aperture of light that was the distant conservatory; the rim of the instrument's eyepiece and its cool lens all the while tight to the intense pink pupil of Brontë's right eye.

Come evening Mrs Vaughan would summon the kingfishers to her from the lily-padded moat by means of gently piping on a whistle: the birds returning, every one, via the open French windows, accompanying her through the doors and rooms of The Fosse to Brontë – this inward flight being conducted in precise reversal of their earlier liberation and to a gradual, but definite, extinguishing of the light.

The Fosse was the first place Theaxton made for after stepping from the train. Even after all these years it would still be there, he told himself; Brontë, too, though she would be older now, of course. He cut over the fields, beards of wheat sticking to his trousers, dust powdering the laced, black-leather uppers of his shoes. In a copse he scattered rooks from the fly-blown corpse of a rabbit. Emerging from its trees he looked for The Fosse. But it wasn't there. Not the house. Not the moat. None of it.

He stopped on the edge of a pasture that was corralled with barbed wire. The land seemed familiar, and yet... He went over his route in his head: the station (no one had taken his ticket and there

4

was no tea-room, no kiosk selling newspapers, but the buildings were otherwise the same), the main road (busier than was once the case – a woman in a red car had hooted at him – but running, so it seemed, where it always had), from the road to the lane that used to flood (it still had its dip), and then, where he stood now, the fields (whose quiet emptiness, apart from the wheat, had surprised him).

Yes, it all *seemed* right. And yet... no Fosse, no Brontë. He looked behind him, saw the distant pitched roof of the station, blurred in his eyes, but there, on the edge of the town, as it always had been; west of it, the rest of the place, bigger than he remembered, but the tower of the old abbey quite visible.

He told himself he'd made a mistake, that he'd crossed the road too soon... or too late. He began to walk back the way he had come. Amid the wheat he saw a scarecrow. It slumped forward on its cross, like a reprobate in stocks.

What he needed now, Theaxton told himself, was a room; everything would become clear in the morning. The Goat: they would know him there. There would be a fire, men playing darts. He pictured it: the panelled interior, the frosted windows, the horned head with its superior stare that had so intrigued him in his boyhood, etched in the glazing.

Besides, it was turning cool. The sunset had the heavy, mauve look that he knew spelled a storm in that part of the country. It would be good to get in.

He passed through an estate of houses that was new. A man in a garage with its door up eyed him. Theaxton nodded. The man wiped his hands in a rag.

A mews of cottages in a cobbled lane seemed more familiar.

Soon he was in the old square. He had his bearings now, or so he thought. The Goat, in the same way as The Fosse, wasn't there. A shop selling phones stood in its place. Next to it was a bookmaker's. In the window a cardboard greyhound lunged at a life-size cut-out of a footballer who was holding a ball, grinning. A woman who looked to be an employee emerged, lit a cigarette. She stared at Theaxton as she drew on it by a drainpipe. He forgot about The Goat, and moved on. Businesses were closing for the day. Shutters came down behind him, voices bade goodnight. He crossed a small park where some youths who were too old for them were sitting on the swings. They stared as he passed.

It was only when he found himself on the hill, having left the park through some gates on its far side, that he realised where he was and remembered what he was doing, what this day – the train, the journey – had been about: the fact that he was going home, at last.

The house was still there, halfway up the hill, not quite as large as he remembered it, but, in its way, imposing: detached, steps to the porch, the architectural flourish at one end of a red-tiled witch-hat. *Halfway*. Not right at the top of the hill where the more moneyed solicitors and doctors had, in his parents' day, resided, but distinctly above the tradesmen: a goodly climb. His father, the headmaster of the junior school, had been happy with that.

Theaxton stood in the entrance to the drive. He looked at the house, the garden. Tamarind. The plate on the wall was different, but the name remained. He remembered his father – sleeves rolled-up, pipe in his teeth – mowing the lawn with an old push-and-puller. It sounded like the propeller of a plane: starting up, giving out.

A woman came to the sitting-room window. For a moment he thought it was his mother. He raised his hand, waved. Then he saw it wasn't her at all, felt foolish, put his hand in his coat, stepped back.

A boy sped past him on a skateboard. The grind of its wheels on the pavement brought Theaxton to his senses. He took a last look at the house and began to walk back down the hill. It was turning dark now. He knew he had to find somewhere to spend the night.

Between the hill and the square Theaxton found himself in the small quarter of lanes that in his day had been called The Streets. Cobblers, tailors, barbers, printers and similar artisans had had their shops there (and homes above). Like the square, the area had changed, but in a different sense. Now the frontages were those of antique dealers, galleries, coffee shops, boutiques. Outside a delicatessen were trays of plants, a faux milk churn and a blackboard chalked with things he'd never heard of. A young man emerged from the shop and began to gather the items up. At the entry to a passage at the side of the premises the man looked at Theaxton, who turned away. In doing so Theaxton saw it: the horse.

When he first caught sight of it, in the corner of his eye, he felt sure its presence must have been another of the day's deceits (along with the absent Fosse, the disappeared Goat). Yet its small figure persisted.

Theaxton stepped away from the delicatessen, whose lights were now going out. He walked further down the footway overhung by the upper storeys of the old buildings either side of it. There, in the window of what called itself an antiques shop (whose contents appeared mainly to be junk), was his horse: the wooden equine on wheels he'd ridden throughout his infancy wherever he'd been able to roam. Its shape was lit by a street lamp. Theaxton's image fell over it on its low ledge on the other side of the glass. He was amazed. He remembered it... all of it: the hooped bar at the back that his mother (and sometimes his father) would push, the odd barrel-shaped body, painted black-and-white, on which his legs would swing, the handles he had gripped at its ears, the mane of carpet-brush bristles best avoided with bare arms and legs... the black button eye. Looking rather worn now, yes, but unmistakably... *his*. It stood there as if waiting to be reclaimed.

It started to rain. Theaxton felt the drops on his head. He turned from the window, wavered, began to walk back the way he had come. After a few steps he stopped, looked again for the horse. It was still there... in the lamplight.

He spent the night in the porch of the abbey on the rough bench under the parish notices, coat buttoned to the collar. He tried to remember when he had last ridden the horse, why he had stopped riding it. An ancient yew swayed in the wind, its squat shape darker than the sky.

In the morning Theaxton went back to the shop. He had no idea of the time. On the train the previous day he'd felt for his watch and had found his wrist empty... leathery... as if it belonged to someone else: a passenger seated next to him.

It was light now albeit that the sky sagged with clouds. Theaxton hung by the drizzled window, looking at the horse.

A woman hurried to the step, bringing down an umbrella as she did so. She thrust a key in the lock. The door of the shop shuddered open as she pushed. Theaxton was behind her, inside before she knew it.

'The horse,' he began quickly. 'How much is it?'

His intrusion startled her. 'I'm sorry?' she said. She was fair-haired: in her forties, Theaxton judged.

'The toy horse,' he began again, 'in the window.'

'Yes?'

'How much is it?'

The woman took off her raincoat, hung it on a stand. She wore a pale-blue sweater, check skirt, pearls. She lifted her fingers to the collar of the blouse beneath her sweater, flicked out her hair.

'Oh that,' she said. 'That's sold. Lovely little piece. Edwardiana. Great market for that sort of thing these days. Hand-made.'

'But it's in the window,' said Theaxton.

'I think you'll find there's a "Sold" tag on it.'

'I haven't seen one.'

'On this side... maybe you couldn't see from the window. I think you'll find there is.'

'It's my horse,' said Theaxton.

'I'm sorry?' said the woman.

'How did you get it?'

'What?'

'The horse! How did you get my horse?'

'By wholly legitimate means, I can assure you. Now if—'

'How much?' he said.

'What?'

'For the horse. Name your price.'

For a moment she hesitated, glanced at the window. Rain squalled at the pane. Amid the lumpen furniture, chipped crockery and shabby canvases Theaxton was suddenly aware of the reek of decay: a dirty, sickly odour that he remembered from those places where he had hidden while playing at The Fosse with Brontë: the wall hangings he had gone behind while she looked for him in the weak light of oil lamps lit by her mother and, later, low-wattage bulbs that glowed feebly in her rooms.

'A lady's coming to collect it,' said the woman.

'I'll be back...' said Theaxton, '... with cash.'

In the bank a girl stared at her computer. 'Nothing's coming up on the screen,' she said.

'Theaxton... Tamarind,' he said. 'My family's banked here for years.'

A young man not much older than the girl introduced himself as the deputy manager. He led Theaxton to a side room, tapped at a keyboard

'Uh-hum...okay,' said the young man. 'We have *some* records and, by the look of it, a debt.'

'Debt?' said Theaxton. 'What do you mean *debt*? I've never had debts. My family has never had debts.'

'Pounds, shillings and pence,' said the youth. 'Been there a time, obviously.'

'*Time*?' said Theaxton.

'Still...' the young man continued. 'You've no cards with you, but you have a cheque book and a driver's licence. Is that right?'

Theaxton gave him his cheque book and the licence, a paper one of the kind the authorities no longer issued.

The young man tapped again at the keyboard. 'I think we can help. How much would you like?'

'£100,' said Theaxton.

The young man came back with the money in tens.

'Anything else today, Mr Theaxton?'

'Yes,' said Theaxton. 'You're playing music in here – of a kind. What sort of place is this? A dance hall?' He took the cash, and left.

It was raining harder now. After the stuffiness of the bank Theaxton shivered in the wet square. He hurried down the narrow lanes of The Streets to the junk shop. The horse was still there, in the window.

Droplets showered from the lintel as Theaxton pushed the door. Behind him clouds closed-in on the town. A cumulonimbus with the purple and blue-black of a bruise on an old woman's knee welled over Tamarind and the other houses on the hill. A growl of thunder followed him in.

The woman was fiddling with the hands of a longcase clock whose glass was ajar. Little slicks of sweat and rain pooled behind Theaxton's ears. He felt them run down his neck inside his shirt. She turned to him.

'How much do you want?' Theaxton asked her.

'A hundred,' she said.

'Don't be silly,' he said.

'Ninety, then. It's an antique.'

'It's not an antique,' he told her. 'Not yet anyway.'

'You know,' she began, 'for an *older* man, you're very—'

'Never mind that,' he interrupted. 'I'll give you forty.'

'Sixty.'

'Fifty.'

'Done.'

He took the horse from the window, put the notes on the woman's desk. Without looking up she drew a line through an entry in a ledger.

'You know,' he said, 'this was such a *nice* town – once.'

He walked out into the rain, the horse under his arm.

In the porch at the abbey he lay back on the wooden bench. His throat was dry and it occurred to him that he had neither eaten nor drunk since before the train. He glanced at the horse which he had placed on the seat on the opposite side of the porch. He thought of the tombs of the Vaughans that were in the nave. One of their clan had been with Richard at Bosworth Field. He remembered touching the tomb as a boy: the sepulchre had been colder than a night filled with snow.

In the dull light Theaxton looked again at the horse. It was *his*, of that he was convinced. And yet it was different, but in a way that he couldn't pin down.

No one came to the abbey or left it. Rain curtained the entrance to the porch. Theaxton slept, as if under a waterfall.

It was dark when he came to, and still raining (he could not see it but he could hear it). Thunder kettledrummed in the distance. He swung his legs from the bench, groped for the horse. His fingers fell on its mane. He picked it up, walked the puddled path through the abbey's yard.

Soon he was on the hill: his arm between the horse's belly and the board at its black hoofs. The rain was heavier now. It drove at him as he climbed. The thunder was no longer distant. It erupted over his head.

At the driveway to Tamarind, where the boy on the skateboard had sped past, he stopped, drew breath. Oily pools collected on the pavement. The gutter streamed with brown water, leaves and twigs.

In the orange haze of a streetlight Theaxton set down the horse. He looked at it for a moment, then got on its back.

At first they moved slowly: bumping over the raised edges of paving stones, dragging through puddles. Theaxton pushed at the pavement with his half-brogues, and pushed again. Soon they were flying: down the hill, passing the streetlamps as if these were posts marking-out furlongs. He gripped the handles at the horse's ears, his eyes gleaming.

Next they were in the park, passing the empty swings where

the sullen teens had been. The wind blew a tunnel of leaves around them. Man and toy raced onwards as the chains and seats of the swings rattled and jounced.

Soon they were charging into The Streets, splashing their way through the narrow lanes which, but for them, were empty. Theaxton was startled by their reflection as he and the horse flew past the junkshop and its window. From the shop he looped to the square, where the rain was now pouring in torrents. A sheet of lightning filled the flooded precinct with a glare. The little horse parted the rainwater, waves sickling from the sides of its board as rider and steed pressed on.

It was when they entered the byways of The Streets for the second time that Theaxton noticed the strangest thing.

Rain had washed away the frontages of the buildings as if their facades had been mere painterly brushstrokes. Those homes and businesses that had preceded the boutiques, the galleries and the coffee shops stood unmasked, like bones unpeeled beneath rouged and powdered skin.

Heffer's, the paper shop from which he'd had comics and colouring books as a boy, Theaxton recognised immediately. And, next to it, *Coronation Confectionery*, which had been the pride of two spinster sisters, the Misses Pearce. As he passed, Theaxton thought he saw one of them... drawing down a blind.

A flash from a dark doorway drew his attention to the opposite side of the lane. Arthur Beard was standing on the step of his barbershop, opening and closing a pair of scissors.

Theaxton kicked at the lane with his heels. But, rather than quickening, the horse lost pace. It was barely crawling now, the back of the board snagging and scraping, as if a wheel had flown off or become caught in the grille of a drain. Theaxton turned away from Beard's glinting blades.

The last of the delicatessen, with its white-framed window of meats, cheeses and pickled delicacies in jars, was slithering into a sewer. In its place the frontage of its former occupant *Harold Hook, Cobbler* showed its drab face. Hook's leather-aproned figure loomed over Theaxton in the lane, the jaws and claws of his tools protruding in a line from his apron's front pockets. A sheet of lightning illuminated their tips.

Hook raised a hammer in one grimed hand, a fist of nails in the other.

'It's no good looking at me like that,' he snapped. 'I want paying – and I'm not the only one. You can tell your father. If he can afford to live on the hill, he can afford to pay his bills. I'll have the bailiffs on him, so help me. Now go on! Get!'

Theaxton wasn't so much riding the horse now as forcing it, beseeching it. He felt the rain in a way that till then he had not: his soaked clothes clinging like the leaves of a sodden book; such hair as he had stuck to his skull as if it were weed that had been slung on a dump. As he strained onward he heard a voice ahead of him: the sharp tongue whiplashing its way through the falling rain. Theaxton knew its scold instantly.

'I'm not one to gripe,' Mrs Cockitt, the washerwoman, complained to the audience at her step. 'But they owe money all over town. Shillings and pennies it may be. But it mounts up. A headmaster should know better. That's what happens when people go taking themselves up the hill. "Kippers 'n curtains" my ma used to call it. And him in his soldier's uniform... bossing the cadets. I'd like to give him a bullet, I can tell you. Two years my Joe's been serving. Wounded 'n all. What thanks will *he* get?'

Theaxton threaded through the crowd's outer ranks, praying none of the dark figures would recognise him.

Finally, he reached the junkshop.

In its doorway, standing out of the rain, chestnut hair at her shoulders, still young, still beautiful, was Brontë's mother.

'Clive!' Mrs Vaughan called.

He pushed his horse towards her eagerly over the wet stones, looked up to her on the step.

'What have you got in your pocket? I want to see what's in your pocket.'

Theaxton looked away.

She began again. 'Look at me, Clive! I'm not standing here for the good of my health. Show me what's in your pocket! Empty it, Clive Theaxton! Empty it!'

Beneath the damp flap Theaxton again felt... the feathers... the fine bill (which had so intrigued him) almost equal in length to the rest of the bird... the tiny, orange legs (too insubstantial to even be called twigs). And he remembered, he remembered... Brontë hiding behind a tapestry: her white pumps poking from beneath it (even in the dimness of The Fosse they had been in plain sight)... the kingfisher, its claws wrapped around the edge of a desk, its eyes watching him... the scene in the conservatory as he left... Mrs Vaughan stopping him in the long room's harsh light... slapping his hand... his weeping escape from her across the wheat field... her cry coming after him through the waving stems... that he was 'Forbidden! Forbidden! Forbidden!'... to ever go back.

Theaxton knew now that *that* had been the word that (before the bus, before the train) he had heard in his flat. Not the *forgiven* that – above the quarrelling couple and screaming child next door, the barking dog in the yard, the traffic in the street, the jackhammers, the sirens – he had thought or even wished the word to be.

Suddenly he remembered his image and that of the horse – its tail flying – as they had ridden past the window.

'Its tail,' he whispered.

His horse had never had one.

He remembered holding his mother's hand, his father wheeling it from the shed: the horse that Jack had built from odds and ends, shavings and scraps.

'But where's its tail, Jack?' his mother had asked. 'It hasn't got a tail!'

'It's not my horse! It's not my horse!' Theaxton shouted now.

Even as his cries rang out, the old town melted in the rain.

Its rotten world dripped to nothing, and the little horse pulled him deeper and deeper, as if he were bound to its saddle, like some prisoner, into a blackness which was only broken by the unrelenting stare of a single, pink eye.

The Service at Plas Trewe

Almost like a lover I know when he is near.

The aroma of cigar on the empty terrace in the evening that I alone seem to scent. That normally comes first. Then the change in the character of our clocks: their strikes and chimes so vigorous and urgent, a chorus of quickening hearts, all through the house. That, usually, is next. After it, the sudden draw that re-lights the library's dying fire with a roar, signalling him there: warming himself, grinning, holding court. Finally, at breakfast, the clatter of cutlery on a plate pushed aside when everyone else is still eating, reading, or contemplating their day. Proof, as if by then it were needed, that yes, oh yes, our wanderer is with us, our rotten apple has rolled back.

Of course, there are his other, theatrical tricks: creaks of floorboards, turns of doorknobs, clicks of billiard balls on tables in the dark. Not to mention groans from our weather vane on frosted nights when I know full well that the air hangs still. Frightening at first, I concede. But I've grown wise to these taunts of his. I know him intimately, as I have said. Yet, let me make this clear, he is definitely foe *not* friend. So if I do hold him close, as I suppose that I must, it is as enemies and *not* lovers that we embrace. And now I'm getting carried away. Emotions, you should be aware, are not my thing. Particulars, details... it is in these that I both find and lose myself: cushions for the terrace, flowers for the halls, adequate mallets for the croquet lawn, lemonade – fresh-made – for the tennis courts.

The one thing that I don't do is bother Mr Penry Davies. As our manager, Mr Penry Davies has enough to do without being bothered by me. That is not to say that he would be unreceptive to enquiries from me on a great many matters. It is simply to make the point that, on a matter such as this, the return of our... *guest*... Well, he – Mr Penry Davies – would expect me to use judgment, to take responsibility. Anyone with half an eye on one day succeeding him would see the sense in that: the need to show their mettle, to prove their worth, to demonstrate their ability to... *manage*.

Mr Penry Davies and I go back a long way. But my relationship with our guest goes back further, much further, than that. I shall explain. But before I tell you *his* story you ought, perhaps, to know a little more about mine: how I came to be here, in Wales, in this gracious, old house called Plas Trewe.

I wasn't born to this life. I was a city boy: a Liverpool lad, in fact. Left school at sixteen, signed for an apprenticeship with *Kings Crown Inns*, mostly served in a motel on Merseyside, the haunt of young men and women not much older than me who fell in from taxis when the clubs closed. All of them off their heads. Hell would be too kind a word. I gained one star for the lapel badge on my waistcoat, and left.

It was in 'guesthouse land' on the north Wales coast that I found my feet. One small hotel, in particular, that boasted sliver-like glimpses of the Great Orme: the *Headland View Gardens* was its name.

The frontage of *The Gardens*, as we called it, consisted of dwarf conifers, concrete terraces and gnomes. These latter were splattered with gull shit, their suits and beards in sore need of new paint. But, for three years, its pebbledashed facade was a happy hunting ground for me.

The *chatelaine* – as she styled herself – was Vera, a dried walnut of a widow, already well past seventy, who took a shine to me at the tea rooms where I worked. I was not quite eighteen when she placed her thin, spray-tanned hand on mine and told me she had a position that she was keen to fill.

It's on your mind, I know, so I'll admit it: yes, we had sex. Not often, but it occurred. My desires have never really been carnal, but with Vera I found that it paid to perform. After our encounters she'd float through *The Gardens* high as a kite. In return, my fees were met for a course in silver service at the local technical school.

Her stroke came suddenly. I'm still less than sure of the cause: the high heels she tottered on, the corset she wore even though stick-thin, or maybe some confusion with all of those medications that littered her dressing table in their bottles and strips. I found her on the carpet in the lobby: glassy-eyed and gaga, scarlet lips lopsided, skeletal right leg oddly twisted at the hip.

She stared up at me: her claw-like right hand clenched into a purple fist. Her familiar bracelet of gold-plated charms had come apart in her fall. Its trinkets – a miner's lamp, gipsy wagon, Scottie dog and the rest – lay strewn on her scrawny chest.

For a moment I wondered about what might be done: in terms of finishing her, I mean. I pictured my hands – tight – on her twig neck. But there was no need. One good look at her told me all that I needed. *The Gardens* was under new management now. Mine.

I never had to tie her down or lock her up. Vera had nothing left in her to warrant anything like that. I just stuck her on a chair in the kitchen, or, if she misbehaved, I left her inside our private loo: light off if she'd been naughty. Not that she knew.

There were big changes at *The Gardens*, of course. I ran the place alone: seven rooms, a handy size. My alterations paid off. Higher ratings in the guides, warm endorsements on the internet. No more of Vera's beery, black-nailed navvies making themselves at home 'on contract'. *The Gardens* was on a better class of map. I upped the tariffs, too.

And then... pear purée... as quickly as it began. Wet October evening, blowsy female in the hall: smudged mascara, big ear-rings, fake furs, rain – or was it sweat? – trickling her thick, orange neck. I knew the look: Lady of The Night. And one who, I was about to inform, was very much in the wrong hotel. But *I* was wrong. A niece of Vera's – or so she claimed – fresh back from Dubai, and wanting to see her Auntie V. Brushed past me into the kitchen as if she owned the place... saw Vera in her chair. I followed, took a cloth, wiped dribble from the old girl's chin.

Why was she like... *that*? stammered this niece with no name.

A stroke, I said.

What was the doctor doing?

Doctor? What good would that be? 'Look at her!' I said.

'Who *are* you?' she demanded, turning on me.

And that's when I snapped.

Beyond her shoulders I saw the knives, on their hooks, by the sink: all lined up, either side of her head. Exactly what I needed, to gut and fillet. Cellulite thighs, rubber nose, polyfiller breasts: oh the dainty dish that beckoned, the exquisite carvery that called.

I felt like screaming. About all that I had done at *The Gardens*: the wallpaper, the menus, the Egyptian cotton sheets.

'Look around you, bitch!' That's what I wanted to yell. But I said... nothing. I just looked at her, and I knew... I knew that in the morning I'd be fired. And if I couldn't find it within myself to wring the neck of an old boiler like Vera what on earth was the point in pretending I'd slice a strapper like this poisonous piece of a... *niece*? So I left her there, with Vera, and I went and packed my things.

At the bus station I caught the first one that came in.

'As far as you can take me,' I told the driver.

I flung myself down in the back and sobbed.

It must have been three hours later when he pushed me awake. I stepped off with my bag into the dark. The bus turned back the way we seemed to have come, the driver glancing as it lumbered off.

And then... silence. Or so it seemed to my city boy ears.

The blue-black sky was full of stars. Near me, I made out the shape of a shelter. I curled myself up on the bench inside.

As I lay there I heard the sound of a river, not rushing but moving in a calm and purposeful way... a whisper of water... into the night. I found myself imagining its reaches and pools, and, in doing so, drifted to sleep.

It wasn't the cold or discomfort that caused me to wake or even the day's early light. It was the bewildering, almost deafening, sound of the birds. Never before had I heard anything like their song. It seemed to me an anthem. I wondered if it was real.

I picked up my bag and followed a lane that took me to an ancient bridge. Below its tall arches a misted river flowed. A squirrel scurried along the parapet. A violet light rose around me, illuminating the dewed pastures that tumbled to the water. I crossed the bridge and, as I did so, I sensed something different inside me: the feeling that, in the same way that the river, even in darkness, knew its course, I also now had a path and a purpose.

When I first saw Plas Trewe its beauty moved me. The mansion stands in its own wooded valley, and autumn had turned the trees to the colours of flames. It was as if the house were surrounded by fire. Immediately I felt the urge to protect it, a feeling that I have had from that day to this.

The cries of peacocks lured me. I reached a lodge beside a pair of iron gates between pillars that bore the sculpted forms of leaping fish. Through their ironwork I saw the wonderful form of The Plas. I opened them and began to walk towards the house.

The peacocks eyed me from a lawn where brightly-coloured dragonflies hovered over the lily pads of a circular pond edged with mossed stones. A weather vane in the arched shape of a golden salmon glinted in the rising sun at the top of a conical tower. Smoke curled from a chimney as I approached.

A smiling figure – Mr Penry Davies – drew open the front door. He told me to put down my bag. 'You've found us,' he said. Later that same day I began work as a porter. I didn't ask if it was all a mistake.

And that, more or less, is how I came to be here. Ten years have passed. In March I was made under-manager. This technically ranks me as Mr Penry Davies's deputy. In the fullness of time I'd like to succeed him. But I fancy we need his experience, at least for a while. I've gone *some* way towards it, but I feel I've yet to fully earn my spurs in a house as historic as this. For centuries it was the seat of the Trewe family, one of the most quietly ancient in Wales. When the last of their line perished in a shipping tragedy the house and its estate passed to a trust (on whose board, I believe, Mr Penry Davies sits).

It's a hotel now, of course. Not that we use the term. We leave that sort of thing to *Kings Crown Inns*. The Plas, as we call it, is a house, and, as well as being its servants, we are its defenders, its keepers. Guests come and go. But *we* are loyal. This is our home. As much as its slates and stones, *we* are The Plas.

All of which brings me to our guest, the one I spoke of at the start. I first encountered him here, in our library, among our volumes, in 1913. Not man-to-man, of course – I'm not *that* old. No, I discovered him in our Domesdays, as I call them, those volumes that are generally considered our most noteworthy books. Not many people seem to bother with them these days. Perhaps their significance is on the wane. Still, they fill three glass-fronted cases that occupy most of the library's west wall. I opened one out of curiosity about a month after settling in. As I turned its handwritten pages I was less than sure as to the meaning of certain of their particulars.

... six salmon & eight trout before luncheon to Mrs Winston-Whillians. From a boat with gillie Pryce at Black Reach. 'Never fished before,' Mrs W-W avows. 'Beginner's luck.'

... Major Hughes lands lively pike* in colourful episode at Pwll Gwyrdd (courtesy of a tumbler tied only that morning by his man, Evans, using feathers from the peacocks at Plas).

Pike nearly has one of the major's fingers. Dr Pritchard summoned. Three stitches in wound before dinner. M. Hughes regales table – 'All in a day's work' – and displays his bandaged digit to general applause. *19lbs.

Those were among the first entries that I read in our 'Books of Catches', our journals of life and death on the river that winds here in (mostly gentle) *esses* beneath Plas T. The books span two centuries: one for each year. Yet those stories were – how shall I put it? – small fry compared with what occurred in 1913.

That year occupies not one but two volumes in the records of The Plas. And they are bigger, *much* bigger, than all of the rest: the sturgeon – yes, I have come to know my fish – of our shelves, the real monsters of our deeps. Rather than having their binds in dark green leather like the rest, they should perhaps have an alternative colour: oxblood, I suggest. For this was the year in which Henry P— turned our river (and maybe even Wales) red. Certain legal formalities prevent me from spelling out his surname. His descendants are not without influence. But I know who he is and, more importantly, *what* he is... as do they and he. His record catch of that season will never be beaten. And who would want to take his place? Our Marquis de Sade, our Mr Hyde, our Jack the Ripper of the river.

I can only think that he must have been mad. Why else would anyone have done it? Five thousand fish – an appropriately Biblical sum... most of them salmon – in a season of slaughter that now not only seems repulsive but which somehow speaks of the war in Europe that was to come.

I've wondered how he managed it: physically, I mean. He was an ironmaster, a coal baron, the owner of half-a-dozen pits. I suppose few would have dared stop a man such as that.

It's pure fantasy on my part, but I've pictured him: devouring the river, killing it, his rod a flame-thrower, torching the banks: the burning trees falling upon the water in their oranges and yellows as if trying to save themselves, yet, at the same time, fuelling with their collapsing limbs some kind of molten channel into Hell.

At other times I've seen him holding not so much a fishing rod but a kind of conductor, catching forks and flashes of lightning from the sky, directing murderous current into the river's dark depths, the water convulsing under a light that switches between phosphorescent white and electric blue... the shape of P— standing there, alone on the bank, furiously casting and casting, under thunderous heavens, whilst all of the creatures in the woods – the rabbits, the foxes, the badgers, the owls, even the smallest voles flushed from their leaf-lidded holes – come to the water's edge to watch, wide-eyed, his carnage and to *wonder* at the animal that stands before them, killing and killing, as the light from the leaping flames of the flaring trees and the firework sparks of those white and blue shocks dances upon his grey, pitiless, tombstone face.

I've seen – in these *visions* – the salmon, the pike, the trout, the eels... all manner of fish... hurling themselves to the shore, and in such numbers that they have seemed not fish at all but great flocks of birds in some strange reversal of Nature that is an omen of apocalypse: thick, dark, arching canopies of scales, these flying then falling shoals sandbagging the bank with horrible, ugly slaps, piling in pyres at his sides and back, as if he is not merely a conductor of electricity but an orchestrator or wizard who has the whole of the valley – every stream, every glade, every dingle – right there, in his dripping, throttling fists.

And then in those moments, those rare moments, when his onslaught eases the fish have seemed to me in their temporarily thinned numbers not so much like birds, but bombs, shells, screaming from one blood-soaked bank to the other, one filthy water-filled trench to the next: every fixed, dead eye in those arcing volleys more alive than his, which glare blacker than the coals of any pit, crueller than the cold steel from any Satanic mill.

Sixty eight one day, three hundred the next, three hundred and fifty the day after that.

'Another fine day for Mr P—,' a trilling entry, for that horrible season of 1913, begins.

I can only speculate as to what became of his butcher's harvest. Eating all of his catch at Plas would have been impossible. Some, maybe, went to Cardiff, or by train to the London markets. Others were smoked, salted or pickled, perhaps. Many, I suspect, were simply left to rot, then scattered on the fields as fertiliser, their blood, brains and bones ploughed into the sucking soil.

But the sickening thing for me, the thing that I have *tried* to fathom, is the hunger that drove him... even in the dying days of that scarlet season.

Towards its end his catches dwindled, turned paltry, pathetic, as if the river were challenging him, scorning him, humiliating him, *spitting* in his face, for what he had done.

That he always had five thousand in mind as his finishing line, his ceasefire, is evident from the entries in those fat, sad books.

'Will he make it? Only two small salmon today. Another difficult innings for Mr P—' a pitiless page near the end of that chronicle of his carnage complains.

In the end he was reduced to snatching out sprats. It wasn't a salmon or a trout or a pike that saw him wriggle past his ghastly winning post, but an eel. And one that tipped the scales at barely half a pound.

He'd run the river dry, exhausted it of fish.

'Will we ever see such a time again?' reads the last line of those volumes, those villainous volumes, of 1913.

In my mind I'd always seen P— as tall, thin, sharp: a sort of fish hook of a man. But he wasn't that way at all. I looked him up in another of our ancient books: *The Gentlemen of Wales*. He looked away from me, the tips of his fingers on a table, in one of those posed *serious* old photographs: short, stout, whiskered, more artisan than aristocrat (at least in looks), black bags under his eyes, a mane of grey hair turning white.

I wondered if something sexual drove him. To slaughter, I mean. A father of fifteen, according to his biography – and a few more, I suspected (on the 'wrong side' of the sheets). Perhaps that wasn't enough? He built a castle that overlooked one of his collieries. At times an image of him *rodding* maids in its chambers enters my head despite my best efforts to keep it out. But maybe I'm wrong. Maybe something else floated his boat. Perhaps the river was his whipping boy. Sometimes I think there is something flirtatious in our dance, the way that he... engages me.

Lloyd-George sold him an 'honour'. A barony, I believe. Never mind the miners who died by the dozen in his pits. He had an estate in Scotland, but seldom ventured there. I expect he scented the coming war early... in the way that rich men do: its sickly odour cautioning him to stay close to his own empire – to be in position... ready for when it should begin. So, for 'sport', he came here to The Plas. That's why he returns now, I guess. That and his record. To see if it still stands. Which it does: the volumes in the library grow thin after 1913. He, of course, grew fatter: thanks to the slaughter when it finally came. Those murderous years were golden to him: ships and trains surging to the Front fired by his coal; bombs and bullets exploding from cases crafted with his metals. Oh, he had a good war. His only regret, perhaps, that – in dying peacefully in his bed – he missed the one that came next.

All of which – hurtling, if you will permit me, like one of his screaming shells – brings me to yesterday, and the most glorious moment of... serendipity. (I've kept up my studies. I've a liking for words, as you can see. Well, it would be a sin not to, with a library as fine as ours.) To be short and to the point, we receive – with warm smiles – a guest who is new to Plas but whose name is as familiar to me as the ticking of the grandfather clock in the library and the cool sheen of the midnight moon on its mullioned windows. The information is laid out for me clearly as Mr Penry Davies hands me the register: passing it into my palms as if it were some medieval warrant, signed and waiting to be sealed.

That afternoon I watch him – the newcomer – from a casement

in the south tower. He's playing tennis with the young woman he's brought. Hasn't that always been their game? Their *set*? Precious little of that on *my* old estate. Plenty of graffiti, stabbings, dog shit and drugs. But not much in the way of barley water, let calls, backhand lobs.

He puffs around red as a raspberry. She tosses him pat-a-cake shots. Through the glass I hear his grunts, her small whelps and shrieks. What *is* she doing with a specimen like that? Perhaps it's in the job description, a willingness to serve: 'new balls, please'. He can barely bend. Maybe she's worse... seeks his... *patronage*, even his scalp. Perhaps that's her game. I move from the window before I'm seen.

At dinner I'm all over him, *playing* him.

'More wine, your lordship?'

'Ah, now that's something I don't actually use. We've done away with all of that. Mr P—, or Bill. Either of those will do.'

'Very good, sir.'

I charge his glass, take his plate. *Bet you kept the cash though, Billy,* I think to myself, *and the property, the shares... all of the treasure, the real plate.*

'I trust the beef was to your liking?' I ask. I don't listen to him, but instead weigh the blonde, his tennis partner – some kind of *aide*, Mr Penry Davies said.

Billy is florid, sweating. A lump of mashed potato clings to his chin. His drone stops. I begin again.

'And how's life without the red boxes, sir?' *He's not a minister now – even I know that. Just a washed-up Westminster bore-cum-barfly.*

'A *political* animal?' he says, feigning interest in my views. The blonde yawns.

'Well...' I begin.

'Don't write me off,' he winks. 'Not yet. I'm still a big beast.'

'River tomorrow, sir?' I continue. 'Shall I arrange a rod?'

The blonde looks at me, takes out a phone, scrolls.

He glances at her, returns to me. 'Yes,' he says. 'Why not?'

'Very good,' I say. 'Your great grandfather is... *was* quite a figure here.'

'Oh I expect so,' he says... does Billy-boy. 'He liked to make his mark. Family thing. We all do. Old habits.'

As I carry their plates to the kitchen I find myself thinking of school. How far I've come: fraternising with the ruling class... still waiting on them though.

I enter the kitchen. Chef is pummelling a steak. A girl from the village who serves here at weekends comes past carrying plates. On one lies a trout. It looks back at me: grilled, jaws agape.

And now... now I'm finishing my contribution. There are just some particulars to put down. Bear with me while I smooth the page of this volume and unscrew the cap of my pen.

'The secret of good service – a task well-executed – is attention to detail,' Mr Penry Davies wisely told me once.

Now let me begin:

Taken mysteriously at Devil's Edge: one former Minister of the Crown. Some terrible mishap causing him to tumble to that cauldron of a pool that boils below it, and into its salmon-like mouth.

And thence down into its dark and awful gullet, scarce touching the sides; the water of that unforgiving piece of river apparently surging into his waders as he sank.

Those being the very same pair with which he'd been furnished after breakfast at Plas; the heavy weight of the water entombing him as fatally as if they'd been lined with lead.

The gentleman's absence was only noticed at dinner: he'd been fishing (so it seemed) alone.

A search party dispatched to the bank discovered his rod – snapped – between rocks. They cast ropes fixed with grappling hooks time and again into the notorious pool. Why he had ever thought to try his luck there goodness only knew.

At length, eyed by cormorants and kingfishers, his corpse – all nineteen stones – was finally snagged and heaved ashore by that persistent party, pestered by the midges of the dusk.

And what a scarecrow sight he was. A mop of green weed like some grotesque wig on his skull, sharp stones skewered into the sockets of his eyes, fat clods of clay clogging each of his ears, and silt – so very much of it – oozing almost like gold-dust, gorged to excess, from his stuffed nostrils and absurdly puffed-out cheeks.

The sad and sudden nature of his passing – albeit obviously an accident – necessitated one further cruel indignity: his bloated body being taken by the police.. every help being afforded by The Plas.. for gutting and study on a slab.

Yes, that all looks quite in order. There stands the record, as they say. I shall just give it a moment, to let the ink dry.

And what now, I hear you ask, of Plas Trewe?

Well, I can report that the house seems settled, that order has been restored. Silly Billy's aide... mistress... whatever she was, has packed and left. I don't like to point fingers, but that 'slip' on the rocks. Well... it makes *sense*, doesn't it? Some fall-out or other, I expect.

And the great granddaddy? Old Henry P—? He'll stop his mischief, for a while. Our ledger has a balanced look. But it's a constant duel. Some night, I know, he'll be back: casting, teasing, trying his hand.

In a moment I shall see Mr Penry Davies. We have a meeting, of a kind, once a week. In truth he does much less than he used to. These are *my* waters now. Still, he's been generous, he gave me my chance, showed me the ropes, how things *should* be done. I... humour him.

He says he likes to know how I'm managing, a young chap like me.

With beginner's luck, I tell him, and we smile and sip our tea

Rain

I remember, on a rare outing, sitting in my father's lap as he drove the two of us on his tractor to the reservoir that supplied The Joy and the other small farms that were near. I remember our long hair flying – I don't think we ever had it cut – as the tractor – an old one with no cab and a *phutting* chimney-like pipe – drew on noisily in the empty, dappled lanes. I remember the coolness I felt on my face and my small, bare chest, his arms around me, his stubbled chin on my head, his big hands on the wheel: the two of us cowboys, I felt, what little I knew of them. And, when we got there, the smell of sweat and dirt that was upon him: I remember that also.

We walked down to where the reservoir *should* have been through a dark and airless plantation of firs whose bark was peeling in ugly crusts and whose lower branches were mud-brown and skeletal; the floor of the forest – soundless except for the movement of the two of us – thick with dry needles that pricked the soles of my bare feet. When we came to it, we stopped, greeted not by the reach of deep, calm water that ought to have been there but, instead, a great bowl of exposed stone and bleached earth, grey as old bone. We walked along an embankment that projected into it, like a pier. Its end didn't even reach the drab pool that lay, like some spillage, in the middle. The feeling I had was one of being inside something enormous that had died: *there*... at the top of our valley. I would describe it now as like being in the picked carcass of a dinosaur or elephant.

The two of us walked back to the bank. I took hold of a stick, so parched it seemed hollow, and threw it. It bounced with a light tap on the dry bed beneath us. My father and I got on the tractor. At a break in the sickly-looking trees that lined the lane, I remember him slowing – to look again. It was as if our exploration had not been enough and that he had to absorb the reservoir's emptiness with his eyes once more to know that its death was real.

We rode back to The Joy without speaking. I knew it wasn't a time for words. I sensed that he was struggling to comprehend the same thing as me: how we had been to, and seen, the edge of the world, even the *end* of the world: how Death had crept up on us when we hadn't been looking.

That night, in the warm dusk, my father began divining.

Although they didn't like to admit it my parents came from families with money. That's how they came to buy *Y Llawenydd* (which in English means The Joy). They had ideas about how they wanted to live and bring up kids. Above all this meant having nothing to do with the businesses they were heirs to: on my mother's side a food-processing concern that had interests in battery farming, and, on my father's, a producer of pharmaceuticals. You might say that what they wanted, as far as the arrangement suited them, was to have nothing to do with the world. Hence The Joy, my parents' small piece of Wales.

They turned the house, barns and land into a market garden; their aims being, I think, self-sufficiency and to foster a colony of similar types who wanted, and had the financial means, to 'opt out'.

At first things went relatively well. As a business, of course, it could never really have added-up. But, occasionally, people called for produce – the place wasn't easy to find – and my father took boxes of vegetables to neighbours and sometimes into town. Money wasn't my parents' main concern. Happiness *was*, and they seemed happy. I suppose my sister and I must have been happy too. Most of the time she and I ran around in a way that was more or less feral. More often than not we'd be joined by our dog with a bit of everything in him, Finn, whose distinguishing feature, in the latter half of his life, anyway, was his possession of only three legs.

The private incomes of my parents meant that The Joy could have been furnished with almost any gadget of their choosing. But we had nothing like that. We had no phone, computer or TV. Heating was by way of logs or peat. We did have books though, and a player on which it was our treat to listen to records. *Pictures at an Exhibition* by Mussorgsky was one that, for some reason, my sister and I liked to hear. *The Lark Ascending* by Vaughan Williams was something that my mother liked to put on. We enjoyed surrendering to it: holding out our arms, flapping them, slowly, gently, as if we were birds, climbing skyward in its violin solos, sweetly soaring.

In the evenings my mother would embroider samplers that depicted The Joy. My father would fiddle, without much competence, with tractor parts. We had electricity, but this was not always used. Often my mother would light candles. These filled the house with faint, quivering light. Seen from outside it sometimes looked as if The Joy was on fire: quietly burning within.

My sister and I didn't go to school. My mother taught us, after a fashion, at home. Apart from occasional trips on my father's tractor I knew almost nothing of the world. My sister, younger than me, knew even less. But we survived, at least to begin with. It was when the rain stopped – in Wales of all places – that our problems began.

I can't say to the day when it was that the drought set in, but it was no later than early summer, and maybe even the spring. The water pressure in our taps fell steadily till nothing dribbled from them at all. Our storage tanks, fed by rain that ran from the slate and corrugated roofs of our house, barns and sheds, gradually dried up too. The thermometer that hung on a hook on the back of the house reached ninety, the level seeming to lodge there for days. I remember hoping its tiny red fireball would hit one hundred, also wondering how it might taste if it were tipped on my tongue. Our crops were dying in the fields by then. The soil perished to dust. Those streams that crossed and bordered our land became stinking channels of sludge that baked and then broke apart. Their small fish died in what seemed like utter bewilderment. One day I found a fox dead on its side, its mouth seething with maggots.

Anyone *not* living like us and intent on finding water, would, of course, have gone to their solicitor or bank or council office, and examined deeds, looked at plans, consulted registers, about aquifers, boreholes, wells. But, as I've said, my parents were different, or at least wanted to be. And so my father's instinct was to take hold of some twigs. We – my mother, my sister and me – watched as he padded the yard, holding these sticks in front of him, buzzed-at by gnats in the fading light. When my mother tried to speak he cut her off, telling her to hush. Eventually she took us inside. Later we watched him from the upstairs windows as he stumbled through our dead acres in the orange fire of the sunset: his sticks in front of him, our dog Finn at his heels.

When, after a week of doing almost nothing else, my father reported, in a state of great excitement, that he had finally found water, he took all of the credit for himself. I, however, had seen 'his' discovery happen somewhat differently. In particular, how Finn, who had loped after my father throughout my father's clueless prospecting, more or less forced him to a stop one evening by getting under his feet as they headed back to the yard. As I watched from our back door, and as my father called him to come, Finn thrust his nose at the ground just shy of the yard's concreted splay, following-up with a show of snorting, barking and wagging of his tail. My father – moody after another failed day in the fields – went, grudgingly, to investigate Finn's fuss. And there he found it... the lip of it, poking out, where the dessicated earth had blown away: an old, iron manhole cover... and, beneath it, our well.

When he called us from the house and showed us, my father, as I've indicated, said nothing about the part played by Finn. Regardless of my age, I knew that this finding of the well was a big thing, and I did not want to take my father's moment from him, so I kept to myself what I had seen and knew.

The evening was still warm as we stood at the edge of the well: my mother holding us back, worried that we might fall in. We sensed its coolness, its depth. I had the feeling that at its bottom lay another world. Despite the attentions of my mother I was able to see that its walls were lined with bricks in what I came to know to be a hexagonal shape. The fronds of ferns, green in a way that everything else on our land was not, fanned out into its chamber. My father, who had already gathered a bucket and rope, now lowered them into its depths. We heard a splash as the bucket hit the water. He slackened then swung the rope, left and right, so that the bucket might scoop at what was down there. Then, arms pulling powerfully, one after the other, he drew up the rope and, with it, the spilling, swinging bucket, its handle held in a knot.

As he planted it before us my mother began to cry. Finn (who I knew to be the real hero) barked and spun in an awkward jig. We all knelt at the bucket, plunged our hands in the cold water and then, as my father cautioned us not to drink it – at least not then – we each of us threw it over our faces. My face – I'm not sure when before that I'd last properly washed – tingled. My father picked up the bucket and threw half of its water over my mother, who shrieked and told him not to waste it. Then he tipped the rest over my sister and me as we cried out and skipped-cum-ran in circles.

Everything would be all right now, my father said.

As my mother called us to the house I looked, in the dusty light, at the rope and the bucket that my father had set down where my sister and I had whirled. Beside it, the water lay on the ground in dark and beady blisters – as if the earth did not want it, and would not let it in.

The finding of the well was a time of happiness in our home. On the night of its discovery I'm sure we listened to a record and, though I cannot recall what exactly, there was also, doubtless, an enthusiastic poetry reading by my mother (with lively actions on her part), quite possibly some verse by Edward Lear.

My father put out water from the well for Finn, our hens and even our bony cats, who lapped it with curious tongues. While we ate that evening (by then our meals were mainly eggs and, from time to time, a hen that had stopped laying) he announced that we could forget any crops that summer, but that come autumn we would 'dig for victory'. Ruffling my hair and smiling at my mother, he said he felt sure that we would win.

As the last of the daylight came through the kitchen window my mother used a big pudding-bowl of water to soap and scrub my sister, and then me.

In time, my parents began to drink water from the well unboiled. They did this, I think, in part because of how long it took to heat and then cool, and in part because they were taken with the idea of drawing and drinking water from their own well. I, however, did not. Neither, so far as I could see to it, did my sister. Not after what happened to Finn.

One afternoon he went to the edge of the trees at the bottom of the patch that passed for our garden and threw up. When he had finished he staggered to a spot out of the sun, fell down and then, while stretched out on his side, shivered and panted for the rest of the day.

Next morning he was still there, except now he was dead, bluebottles besieging a brown eye that stared skyward. I reported this to my parents who, owing to the detachment which had by then overtaken them, hadn't noticed Finn's quiet removal of himself.

That evening we had a funeral of a sort near the place of Finn's passing. My father set down a large stone which my mother had painted. It bore Finn's name, a daisy-like flower that had large petals and a childish image of a dog that looked nothing like Finn.

As we went through this ceremony the message I sensed that my sister and I were supposed to draw was that Finn had been buried there. Yet I knew that he had not. For one thing the ground was harder than the stone my father placed there, and it showed not the faintest sign of having been disturbed. For another, my father (I knew) had spent all that day doing other things, fiddling in the cool gloom of one of the barns, disappearing at one point into the woods, with a sack – which had almost certainly contained Finn. My doubts – no, make that *distrust* – didn't end there.

That evening, in our kitchen, I asked my mother why Finn had died. She told me it was because he was old. Yet I knew this could not be so because I remembered us having him as a pup – which made him younger than me, and I knew that I was still very much a kid. For his part, my father said what had happened to Finn sometimes happened to dogs and, in Finn's case, because he only had three legs, which meant that his life had been harder than those of most dogs, his death was actually a blessing.

I heard my father out while discounting his words. The reason for Finn having three legs was something I well remembered: the rusty nail with its sharp, sheared end that he, my father, had carelessly left in our yard, which, had Finn not stepped on it, could so easily have ended up mutilating my sister or me (given how we spent the greater part of that time wandering around barefoot). That nail had rotted Finn's front left leg up to his knee. My father cut off the limb on our kitchen table with an axe, cauterizing the wound with a hot poker as my mother held Finn down: a towel around his jaws so that he, gentle Finn – bucking and whimpering on the table – wouldn't bite. Afterwards my father announced that, because Finn was a right-pawed dog and it was a left paw that he had lost, Finn's future would be fine. The medieval amputation over, Finn proceeded to fall and wobble about our house for several days till he finally found some semblance of balance and the absurd loping gait that was for ever after to be his (a disability which caused my parents at times to rebuke and even forget to feed him, as if he no longer mattered). Yes, as my father told me Finn's death had been a blessing, I remembered all of that.

For me Finn's death changed everything. As our world burned on the outside and was poisoned within, I understood that what my sister and I needed, above all, was water – clean water – of our own.

The cave was not on our land. At least, not those parts of it which contained my father's shrivelled and horribly blighted crops. It hid itself in a cluster of rocks the other side of a dried-up stream which seemed to mark our boundary... the place where my father's failed endeavours stopped. We discovered it one day – my sister and I – by chance.

Although small the two of us roamed almost anywhere we wanted. My parents, I think, had the view that in Nature we could meet no harm. And that, anyway, Finn (at least while he was alive) would come loping to alert them if there were any real cause for alarm.

I was partly scraping, partly beating a stick against the rocks, not really paying attention to what I was doing, when, suddenly, the stick, meeting no resistance, flew from my hand. I stopped to look at where it had gone, and that's when I saw it: the gap. It was low, narrow. I wriggled into and along its dark channel (which, if I consider it now, must have been something like six or seven feet long). At the end I stood up and looked around for a moment in the gloom. I then wriggled back to my sister, who was crouching outside. I pulled her in.

Given our mother's tendency to illuminate The Joy with only candles, the near-darkness in which we found ourselves was not something that particularly unsettled us. Besides, after my sister had finished squirrelling through, a jagged crescent of sunlight shone into the chamber where we stood.

As our eyes adjusted to the gloom we saw the pool. Barefoot and naked, as we almost always were, we stepped into the water. The submerged stone, I remember, was slippery under our feet. The water was maybe a dozen feet in diameter – rising, I suspect, from some kind of spring. It nearly reached my knees: higher on the shorter figure of my sister, who shuddered and took hold of my hand. We stood there like that for several moments, looking up at the shaft of light. Then we stepped from the water and explored the chamber. I ran my hands over the smooth, wet rock, stuck the moistened tips of my fingers in my mouth. My sister watched me and did the same. I shouted something idiotic – Finney! Finnbar! Finnbar! Finn! – and we listened as the words bounced around us. I pissed against a wall as my sister looked, then I told her we had to go. She went through the hole first, blocking the light. I pushed her feet and bum, then I squeezed through after her. Walking home through our dead fields, I looked at her, ahead of me. For a few moments, I thought – for what must have been the first time – about how boys and girls weren't quite alike.

I can't say exactly when my parents fell sick. Their fever seemed to come over them gradually. They attributed it to the heat and the sun, which continued to blaze without so much as a drop of rain. They stayed indoors, seldom venturing outside. They complained about the brightness of the light. From time to time I saw or heard them vomit. They passed their days in armchairs in the cool of our living room, struggling to the kitchen for water to drink. Eventually they took to their bed.

How my sister and I managed I don't really know. I suspect that *officially* the world didn't even know about us. Our mother, as I've said, schooled us. My parents had no friends that I was aware of and, in terms of our neighbours, we lived our lives apart. Although we hardly ever received any, the box for our post stood in a lane that led nowhere and was out of sight of our house. As I've already said, we had no phone.

I remember eating raw eggs and ensuring my sister did the same; also the two of us wandering through what must have been raspberry canes, picking tiny specks of red fruit, finding some bushes with dust-covered gooseberries, which the birds, possibly on account of their exhaustion, had overlooked.

The days were ferociously bright. Our valley was almost completely still; soundless save for the occasional dry caw of some passing crow. Our cats grew so thin that on their skeletal bodies their heads seemed weirdly large, like those of marionettes. A couple of them died, as did a number of our hens. Their remains littered the yard, fly-blown, partially-eaten, presumably by the rats which, because of the lack of all other activity, went about their business more or less as they wanted.

Most days my sister and I went to the cave. To begin with we just stood there, in the pool. But after a while I began to bathe both her and myself, and, of course, we cupped water to our mouths and drank.

One evening, in the house, when it was still light, I put on a record: Mussorgsky, probably. The music drifted through the still rooms. My sister and I were sitting on the floor of the living room, sketching, when my mother, who we hadn't seen for days, stumbled in. I remember for a moment being frightened, as if we no longer knew who she was. She half-fell, hitting the player, so that the needle ripped over the record. Then she righted herself and said that she was sorry... so sorry... patted each of us and left. Some moments later we heard her retching. I walked to the kitchen doorway and saw her slumped over the sink. I returned to the living room, put Mussorgsky back on. My sister and I listened to the record, the needle jumping on the scratched vinyl, as the house grew dark.

We stopped going to bed at night. We slept in the armchairs in the living room. Sometimes I would hear my parents moving awkwardly upstairs, coughing, being sick. The light and the warmth of the mornings would wake me. I'd rouse my sister and we'd either eat what scraps there might still be in the kitchen or wander in search of something outside. Days and time meant nothing to us. I can't remember there being a clock in the house. Often I was glad of the daylight. Nightmares visited me. In the worst, the one that I still remember, my father would be drawing up the bucket – all smiles – from the well. In the bucket though would be not water, but all of the dead creatures of The Joy: Finn, the fox with its mouth of maggots, the cats, our hens, their heads all lolling over the rim. I'd wake, sweating, and look at my sister, who'd be asleep in one of the chairs: her head on its arm, mouth open as she breathed (not unlike one of the dead creatures). I'd study her in the gloom, wondering what was happening in her dreams.

One night there was a thunderstorm. White light flashed through the house. My sister climbed into my lap. We held on to each without speaking. I saw a figure moving in the gloom of the hall and then in the living room doorway. A sudden burst of light illuminated the bearded stranger, who looked at us and grinned. It took some moments for me to comprehend that it was my father (who I hadn't seen for days, maybe weeks). He shuffled away. I heard him stagger up the stairs. I let go of my sister and went and stood on a stool by one of the windows. I watched the storm: its sheets of light gradually moving further away... striding off, like a giant. In time it disappeared... all without shedding a single drop of rain.

The gap to the cave grew smaller. I wasn't (and I'm still not) sure how. I wondered if it was because my sister and I were getting bigger. But that seemed impossible. In the cracked bed of the stream at the end of our land I ran a finger over the bony ridges of my ribs. My sister watched then copied me.

The rocks chafed us now as we wriggled in and out. Over a period of days the gap seemed to narrow to a slit. Maybe it was because we were sick and therefore weak. Once, at this time, I remember emerging into the light and being dazzled and feeling dizzy – to the extent that I lost my footing and fell.

In time, the entry reduced to the merest crack, so that the stone grazed our shoulders and our sides. On our final visit we had to force our way in.

Normally a shaft of sunlight lit up the chamber through the aperture in the rock. This time it was so dark we could barely see. It was much colder in there too. As I bathed her in the pool my sister shivered. I cupped water to her mouth, then drank some myself. I decided we should leave.

When I looked for the hole I struggled to see it: our exit seemingly reduced to the breadth of a hair. I pressed my sister to it. She wriggled into the closing folds of rock, then stopped, as if stuck. All that I could see were her feet, kicking – like those of a child in a rubber ring, learning to swim. Finally, tough little girl that she was, she began to move, and pulled herself out. I now forced myself at what remained of the gap. In my eyes it seemed no bigger than the tiny mouse-hole my mother had once shown us – her face a picture of delight – under our kitchen sink.

The way out seemed not only much tighter, but much longer. As

I struggled I wondered how this could be.

It was against my head that the rocks closed first. Two rough sides of stone: scraping, then squeezing, then sandwiching my skull. I felt incredibly weak. I could barely breathe. It seemed in my body as if the summer and the drought that had consumed everything else at The Joy had also secretly and steadily been draining me. I stopped moving. Then I sensed the stones closing on my elbows... my hips... my knees... my feet... so that I was held fast, locked-in. I was able to move my head just enough to see my sister – no more than a segment of her face – outside, peering in. Then I passed out... I think – because what happened next was unclear to me then, and is unclear to me now, and difficult, if not impossible, to explain. All I know – that I *think* know – is that I heard Vaughan Williams... *The Lark Ascending*... those final bars in which the lead violin rises so serenely. And with it my mother's voice, as it was when she played the record to us and the three of us – she, my sister and I – responded to the music, spinning and waving, as she told us, 'You are larks! Let me see your arms! Let me see your wings! Lift them! Let me see you... fly!'

In the white glare of the field I took my sister's hand and we walked back to the house. As we did so I thought I heard voices and the word *children*. But all I knew, definitely, was that I was very weak.

That evening they came for us: doctors, social workers, police. We had apparently been seen by some walkers, bird-watching, who'd reported two children, naked and thin, walking a dirt track, 'like pygmies'.

Someone wrapped me in a grey blanket, likewise my sister, carried us to the back seat of a car. Our parents were taken away separately. I haven't seen them since. They weren't bad people. They meant well. Even now there are times when I long to feel my father's arms as they were that day on the tractor to the reservoir – cowboys, the both of us – and to dance like we did with my mother.

Their crime, if there was one, was that, really, they were children too. Maybe it was also the time, the place and, certainly, the weather.

Occasionally I hear from my sister. She's studying at a university in Canada. (A Christmas card, sometimes a photo. That tends to be all.)

As we were driven away a sludge of bugs smeared the windscreen. The wiper blades raked stickily over the glass. I turned and – kneeling on the back seat – I looked through the rain-spotted rear window. The road to The Joy had the look of a black river.

Rain, Welsh rain, was falling at last.

Dragon Hounds

When Denzil James told me he wanted to wager his teeth I knew things had gone too far. 'What's wrong with them?' he said. Or something like that: his speech kind of soupy on account of the way he was holding them – his teeth, I mean – for my inspection... in the palm of his right hand.

'Nothing's *wrong* with them, Denzil,' I said. 'But it's kind of... kind of...'

With the speedy finesse of an artiste in a cabaret act, spotlight on his wand and cape, Denzil slid the dentures back onto his gums.

'Full set,' he said. 'Good working order. And only one *previous* owner.' His lips parted in a wolfish leer.

'Denzil,' I said. 'When people bet it's generally with cash. Or watches. Or jewellery. Cars even. Merchandise like that.' I thought for a second. 'One *previous* owner. That's you... right... Denzil?'

'Tom Watkins – my cousin,' he responded. 'Got home from work: heart attack. Outside his front door. Nurse from the corner – nosy thing – tried to administrate the mouth to mouth. But gone he was – right there – poor bugger, on the crazy paving he'd laid not three weeks previously. Well, of course, I got there as soon as I heard, to pay my respects. And I saw them – shining – in the flowerbed. I put them in my pocket, then went in to comfort his wife Myfanwy. Good woman... too good for him. Miserable sod, he was.

'The fact is, Gar, he'd have wanted me to have them. You know, to keep them in the family. An heirloom if you like. It was as if he'd put them on that pansy personally. *To Den, With All My Heart, Tom*. Tailor-made by a chap in Cardiff. Lovely fit. Now—'

'Whoah, Denzil! Whoah! Hold up!' I said.

'Want another look?'

'No I do not. Anyway, what if you lose? I mean, how will you eat?'

'I won't lose, Gar. I know it,' he said.

'That's what you always say. Before you lose.'

'Not this time,' said Denzil.

'Anyway,' I said, 'everyone here has teeth, don't they?'

'Olwen Davies. Room 13. Nothing to her name but one single stump. Don't ask me how I know, but I know. Anyway, Gar, think of it. Spare pair for a rainy day... coach trips, chapel, Sunday best.'

'What do *you* know about chapel, you old goat?' I said.

'Oh come on, Gar. You've *got* to let me,' said Denzil. 'It's my last chance. To get even with that bastard Morgan, I mean. I can't give him the satisfaction, Gar. I can't.'

His eyes were suddenly watery. He wobbled on his frame.

'*E-a-s-y*, Denzil. *E-a-s-y*,' I said.

He gripped the tubing. The joints in his liver-spotted hands glowed a yellowy white.

'Look,' I said. '*If* I take the teeth – as a once-only – will you bury this thing that's between you and Morgan? It's gone on long enough.'

Denzil said nothing (which I knew was as good as it was going to get).

'Anyway,' I said, 'this one's going to be the last. There'll be no more after this.'

'Suits me,' said Denzil. 'All or nothing. Death or glory. These teeth are the last of my liquidity anyhow.'

I sighed.

'Want them now?' Denzil asked.

'No. Enjoy your supper,' I said.

'You're a good man, Gareth.'

He clumped off, muttering, into the bottle-green gloom.

'Death or glory, Tudor Morgan. Death or glory.' And then, knowing I was still listening, 'Myfanwy Watkins. Nice ass.'

Dragon House. The place was like a rock pool: cut off and forgotten. I should never have been there. For one thing, I was about a thousand years too young. For another, I still had my marbles (and my teeth, for that matter). And yet, somehow, *there* I most definitely was. The place belonged to Miss Gwendoline Glynne-Beynon, an octogenarian spinster who took in paying 'guests'. It was a big, old house that had seen better days but which still possessed a certain elegance. It stood on its own overlooking a saltmarsh beyond which lay dunes and then smooth reaches of sand that finally gave way to the sea. In times past, when the more mischievous locals were given to inciting wrecks on the coastal reefs, the waves practically lapped against the boundary walls. Since then the house had been engaged in a sort of strange, silt-induced retreat from the sea. My theory was that its stones crept backwards beneath us as we slept.

Miss Glynne-Reynon's guests were, for the most part, a bundle of befuddled crustaceans. Occasionally, in a storm or on an exceptional tide, a drifter like me blew into their backwater. I was walking the coast roads at a tricky time in my life when I discovered it. A peeling sign at the foot of the drive said *Vacancies*.

Miss G.B. (as she was known) interviewed me in her apartment on the first floor. She was as delicate and exact as a piece of fine glass. I told her I was a painter, mainly of portraits. She showed me a photograph of herself as a young ballerina. That was the last time I entered her rooms. Later, when passing, I sometimes heard her at the piano. Every so often the arthritis in her fingers caused her to scuff a key. She'd pause for a moment then begin again.

Unlike the other residents, who seldom strayed beyond the veranda, I was in the habit of going out and doing things. In the summer I picked peaches, and in the early autumn pears, from trees that grew against the flaking walls of the mostly derelict kitchen garden. I also fished: stringing lines from one boot-sucker bank to the other of the muddy river that cut through the marsh. Most of all I combed the beach. And it was there, on the sandbank, that I first met him: the stranger.

I'd been examining the entrails of a washed-up jellyfish. I heard him before I saw him: his boots scrunching over a ribbon of dry shells. The low evening sun danced at his shoulders, flashed in the gaps between his arms and his sides. The way the light loomed behind him meant I could make out almost nothing of him, not even the colour of his skin.

When first he said, 'Will you hold them?' I hadn't even registered the dogs. These, I realised after a moment, stood at his feet with a sculptural stillness, as if vesting all of their powers in the act of listening.

He held up their leads, which were more like reins: long strips of dark leather that curved from his hands like crescent moons. They were greyhounds. The one furthest from him had the grey-blue colour of a storm cloud. The coat of the smaller, closer one was much lighter, like sand or even gold. They wore collars which were tall, smooth and had the patina of grandfather clocks. Though listening to us, the dogs looked along the empty beach to I knew not what.

'Will you hold them?' the stranger said again, this time raising and definitely offering me the leads. I took them, and the dogs stepped to me. With that, he turned and walked back into the sun.

His figure veered from the light into the fattening dark. I heard his boots on the shells once more, the sound getting thinner, and then he was gone.

I led the dogs through a gap in the dunes. They moved quickly and quietly... as if they knew the way, and had always known it.

In contravention of Miss Glynne-Beynon's rules on pets – 'We like things quiet here, Mr Howells' – I took them back to the house. We watched the moon rise over the marsh from my windows, and then they slept at my feet.

In the morning I fed them fried trout. Then I led them down the backstairs so they could relieve themselves outside. Later we made our way to the beach. We cut through the dunes where the fence posts had rotted: barbed wire put up by the Glynne-Beynons, years earlier, straggling the marram grass in rusted surrender.

I unclipped the dogs' leads. They stood at my feet and stared along the beach. I cupped my hands to their hinds to encourage them, and they edged out a little to the wetter, firmer sand. I turned back to the dunes and sat out of the wind against a slope. The dogs were skittering now. I watched as, for a moment, they reared, nipped and pawed each other, heads sliding down one another's necks. Then the small one – the bitch – ran, and the blue one – the dog – went after her. Their speed amazed me. They galloped like racehorses. With every forward lunge their feet clean left the sand. As they ran their skeletons concertinaed so that their back ends were at times colliding with their fronts. It made it look like each dog was racing with itself. When they wheeled to come back they moved so sweetly that my eyes found it difficult to keep up with them. The light fawn coat of the bitch blurred with the sand. The grey-blue of the dog merged first with the sea and then with the sky. Before I knew it they were with me – standing at my feet, but looking away, as if asking – shyly – for my approval. Their big pink tongues hung, trembling, from their mouths.

They stood still as I sketched them. We left the beach near dusk. Gulls were flying at the water's edge. Oystercatchers gathered in knots on the ribbed sand. On the way home the dogs drank from a pebbled stream.

It was Tudor Morgan – who else could it have been? – who caught me. He was wheeling his way to Eleanor Meredith's flat, a volume that bore his name (seemingly of poems) in his lap, when he saw the three of us sneaking up the backstairs.

'Are those what I think they are, Mr Howells?' he said, applying the brakes of his chair.

'Temporary guests, Dr Morgan,' I said, deliberately alluding to his past career in academia in a way that I knew he liked.

'Nice looking dogs,' said Morgan. 'Breach of house rules, of course.'

'I'm just holding them... for a while,' I said. 'I'm not sure there's any need for Miss Glynne-Beynon to know.'

'Holding them?' said Morgan. 'Sounds rather strange. We'll discuss this further, I think. But, now, if you'll excuse me, I've an appointment to keep.'

Eleanor Meredith was eighty-nine, deaf and prone to forgetfulness. But to Denzil James, Tudor Morgan and most of the other old men in Dragon House she was hot... red hot (though the hounds themselves tended to other terms: 'pleasant company' being one). She was a high cheekboned beauty who, not unlike her friend Miss Glynne-Beynon, had at one time been on the London stage. In her youth she'd starred in a radio serial about a girl who loved her horse. The animal – or at least various sound effects – had snorted and clip-clopped its way through 104 episodes on the *Light Programme* on Sunday evenings about a century before. Memory of it sent the old dogs of Dragon dreamy-eyed, then crotchety at their inability to recall the horse's name. (Gambol, for the record.) Miss Meredith smelt of lavender and wore lipstick which she applied herself. When she moved in it was as if we had Helen of Troy on our hands. A whole armada of tortoise-like advances got under way to her door. Denzil James muscled in hardest, of course. He made sure he always had a seat next to her in the dining room, and came to see himself as her beau.

One day though he was late to the table. When he finally clumped in on his frame he found Morgan in 'his' place... regaling Eleanor with anecdotes of his academic life as she smiled and pushed a small fillet of cod through the parsley sauce on her plate.

Denzil stopped going to lunch after that, hiding sulkily in his quarters.

He thought it would only be a matter of time before Eleanor sought him out. But, tired of all the old men who were hitting on her, this she never did.

Denzil, meanwhile, pictured Morgan sharing chocolates with her, the two of them holding hands, smiling as they watched gentle movies in her softly-lit rooms, fragrant with scent.

At night he couldn't sleep for the torment.

The races were Morgan's idea. To say that he blackmailed me into them wouldn't be that far from the mark. One afternoon he knocked my door and wheeled himself in. He told me that while – as a man of some standing in the community – he could not condone any breach of the *rule of law* in the house, he'd been contemplating how, during the temporary residence of the dogs, some pleasure might be derived from them for the benefit of the populace as a whole.

What I imagined Morgan was leading to, in his nasal, professorial way, was a proposal that I should shepherd the dogs around the oldsters' rooms every so often in order that they might get to pet them and give them names and treats.

But then he said, 'So what I recommend is a weekly race up the backstairs, taking in certain of the landings which might also have on them hurdles or markers for the dogs to jump or otherwise circumvent. To bring some spice to these proceedings,' he went on, 'I submit that you, Mr Howells, should open a weekly book so that those who are so inclined will have the chance to place the occasional wager upon the outcome. If other dogs can be found or persuaded to enter these meetings of ours, well, the more the merrier.'

Morgan handed me a plan that had lots of arrows and notes on it which said things like *Not To Scale*.

'I look forward to it,' he said finally, and wheeled himself out.

And so our races began. To help bulk-up numbers, Windsor Harries, whose room was on the top floor, produced from somewhere – the attic, it was thought – a spaniel named Duke. Harries had in his day been a civil servant with his own office, name plate and a small degree of power. He was another with whom Denzil had feuded – 'Lah-de-dah London lickspittle' – albeit on a lesser scale to the warfare with Morgan.

Harries' production of Duke caused a jealous rage among his neighbours. In the end, for the sake of a contest, they relented (while delighting in Duke's every defeat).

Other dogs quickly came into the reckoning. Trefor, the gardener notionally responsible for the rainforest grounds that surrounded Dragon House, entered his black labrador Quint. Farm dogs, town dogs, fishermen's dogs that went to sea: they all began to show up. Gwyn Walters, a grocer from town, decked out his beagle Benjie Boy with a green and gold vest that said 'Go to Gwyns'.

When Walters first showed the dog in its 'silk' Harries made a sniffy comment about the 'grocerly lack of an apostrophe'. This drew a daggers look from Denzil, a miner all his life who, while professing hatred for 'pen pushers' such as Harries and Morgan, secretly admired their learning in a way that pained him.

Our course comprised the four flights of the backstairs and the second and fourth landings along which various hurdles and obstacles were configured that had to be surmounted or swung round by the dogs. These included commodes laid on their sides in the manner of fences, mops and brooms from the landing cupboards that we laid across upturned buckets like jumps, plus sundry markers and posts in the form of small cairns of Tudor Morgan's many books (which were not infrequently moistened by certain of the less considerate competitors). The races seldom got under way before midnight. I'd tiptoe outside Miss Glynne-Beynon's apartment until I felt sure she'd gone to bed – by which time excitement among the oldsters would be near fever pitch.

The starting line where the dogs were let loose was in the old servants' passage towards the back of the house. A small stuffed bear served as our rabbit. This Trefor soused with a secret potion of crushed seeds from the garden that he rightly predicted would send the dogs wild. The bear, in a checker suit, like some city swell, was tied to four or maybe five retractable washing lines in a spring-loaded rig of Morgan's making. The dogs would dash up the backstairs and over the landings while I took the rickety service lift. More often than not the lift struggled to keep up with them as they flew heavenwards in a tongue-lolling, tail-thrashing, leg-scampering fury. Landings one and three would be secured with tables on their sides in the manner of those festivals where bulls run the narrow streets of certain towns in Spain. From these barricades the watching oldsters would yell and curse and urge on the dogs. On landings two and four the various hurdles and obstacles came into play. If I was lucky, I'd just manage to make it to our finishing post – a dusty aspidistra at the far end of the top landing – ahead of the dogs.

It wouldn't be going too far to say that these races, while inducing palpitations in some of the old boys, gave many of them a reason to keep living from one week to the next. Although it had never been planned that way, the men in the house saw the meetings as very much *their* preserve. The women got wind of them, of course, and towards the end fiery old ladies such as Miss Bethany Evans – whose mother had marched with Lady Rhondda, the famous suffragette – were demanding to be involved.

Positively the last thing I wanted on my hands was some sort of battle of the sexes between rival armies of ancients. On a more personal level something I disliked was the way I found myself lying to Miss Glynne-Beynon. She stopped me outside her apartment one afternoon to say that she felt sure she'd heard dogs, at night, in the dark. That she had *smelt* dogs, in actual fact. I said I didn't know anything. But it was obvious that I did. Miss Glynne-Beynon was a lady who, apart from anything else, had put a roof over my head. She deserved better than that. All of which made me determined to shut down what I'd started (anxious that the whole heated business was spinning horribly out of control).

For Denzil the whole point of the races was to somehow get revenge on Morgan for the way Morgan – in Denzil's eyes – had stolen his sweetheart. He had the idea that if he could only clean-up enough cash *and* beat Morgan at the same time he'd take Eleanor away on a cruise ship, the two of them very probably marrying... on a beach somewhere, flowers around their necks (and Tudor Morgan truly trounced). But the fact was that for Denzil the races had been a disaster from the off. Through side bets with non-residents he blew £500 at one meeting alone. Time and again I tried to turn things around for him: giving dogs I knew he'd bet on head-starts, risking my neck with questionable rulings, holding others back. But no matter what I did, solemn, studious Morgan *always* got the better of excitable, emotional Denzil.

All life in Dragon House – or so it seemed – closed in on that final race. I took Denzil's teeth – he insisted I actually have them (wrapped in a handkerchief) – and, in return, I gave him £20 with which to roll the dice, one last time.

The book I ran was not dissimilar to a sweepstake. How the oldsters and those non-residents who participated chose to mix things up on the side was a matter for them. In the sweep Denzil had – forever and a day – been in the habit of landing lame-duck dogs like Colin, a corgi that belonged to Dai Richards, the dairyman. Little-legged Colin never had a cat in hell's chance, but I let him run to keep Dai quiet after he heard about our races from talkative Trefor.

Another loser Denzil often drew was a brain-dead poodle named Sophie. Sophie belonged to Jean-Paul Pugh, a crimper who called at Dragon once a week to fuss, snip and cluck over the last tufts of wiry white hair that held out defiant on the skulls of residents such as Miss Guinevere Pryce-Powell who, though only two years short of her century, many of the men were nervous of on account of a story that she'd once shot and brought down unaided a rogue bull elephant in the days of White Mischief in Africa.

This time though Denzil drew Goldie. And everyone knew how Goldie could fly. So much so that by that stage I was having to start her from out in the garden just to give the other dogs a chance.

It was my routine to slip the relevant details of the draw – always conducted in the scrutineering presence of Morgan – under the doors of those who were in on it the night before the meet. Next morning Denzil hailed me on his landing as I headed downstairs.

'I've got Goldie,' he said, his hand shaking as he held up his copy of the draw. 'The golden ticket at last.'

Word had got around that this race would be the last. The field was the largest ever: fourteen dogs with big money on their backs. Gwyn Walters brought his brother Wayne who was a security guard of a kind at the indoor mall in town. Wayne brought Wolf, his powerful and serious German Shepherd. Having had a message from Gwyn the night before, I'd pencilled the animal into the sweep as a late entry headed *A.N. Other*. Tudor Morgan drew Wolf. Ken Lu, who owned launderettes and takeaways in half the towns on the coast, turned up with his chow Caesar. To be honest, the number of runners worried me. It was going to be a case of each dog for itself. Even before things started there was a flare-up between Caesar and Wolf. I thought of calling the whole thing off. But so much money was riding on it I figured I'd be lynched if I tried a thing like that.

The dogs were let loose on the stroke of midnight.

Benjie Boy made the early running from the passage to the stairs – before being cannoned-into by Wolf at the corner. Benjie went sprawling to the skirting in Wolf's wake.

I let go of Blue who, as a greyhound, was handicapped to a delayed start at the back door. As he burst away I dashed to the garden for Goldie who stood tethered to a tap. She now streaked into the house in pursuit of the pack. I ran in after her to find Gwyn in the passage, yelling.

'Did you see that? My dog was taken out! By that bloody Nazi beast!'

'No time, Gwyn,' I said, and leapt inside the lift.

He was jabbing his finger and still shouting as I slid the cage door shut.

'I demand an inquiry. You're the referee. Do something!'

'Take it up with Wayne,' I said. 'He's *your* brother.'

Gwyn's yells turned to whimpers. 'How can I? He's the law round here. Threatened me because my fruit boxes were on the pavement. Bastard thinks he's Wyatt Earp.'

Usually I rode the lift straight up. This time I decided to check every landing. The first – sealed-off with tables to create a viewpoint – had the atmosphere of a cockfight. Glassy-eyed old guys I'd never before seen jostled and looked over one another's shoulders as the dogs raced upwards. Duke the spaniel was in front. On his tail came the heavy brigade of Wolf, Caesar and Quint. I hit the lift for the next floor.

The second landing was where the smaller dogs had the chance of an edge. The bigger dogs tended to have to slow to swing round the various posts and obstacles that were laid out there. I rolled back the door of the lift and saw that Colin, Dai Richards' corgi, had the inside lane on both Caesar and Wolf. All three were rounding a cairn of Tudor Morgan's books. 'Go Colin! Go!' Richards was bawling. Meanwhile, Sophie the poodle was running the wrong way into a bunch of dogs who were heading right for her. Pile-up and mayhem all round.

I hit the lift for the next level. As it cranked upwards I began to think about Goldie and Blue.

I only just made it to the third ahead of the dogs. Quint was now leading, with Wolf and Caesar on his heels. Duke had disappeared and Colin the corgi was fading fast. Trefor, who knew Quint had a habit of tiring at the third, was screaming him on. 'Come on, Quinty! Come on!' Thomas Lloyd-Thomas, a defrocked (so it was said) minister of religion, was at the front of the barrier of tables and desks, staring in silence at the onrushing dogs. It was the first anyone had seen of him in two and-a-half years. I hit the lift for the final floor.

There had to be forty guys on that top landing, but it was as quiet up there as it was out on the marsh. Denzil was at the front of them, grim-faced, hunched over his frame. Tudor Morgan guarded the finishing post at the aspidistra, in his wheelchair, a rug over his lap. Ken Lu was down on one knee, rubbing a medallion between his forefinger and thumb. Windsor Harries put on a pair of glasses and snapped their case shut. Wayne Walters chewed gum. The only sound was the scraping of the cage door of the lift as I shut it behind me. All eyes were on the dark mouth at the top of the stairs. It was like the Olympics: the moment when the entire crowd fixes on that one arch through which the lead runner in the marathon will – heroically – come.

Then we heard them. The rumble of paws on the linoleum of the wooden back stairs. Muffled barks. Yelps. Suddenly we saw it: the teddy bear – our 'drag'. Catapulting at head height out of the top of the staircase, bouncing onto the landing and starting to whir its way towards Morgan at the finishing post.

First dog on the landing was Wolf. At his shoulder came Caesar. Some way behind them was Blue. The landing went wild. Oldsters smacked their race sheets and roared as if willing a Welshman to the try-line in a rugby match against the New Zealand All Blacks. Denzil hung onto his frame as if caught in a tornado. The dogs were on the home straight.

Tudor Morgan leaned forward in his wheelchair, determined to be the sole and final judge of who came first, second and third. Despite the tumult around him Morgan held fast against any show of emotion as Wolf, his ride in the race, bore down on the imaginary tape that ran between the aspidistra and a brass mantel clock that had neither ticked nor struck in seventeen years. For all his stony exterior I somehow sensed Morgan's heart *pounding*; his mind wondering if he might die right there, stopwatch in hand, his body falling to the floor: trampled by the storming, marauding hounds.

Then something beautiful happened. Blue, bounding and pushing, somehow carved a gap between the burly flanks of Caesar and Wolf. Having done this he gave way, so that, whether by accident, exhaustion, design... or even a miracle... Goldie, who was behind him and had run by far the furthest, came surging through – her strides lengthening so that, for the other dogs, there was no hope of stopping or catching her. Not now. Not ever.

Denzil won £900 on the sweep. It wouldn't have got him far in terms of a cruise with Eleanor Meredith, but it was enough to pay for his funeral. He was found dead in his bed the next morning: his fiery Welsh heart had finally burned itself out. Vernon Chave, a retired solicitor who liked to dispense unsolicited advice to his neighbours (before presenting them with bills), had called at Denzil's room with a view to doing just that, document wallet in hand, dressed in a three-piece suit. His intention had been to tell Denzil what to do with his windfall (at a fee of 20 per cent plus taxes). Denzil, to his credit, had been one step ahead of his pinstriped predator, and lay on his pillow... white as a cloud, cool as a conch.

He would have been pleased that Eleanor was in the front row for the service at the crematorium (though considerably less so had he known that Morgan was also there: at Eleanor's side). I was just grateful that my friend had passed out of Dragon House a winner at last. What's more he did so in possession of his (or should that be Tom Watkins'?) teeth, which I managed to slip back in his mouth when no one was looking so that he crossed his own finishing line looking his best.

All of which brings me to the here and now. At this very moment I'm walking with Goldie and Blue through that gap in the dunes I told you about. It may surprise you to know that Denzil is with us. Along for the ride, so to speak. To be precise his ashes are in two pouches that I've fixed to the collars of Goldie and Blue. When we get to the beach I'll nick them open with my pocket knife, and send the dogs running... over the sand.

My hope is that Denzil, free of that frame of his, will stream into the salt air from the two of them as they fly along the shore.

When they wheel to come back and stand with me, I'll sketch them... one last time. Then I'll clip their long, soft leads to their collars and hold them till the man comes... out of the sun and over the shells.

And then he can take them to wherever it may be that their beautiful magic is needed next

I've Got You

'Look, Mummy!'

'What is it?'

'It's an ear.'

'A what?'

'I said… "IT'S AN EE-YUR".'

'Bring it here, sweetheart.'

Charlie stomped to her over the sand. He held out his hand, her warrior, her hunter-gatherer.

'Oh that's a lovely shell, Charlie,' she said and then she thought, maybe not *shell.* Maybe… *fragment.*

'It's not a shell, Mummy, it's an *ear.* I told you,' he said.

'Oh, yes, I see,' she said. 'May I?'

She turned it in his palm, ran a finger over its creamy brown ripples, traced a valley to the pearl-white chamber at its heart. To her it had the shape of a pear. To her master of the shore it was, unquestionably, an ear.

'Look!' he said, putting it to the side of his head.

'And what can my lord hear,' she asked, 'with his new ear?'

'Whispers,' he said.

'Whi…'

'Shush, Mummy! They're talking,' he said, 'and now they've gone.' He gave her The Charlie Scowl.

'I'm sorry,' she said. She wrapped him in a hug. He resisted in the way that he did... sometimes: her soldier boy, her little man of stone. She took away her arms.

'Look,' she said. 'Maybe you can find the *other* ear. Where there's one ear there ought to be two. Yes?'

He looked up: thinking, examining her, his fringe almost over his eyes. She wondered how it had got so long. She parted his hair with her fingers.

'With that second ear,' she said, 'you're sure to hear, don't you think? Two ears are better than one. That's what they say. Isn't it? Charlie? Charles? My Charlie boy?' She kissed his head. 'See what you can find,' she said. 'For Mummy.'

He slipped from her, skittered over the warm sand.

'I mean, who has *one* ear?' she called after him. 'There have to be two. Don't there?'

He stopped, looked back.

'A pirate!' he shouted. 'A pirate can have only one ear. Sometimes.' And he was gone. Her beautiful boy.

She crumpled to the sand.

When they came, she wouldn't let them in. She refused. She heard the swing of the gate, the lift and drop of the latch. How she'd come to *hate* that gate. Their anthracite toecaps were enough. She needed nothing else. Not the khaki creases on which you might cut yourself, on which you would *want* to cut yourself. Especially not the briefcase, booby-trapped, as it would be, with those bald letters and signatures, underscored, in ink. She refused them. She would not *permit* them to bring their news – *that* news – to her door. Only when two of the women – ashen, shattered, ancient – came with them would she... unlock.

A bomb, they said. Something... improvised.

Improvisation. Wasn't that something actors did... comedians? Maybe this wasn't real, maybe it was a mistake.

There'd be a coffin, they said, then warned her not to expect... too much. He wouldn't have felt anything, they told her. He couldn't have suffered. She could, they said, draw some comfort from that.

She rained her fists on them.

She would *suffer*, she said.

Charlie tugged her: boy stretcher-bearer raising the not-quite-dead. 'Wake up, Mummy! Wake up!' Sun danced on his shoulders, her angel. 'I want you to see something,' he said and took her hand. 'Shut your eyes!' he commanded.

'But Charlie I've only...'

'Shut your eyes, Mummy! That's an order! *That's* better. Okay. Left Right.' He led her across the sand: her guardian, her rock, her funny mini-man.

'Charlie, where are you taking Mummy?' she asked. She felt the beach change under her, the soft sand of the dunes giving way to the ribbed surface of the mid-shore, her toes entering a sprawl of dry seaweed: bladderwrack. 'Mummy's not sure she likes this, Charlie.'

'It's all right, Mummy. I've got you,' he said.

The sand became wet. Waves that had been lazy grew loud in her ears. 'How much further, Charlie?'

'Nearly there, Mummy. Just a few more steps. Right. Stop!' He let go of her hand. '*Ten-shun!*'

She stamped her right foot.

'Good,' he said. 'Now. Open your eyes... a-n-d... Look!'

The white light of the beach hit her, buckled her. And in that moment she was back with Will... before he went. He was holding her, telling her he'd be fine; that she'd be fine, too.

'Promise?'

'Promise.'

And she believed him. Because Will had always kept his promises. Hadn't he?

She regrouped. Charlie was calling. 'Look!' he said again.

He pointed at the sand. Urgently, theatrically. Heroic boy-worker on some old Soviet poster.

His marvellous Man of Shells looked up at her from the shore.

The figure – the fabulous figure – had cockle shell eyes and a curved slipper shell nose. A beard of grey limpets bristled at his mouth of twirled turret shell teeth. White razor shell fingers poked from otter shell cuffs. A dandy's dream coat – fit for the pickiest Cockney Pearly King – cloaked him with exquisite swirls of Faroes, peppery furrows, striped whelks and banded wedges. His trousers teemed with tiny curling tops and lovely rayed troughs. From these hung oyster shell stockings and barnacle boots. Meanwhile, on his head, sat a black hat of mussels rakishly decked with a periwinkle plume.

'He's wonderful! How did you *do* this, Charlie?' she said. 'I adore him. Look at his hat, and his coat.'

'It's not a coat, Mummy! It's a tunic!' he said.

'Is he a pirate?' she asked.

'No, Mummy! Look! He's got two ears, hasn't he?'

'Oh yes,' she said.

'He's a soldier, Mummy! A soldier! Like Daddy!'

He paused.

'What shall we call him, Mummy?'

'How about... Mr Shelley?' she said. 'Mr Percy Shelley.'

'Yes!' Charlie said. 'That's his name: Mr Percy Shelley!'

'I wish we had a camera,' she said. 'I think the tide's going to take him.'

He held his chin, gave her his I'm Thinking look. 'I don't think so, Mummy. I think he'll be here... for a while,' he said.

They walked back to the house. She kept his shoulders from the nettles that hemmed the path. They stepped over a rusted barbed wire that sagged between fence posts.

'Careful, Mummy,' he said.

After supper she tucked him in. He slept better, now, at least. She'd worried about that. She'd worried about... so many things. At the funeral he'd wanted to salute. They'd practised it together. When the time came he hid his face in her side, and sobbed. On the table by his bed was the ship-in-a-bottle that Will had built. She remembered his freckled fingers raising its little masts with a white cotton thread, squeezing home the cork that smelt of Scotch.

Charlie: 'Yes, but how did you *do* it Daddy?'

William: 'Magic, Charlie. Magic.'

Next the two of them were lapping the table in a riot of pirate *yarrs* and *narrs*, Charlie yelping from a flurry of tickles, jumping on Will's back: 'Aye Ayes' and 'Cap'ns' and false reports of crocodiles all round.

In her bedroom... *her* bedroom (that's what it was now)... she lay awake, taunted by the silence till soothed to sleep by the birdsong of the dawn.

Sun was in the house. Charlie was still in bed, curled-up like a shrimp. 'Come on, Matey. All hands on deck,' she said.

The house had been her mother's, her grandparents' and the home of several ancestors before that in a family which had always drawn its living from the sea: Carmarthenshire cockle-women, fishermen, lobster-potters, crab-catchers, mongers and sailors. She'd gone away to university, left Wales, met Will. He picked up a glove she dropped leaving a rugby match, came after, gave it her back. That was the start of it: her right hand. Two years later her mother had died. And then...

The house stood alone, down a track. You had to know it was there.

She and Charlie scrubbed floors, threw open windows, captured cobwebs and beat rugs over the back of the bench in the garden-gone-wild.

'Let me do that, Mummy!'

'Good hit, Charlie boy! You teach that rug. We'll give him some stick.'

'Take that! And that!'

'Good lad. He won't be getting dusty in a hurry. Mummy's turn.'

How they beat those rugs. Only her tears saved them.

She lit the stove. They ate beans and bacon. Afterwards she sat in the rocking chair and, big as he was getting, he climbed onto her. They sat there: rocking not talking. She stroked his hair, kissed his head. He snuggled close and listened to her heart.

'It's working, Mummy... I think,' he whispered.

'Good,' she said.

His breathing turned heavy and deep. She let her head fall back. Suddenly he sat up, all wriggle and surprise, like those trout she and Will had fished for (and sometimes even caught) in their L.B.C. (Life Before Charlie).

'Mr Shelley, Mummy!' he said. 'We nearly forgot!'

She let him run to the beach ahead of her, smoked a cigarette as she walked through the trees. One of Will's. She'd found them, by chance, in a drawer. Nineteen left: his trademark. He'd puff on one, discard the rest, guilty, disgusted. No wonder they were always broke. If she smoked one a year they'd last till... their silver wedding.

How about it? she thought. Will? William? D'you hear me, husband? Ready for the long march? I'll yomp if you will... Will?

The trees parted to the scrub that came before the dunes. She loathed its dustbowl look. Useless ground.

Husband... how strange that sounded now.

On the beach she called to him. 'Charlie! Charlie!'

He didn't come. She tried again.

'Char-lie!' And louder: 'CHAR-LIE!'

Gulls – agitated... perhaps by her calls – wheeled over the shore. A breeze beat at the stiff grass of the dunes.

She started to run in a way that she hadn't since school.

Madly, wildly.

Sand flew from her feet. Her skirt swept at her legs, the loose cuffs of her shirt slapped at her wrists.

She called as she ran, looked left and right.

She rounded the point where the woods jutted at the water on a cliff of black rocks.

She begged for her voice to swell and boom and echo. But the more that she called the quieter it became, till her 'shouts' were little more than whimpers. 'Charlie?'

And then she saw him.

He was near the water: standing still, his back to her, head lowered, all of his attention on the sand. She ran to him, clasped his shoulders, kneaded his lovely collarbone with her fingers and thumbs, locked them under his downy chin.

She closed her eyes, relished him.

'Look, Mummy!' he said. 'Mr Shelley... and Mrs Shelley!'

Her hair... her hair was a mane of jet black mussel shells that tumbled to shoulders of winkles and whelks, her gown a marvel of flamboyant conches, fluted clams, speckled mitres and Neptunes whose lovely spirals seemed to go on for ever. Matching scallops hung from her oyster shell ears. Dainty bonnet shell boots with barnacle buckles peeped from beneath her skirts. She and Mr Shelley held razor shell hands. Her petite periwinkle eyes stared up at them from the sand.

'What do you think, Mummy?'

'Charlie, how did you do this?' she asked.

'Magic! Like Daddy,' he said.

She split logs for the stove. As she swung at them she wondered how long she'd manage to hold onto the house, now that she was... a widow. The place was an indulgence, she knew. They still had their Army quarters, at least for a while.

No, dammit, she thought. Why *should* she surrender? And to some sleazebag of an estate agent, all tie and talk, wondering if *she* might be 'available' along with the house.

She drove the axe through a piece of ash.

Hold your nerve girl and your ground. That's what Will would have told her.

She buried the axe in its block, drew back her hair with her hands.

Weren't widows supposed to be old? Why *had* he died? She cursed him, without meaning it.

Before bed she made Charlie take a bath. '*You* are smelly,' she said. The pipes knocked and groaned. She rinsed his hair as he scrunched his eyes.

She tucked him up. She wanted to ask him about the beach, the shells.

'Charlie,' she began.

And yet she was afraid of what he might say.

She wondered if she was... all right... so soon... after Will.

'Want a story?' she asked.

'No. I'm all right,' he said.

'Good,' she said and kissed him. She walked to the door.

'Do *you* want a story, Mummy?' he asked.

'Maybe,' she said. 'If it's a nice one.'

'Mr Shelley married Mrs Shelley and they had lots of children and they all lived happily ever after,' he said. He pulled the bed cover to his chin.

'Thank you, soldier,' she said. 'But maybe we need a break from Mr Shelley. For a while. Now... sleep.'

She turned off his light, trod softly down the stairs, and sat in the rocker. She tipped its runners and went to and fro in the chair till it slowed and it stopped, and everything in the house fell still.

The words began as barely a whisper that crept through the cottage like a cat. She woke in the rocker and joined the recitation.

She sells seashells by the seashore.

Then a second whisper came sidling and hissing.

The shells she sells are seashells, I'm sure.

It flung itself after the first: the words chasing each other like a musical canon. The whirl grew faster and faster. It baited her to keep up. She rocked the chair, gripping its arms, made stumbling, spluttering attempts to stay in step. She tried to speak and then to sing and then to preach and then to chant her way through the lines that circled and closed in on her, then wove themselves together and coiled around her – tighter and tighter – like the rough, grimed rope of some devilish Jack Tar.

When she came to she was on the floor. She lay there and listened. The house was quiet. And then she heard Charlie, who began to speak (softly, at first):

So if she sells seashells by the seashore
Then I'm sure she sells seashore shells.

He was word perfect.
She ran up the stairs.
By the time she made the landing, he'd begun all over again: only now he was shouting, bellowing.

She sells seashells...

She put on the light. He was sitting in the bed... yelling... his face a horrible knot of rage.

... by the seashore.

'Charlie! Stop it!' she shouted. 'Stop it. STOP IT!'

She took hold of his shoulders. He fell silent, and flopped back on his pillow.

She lay on the bed, listened to him breathing for a while and they stayed there like that till the dawn.

For breakfast they ate honey sandwiches in the small courtyard that caught the sun at the side of the house. A jungle of poppies and thistles enclosed them. Charlie ate one-handed while attempting stretches and bends he remembered from Will.

'Charlie,' she began.

'Hmmm?'

'That rhyme you were saying last night...'

'What rhyme, Mummy?'

'The one you were saying last night, darling. Where did you learn it?'

'I don't remember saying any rhyme. Are you sure, Mummy?' he asked.

'Maybe not, sweetheart.' She paused. 'Look, I've an idea,' she said. 'Today Mummy's going to teach you how to...

'Yes?'

'... tickle a trout.'

'Don't be silly, Mummy, you can't tickle a trout.'

'Who says, Charlie boy? I'm an expert tickler and you and those trout had better watch out.'

He threw back his head, laughed as she pretended to chase him over the flagstones of the yard.

The stream was the boundary with the farm next door. It cut under a canopy of hazel and alder. The water was cold, quick, delicious.

Their pale feet slid over smooth pebbles and into the soft, silty bed. Tiny fish darted at their ankles and toes.

To her amazement she charmed a small trout out of the water. It flapped and spun in the air. It came down on an old piece of fence that was half in the stream. The trout snagged on a barb. The more it wriggled, the deeper the barb bit.

She bent over it, pulled the trout free and swung it against a stone.

Charlie watched her, open-mouthed.

He held out his hand as she climbed the bank. He stared at her fingers as she wrapped dock leaves around the trout.

'Daddy's not coming back, is he Mummy,' he said.

Flies buzzed around them. He flung out an arm.

'No,' she said and walked on. He caught up, tugged at her skirt.

'But we'll find him,' he said.

'Yes,' she said.

He skipped ahead, singing. The words fell from him as he ran.

'*She sells sea shells...*'

Back at the house he circled the kitchen table, thumping it with his fists and shouting. 'Beach! Beach! Beach!'

'We're not going to the beach, Charlie.' she said. 'Stop this.'

He turned and stomped in the other direction, banging the table and shouting, 'Bored! Bored! Bored!'

As they walked through the dunes she told him, 'You are *not* to let go of Mummy's hand.'

The beach was empty, as always. For holidaymakers there were easier, bigger bays, places with cafés, car parks and stalls. Her beach –

that's how she'd always thought of it – was out-of-the-way, awkward-to-reach, just a beach.

Charlie hauled her across the sand, like a little puffing tug.

'The Shelleys, Mummy!' he said. 'We must see the Shelleys!'

'They won't be there, Charlie,' she said. 'They'll have been washed away by now.'

'No they won't! They'll be there! I know they will!' he said.

As they neared the water he yanked at her hand.

'Look! Mr Shelley, Mrs Shelley and their children Charlie and...' another yank '... his sister. What shall we call her, Mummy? She's ever so pretty!'

She pulled him back to her.

He wriggled and wrestled, like the trout on the wire, but she held onto him. She turned to the dunes, pulling – almost dragging – him with her.

'You naughty boy!' she said. 'You *wicked* boy! After all your poor Mummy's been through. When we get home you're going straight to bed. And tomorrow we're leaving. You hear me, Charlie? We're leaving!'

She hurried him back to the house. Behind them a storm closed in. Wind whipped over the beach and rain spat into the sand.

She put him to bed.

Afterwards she went to the landing window and looked out over the bay.

Jags of lightning were switchblading from clouds that were burly and blue-black. Thunder growled after the flashes, like some moody dog.

She went downstairs, curled up in the rocker and fell into a fitful sleep.

When it came the storm moved quickly: grappling its way from the beach, finding strength in the woods, surging over the fields till the house was at its very core. Water and debris – heavy branches, lumps of rock even – hammered the roof. It was as if the entire shore was being swept-up and hurled on top of the house in a great tidal wave that was determined to claw back to the sea a shoulder of the land and anyone and anything that stood upon it. She tried switches, lamps – all useless – turned out drawers for a match or a torch. Papers, coupons, old photographs flew to the floor. Lightning flashed – as if in mockery – around the house. Rain didn't so much spot the windows as cling at the panes in glutinous slicks. She saw Charlie in his pyjamas at the foot of the stairs, and then the knocking began.

The first strikes were gentle, no more than taps. Almost impossible to hear amid the rain's fat splatters, the angry pushing and pulling of the windows against their jambs. But then the taps turned to raps that fell – persistent, insistent – against the front door.

Charlie stared at it and began to recite.

She sells seashells by the seashore.

'Stop it, Charlie! Stop it!' she shouted.

The blows on the door became huge, pounding.

The big, old-fashioned key jumped back from the lock with every juddering smack till it fell to the floor and lay there.

After one almighty bang the door swung open, and there they stood – silent, dripping, the moon at their backs.

'Look, Mummy!' said Charlie. 'Mr and Mrs Shelley! They've come to call!'

Only they weren't the shimmering, beauteous figures of the beach. For the storm now cast them in a different and grotesque light. Mr Shelley's razor shell hands, which on the sand had shone like silver, had now spun around so that it was their long, dark exteriors that reached from his cuffs. They twitched and turned in the kitchen's gloom. As for Mrs Shelley, her mane of mussels, so bewitching on the beach, was now a crone's tangle of ripped-apart shells. Her dress sagged with seaweed. Only one of her scallop ear-rings remained. She hung from him like some harbour tavern whore.

'It's *magic*, Mummy!' Charlie said.

That word again: Will's.

Show yourself, husband, she yearned. I *need* you. They wouldn't dare. Not if *you* were here. Not with that axe of yours.

Axe? Her mind raced. Where was it? *My* axe now.

In the block, she remembered. In the yard.

'Charlie! Bedroom!' she shouted. 'Now!'

He started up the stairs. Mr Shelley went after him, the whites of his rotating razor fingers glinting in the dark.

She feigned for the staircase, but cut behind the stove and ran into the yard.

A sheet of lightning showed the axe, buried in its block.

'Stupid woman!' she cursed, remembering how she'd driven it hard into the wood, wild with Will, angry with Life, furious with Death.

Finally, the blade came free.

And now she marched on the house – the axe in front of her – like some Viking warrior.

As she reached the door it slammed in her face. The bolts slid shut.

She stepped back, swung into the oak, yanked the blade out and went at it again.

'Two, three, four. Okay door, you can have some more!' she shouted. And then: 'Are you watching, Will? Are you?'

She smashed the door apart.

The Shelleys were on the stairs.

She took out the hag first: splitting her in two, from her skull to her shoes.

'Pick on a widow would you, bitch?'

Shells cascaded down the stairs.

She was on them now, striding through the scattered remnants of Mrs Shelley, slipping, getting back up.

Mr Shelley hurried on ahead of her.

Lightning threw a sickly glare over the landing. Now he was opening Charlie's door. Through the gap she saw Charlie: sitting up in bed, reciting, faster and faster:

> *So if she sells seashells by the seashore,*
> *Then I'm sure she sells seashore shells.*

Shelley stood over him, soaking, stinking, razor hands whirling, whirling, whirling.

To start with, she took off his head.

Her first sensation was of the shells – like glass – under her feet, at the bottom of the stairs.

'It's all right, Mummy. I've got you,' Charlie said.

Then the two of them were outside, on the path through the woods. She felt she could taste their sweetness, hear every insect's hum or buzz.

With a wobble she slipped over the barbed wire and into the dunes. Sharp grass caught her ankles and calves.

Soon their feet swam in the lovely soft sand of the upper beach. And next they were crossing the brittle weed and nudging the bleached driftwood that lay scattered in the strandline. Then they were on the mid-shore where tight little cockle shells and pyramid limpets prodded their soles. Wet sand squeezed between their toes as they neared the tumbling water. They felt its spray on their faces and arms. The sea sucked back shingle with a sound like a sigh.

Charlie's hand was hot in hers.

For a moment she thought of Will's fingers pulling at the masts of his ship-in-a-bottle – rolling out its sails – with his white cotton thread.

Her skirt spread around her in the water.

They walked further and further out. Waves folded over the two of them.

Eventually she heard Charlie telling her that she could open her eyes now, if she wanted to.

'I've got you, Mummy. I've got you,' he said.

Horsemen

'Will they bite?' I asked my father.

'Not the hands that feed them. You'll be all right,' he said.

We showed our palms over the mossy stone wall. On them the wretched windfalls we'd found in the lane.

My father held me. I remember being fearful that, after the apples, I'd be next.

'Do they know you?' I asked him.

'Oh yes,' he said. 'That's Bronwen,' he pointed. 'And him, shorty, over there, he's Hercules.'

'What's *Hercules*?' I said.

'Strong,' said my father. 'More muscles than Swansea Bay.'

The horses showed no interest in us, kept to their side of the field.

'They won't come,' I said to my father.

'Patience. Give them time,' he said.

We looked a while longer. Some of the horses lifted their heads, studied us, went back to pulling at the grass.

'They're nervous. That's all,' said my father.

'What's *nervous*?' I asked.

'Scared,' he said. 'Give them time. They'll come. You'll see.'

We let our apples fall. My father set me down.

That the horses were *nervous* emboldened me.

'Next time: carrots,' I said.

'Oh really?' said my father.

'Yes,' I said. 'To help them see.'

'We'll see,' he said. 'Come on.'

We walked back down the lane – my small hand in his shovel paw – passing the milk churns outside Meredith's farm, the leaves on the hazel above us already turning brown.

That evening – being a Saturday – we had sausages with onion gravy for our tea. Three for my father. One each for my mother and me. A sixth sat on a saucer in our pantry – part of his snap for the week.

With sausages I'd always watch till my father had a mouthful. Only then would I stab at what my mother had sliced on my plate.

Our meat – bar rabbits from the mountain – came from the same place as everyone's: E. Jones, Butcher High Class. Of course, if we hadn't liked *his* cuts or prices we could have gone to the next village and the shop of his brother, C. Jones, also Butcher High Class. Or to their cousin, D.B. Jones, *Quality* High Class, in the village after that. No meat moved in our valley without the thumbs of the Joneses being upon it, my father more than once remarked.

But in my and other young minds, at least, E. Jones's shop possessed a curiosity that set it apart. For to us it was the seat of our village's one, big mystery: the missing finger of Teilo Tully.

Teilo was E. Jones's boy. Not in terms of being his son. His real son, Edgar, was killed in the war. Teilo was E. Jones's assistant – his lad – in the shop. To call him a boy seemed strange to me back then. He had thick, greying hair, was as tall as my father and was well past twenty-one. Teilo winked, whistled and hefted big sides of meat in and out of the gloomy back of the shop. Sometimes when waiting with my mother I'd glimpse the animals there: on hooks, minus their heads, yellowy and still. It looked as if Teilo was waltzing with them as he heaved them to and fro in his arms. When it came to serving, only E. Jones did that, and in an apron that was always clean. Though the word made no sense in ages and years I could tell, young as I was, that

Teilo *was* the boy, and that E. Jones was the man.

The digit that Teilo lacked was the forefinger of his right hand. Where it should have been, a scar-tipped stump suddenly stopped. The stump sat there as if all that were needed was something – tweezers or teeth – to pull it out and into place, like the stuck finger of a glove.

According to one story in our village the Germans cut it off in the war. Another, whispered among boys, held that Teilo *was* a German, a Nazi spy in fact: this lack of a finger being the common sign that all those swines had.

The story most commonly advanced was that Teilo's finger was a casualty of E. Jones's block. That it had joined a string of sausages – never to be found – after tumbling from the block's wooden, bloodied top.

The truth, of course was that – at that time – its loss could have occurred anywhere: the railways, the canal (some were still going, just), in the factories, the steelworks, the pits. And anyway, to adults, as I was to learn, one finger was nothing in a land of lungs, limbs and lives lost or wrecked.

Still, boys weren't to be dissuaded. That night, in bed, after our visit to the horses, I nursed a new theory, which was this. That through drunkenness, stupidity or Nazi skulduggery, he, Teilo, had called the horses – whistling, quite likely, in the way that he did. But that – crucially – he'd been empty-handed, holding not even the crabbiest apple from the lane, when they looked to him and came. There ended Teilo Tully's finger. Of that I was convinced.

The horses worked in the same mine as my father, 2,003 feet below our village. They were called pit ponies and, apart from those times when the men were on holiday or strike, they were down there all year, fifty weeks. Their job was to haul drams of coal cut by men like my father from the face to the shaft to go up in the lift. They did this from the time they were strong enough to the time when their strength was gone. For two weeks in late summer when the miners went on holiday the horses were brought to the surface, and got to see the sun.

Johnson's Field at the back of our village was where the horses went from my father's pit. These weren't horses of the pedigree kind that you see show-jumping, racing or decked in brasses at fairs. These were workhorses: strong, barrel-shaped, broad-backed, in many cases their tails docked. Not abused though. They were too important for that. Worked hard, yes. But looked after, or so it was said.

For me to gush about them gambolling in the light just wouldn't be right. In that first week above ground they'd be nervous, lively, would allow no one to get close, only their handler when he brought their hay. In the second they'd be a little calmer but still frisky. I suppose it must have been the space, the light, all sorts of things: trees, birds, the wind, the quiet.

Three summers I went to the field. At first with my father, then on my own. We always seemed to meet Teilo Tully in the lane. My hand would tighten around my father's as Teilo winked and stopped. Almost always he'd be smoking, cigarette in the mid-fingers of his right hand. My eyes would fix on that small, ham-coloured stump no matter how I begged that they would not. They watched Teilo's every suck and puff so closely it somehow seemed as if the cigarette had passed to my own mouth. In between talking to my father he'd let out a throaty cackle of a laugh. Eventually he'd walk on – whistling – down the lane, back to the village. Only then would I ease my hold on my father's fingers, counting in my head the number he still had to his hand.

I'd ask my father why Teilo had been there. My father said he went to see a lady in her cottage further up our mountain.

'Where?' I'd ask.

A cwm I didn't know, my father would say.

'Why?' I'd ask.

To chop stick and warm her fire, and other things, he'd tell me as we walked on.

'What *other* things?' I'd ask.

'Never you mind,' he'd say (in the way that meant that *that* was the end of that).

But being a boy I knew better. Even than my father. As far as I was concerned Teilo went to the field for one reason. And that was his finger. To my mind he went there hoping that even if the horses *had* taken it that by now they'd somehow rejected or ejected it. That it lay there, somewhere: under a dock-leaf or poking from a dropping. And that he might see it – nail shining in the sun – and scoop it up.

Most summers we went to the seaside. Pretty much our whole village did. We lodged with a landlady – Mrs Herbert – who had family in our valley. She cooked food we took with us on the train. In a way it wasn't really like being on holiday because all of our neighbours were there, the men all being miners who worked at my father's pit. My father wore a black swimming costume that had straps over the shoulder like a circus strongman. Donkeys took children for rides on the beach. Despite my fears I went on one: a man in rolled-up sleeves led while my mother – at my side – held my hand. The rub of the donkey's coarse coat against my bare legs is something I've always remembered. The donkeys made me think about the horses back home. And whether, one day, I might perhaps ride them.

I'd visit them before the village departed, go to them again as soon as we were home. By that time they only had a day or so left on the surface before – like the miners – they went back underground.

As I got older I went to the field on my own, taking vegetables in secret from my father's patch. I'd climb the wall at the field and stand on it, holding carrots or parsnips and early fallen apples (sour as hell) in my hands. Most of the time the horses just looked up then went back to their hay or grass. One time Hercules took half a dozen steps towards me, but then stopped and returned to the rest. I'd end up dropping the apples over the wall. The vegetables I'd take back to my father's patch, re-planting them in the dirt behind the outhouse, wondering if he knew.

Although only a small boy I suspected our ponies weren't the world's most handsome horses. A photograph in my father's paper showed a jockey on the horse he'd ridden in a big race. A thoroughbred, my father said. It looked totally different from our ponies. Yet to me ours were beautiful all the same.

After all of my waiting the horses finally came. I was nine years old, nearly ten. And though it's long ago and I've never had any choice but to live with the events of that night, I still wish that they had not.

Our school was closed and all day my mother had been to and from the pit. Come evening women from our street held her hands in our back parlour, and none of them said a word. My father wasn't there, of course. I didn't need to be told what it all meant. I lay on my bed, weeping and furious. Cursing the coal that even then I could hear being shovelled from a bucket onto the range downstairs. I hated it. Every last lump. When I grew up there would be nothing but wood on *my* fire. Starting with the useless apple trees by Johnson's Field. I'd fell and burn every one.

And then they came... as I've said... the horses: jumping over Johnson's stone wall, bumping each other beneath the trees of the lane, running along the dark streets of our village, rounding the corner, climbing our stairs, gathering... at the foot of my bed. They bade me go with them, with whinnies and turns of their heads. Hercules carried me, Bronwen and the others at our flanks and heels. We galloped past the still terraces in a thunder of hooves. I held on to Hercules by his flying mane. Where they were taking me, I knew, of course: the black tower of the colliery loomed ever closer as I rode.

When the moon and stars vanished I realised we were there, underground, at last. And now the horses were calmer, steadier, as if knowing they were home. Onwards we went, the group of us, through the warm and dust-filled dark: our tunnel worming... ever tighter... so that my head now pressed against Hercules's neck. Deeper and deeper we journeyed, more like a train of mules now than the cavalry charge of the start. I felt at one with the horses, as if I'd been among them for ever: *before* our village, *before* our pit, *before* even Wales. From the era, in fact, when all of our valley had been nothing but trees and rivers and waterfalls, and no one had ever thought of sending live, breathing men and horses into the earth, underground.

A thin sound caught my ears between our steady steps. Faint at first, but definitely there.

Whistling.

The whistling of a man: the notes of its rises and falls turning the corners of the tunnel towards us, getting louder as we neared the source. With it the sound of a tool of some kind.

Thud... thud... thud.

I was hot and wet now, my shirt clinging to my chest and back; my hair dripping at my temples and neck.

Finally a figure stood before us: Teilo Tully... in his apron. A cleaver on one side of him. And on the other: E. Jones's block.

He beckoned me, curling his forefinger, the one that should not have been there.

It bent and straightened, and bent again in the dark.

Behind him a huge fall of rocks blocked the tunnel, like boulders over a tomb. But then Hercules – 'More muscles than Swansea Bay' – advanced and passed through first Teilo and then the stone, as if neither were there. Bronwen and the others followed.

We entered a cave-like chamber. It had a flickering half-light. Men who were stripped to the waist swung picks and scraped shovels and drove drills at its dark walls; some whistling, some coughing, some spitting, some talking, some even singing, as they worked.

And then I saw him, my father. He walked to me, smiling, sweating, looking even stronger than he had in his bathing costume on the beach. He patted my leg, stroked Hercules's head.

'I told you they'd come, if you waited,' he said.

Then he leaned close and blew over Hercules's nostrils in long, slow, deep breaths.

Bluecoat

She first asked about *Y Diwedd*, which in English means The End, that day when she and Tom had been going through all of the paperwork at their apartment. They were about to take over his parents' farm – a new and different life in the uplands of Wales – and she and Tom were sifting and studying deeds, maps and various other papers on the kitchen table of their loft: documents that related not only to the farm, but to the land that surrounded it. This included the mountain on which Tom's family had rights to run horses and graze sheep, also the big dams with their reservoirs shaded blue that kept the western side of England in water.

She was tracing a tight whorl of red-brown contours with her fingers, absorbing – properly... for the first time – the land's impressive height when, suddenly, she found it: the small, black block and the abbreviation, in slanted lettering, underneath.

'What's that?' she asked Tom.

'What?' he said, his mind somewhere else.

She planted a finger. 'That.'

He looked. 'Oh that's *Y Diwedd*... The End,' he said.

'It says hospital.'

'It was,' said Tom. 'Once.'

'Up *there*? What kind?'

'Military... in the wars. It was one of those big houses that got requisitioned. A mansion... quite a place. Belonged to the Bowen-

Prossers. Our farm was part of the estate.'

'What happened?' she asked.

'Second time around the family didn't want it back. Too expensive, I suppose. Army must have made a mess. The children moved away: London, Italy... townhouses, villas, you know the thing.'

'It's nice that we're going the other way,' she said. '*Back*, I mean. Don't you think?'

'Mm-um-mm,' Tom responded (absent again).

He moved the map that she'd been studying. He smoothed and then looked at some sheets that had been underneath.

She looked out of the window. The Thames was choppy. A boat rose on the swell. She thought again about how high it was, Sara and Elwyn's farm, the home she and Tom were inheriting, *Golau Lleuad* ('Moonlight' when his parents used the English), 1,000 feet above the sea.

He'd felt nothing, probably through shock. No, it would be wrong to say *nothing*, because he had felt *something*. And what he'd felt was contentment... a woozy contentment. It wove through him – delirium's warm fever. And after the madness of the charge, the hell of getting even *that* far, it was bliss.

The flares had spiralled above him. He remembered that. Like fireworks at a show. The sort where people queued, stood inside the ropes, looked up together, did as they were told. All of it... *choreographed*.

As well as the flares there were shells. These exploded, burned – in the corners of his eyes – yellow and red, like stubble after harvest. Oh those torchings. He well-remembered those. How as a child he'd watched: fire-lit faces, unshaven men, swirling smoke, fields dark, demonic. But now it was soldiers not farmhands (though some had been that once, no doubt) who ran, scrambled, fell around him.

As he lay there another memory unfurled. This one happier: a bar, wine-soaked, tobacco-fugged, far from the Front, a shadow play in progress in a large back room: silhouettes of Allied troops, boats, cavalry, Kaiser Bill... in his *pickelhaube* helmet... then Bill scarpering, fleeing the field. His exit to clapping, cheering... soldiers stamping on the bar's wooden boards, whistling... whistling. Oh, how he longed to be back there. And then... a waitress... pretty, setting down jugs and glasses, picking up empties... long, dark hair, bright eyes, the faintest hint of a look... at him. Oh how *he* was empty now and longed to be picked up. By her though, only her. But then, something else... something *not* right or good, something... bloody... in his eyes... as if it were raining. Except that it was not – apart from the shells and the great showers of earth and wire and pieces of men that fountained and fell all around him.

The bar's shadow play faded... the waitress too. The noise of the charge, muffled since the time of his final stumble, ebbed till it also was gone. His mouth was dry. How nice it would be if one of these passing fellows – there were fewer now – were to stop and stand him a drink. But they were busy... so busy in the moonlight.

The move to the farm went well, and she was relieved. She had sensed Tom's scepticism about returning, the business of going *back*. They'd met at university, graduated together, entered the same architects' practice, taken it over, sold it, made a bit. After that it had been a matter of doing the projects *they* wanted. They operated alone: boutique.

One of the first things they did on arriving at the Moonlight was to buy a ram. They had him from a neighbour who'd known Tom as a teen. Their ewes scattered as the new boy made himself at home. She and Tom laughed. They christened him Rimbaud, after the French poet and libertine. She remembered – from a short course at university – a collection he'd written, partly in London, in his creative period while with Verlaine: *Illuminations*. Yes, she thought to herself, accenting the word in her head, *Illuminations..* up here... at Moonlight... where things might become clear, where special things might be found.

A noisy, blue morning saw the arrival of new hens, ducks and geese. Meanwhile, the way his parents' sheepdogs took to her and she to them pleased Tom greatly, the black-and-white collies soon hanging on her every whistle and word.

What she really liked was the new closeness she felt to him. All through that first summer they hardly stopped smiling. They kissed, and more, in a way they hadn't since their student days. Early in their marriage they'd been told that having children would be a problem for them. But up there everything seemed different, greener, possible.

The summer months were warm. Their faces and limbs burned red, then bronzed. On long, insect-buzzing days when it was too hot for work – or anything else – they swam naked in the high, cold, peaty streams. At other times they picked whinberries, lay listening to skylarks... walked home to the farm, like sovereigns, in purple heather crowns.

London's halter had been lifted from her.

A mirror was not permitted. He'd asked for one after the first operation, and the second, and the third. He thought that they might have brought him one... out of mercy. He cried like a baby when they peeled him of his bandages. But the nurses always somehow turned the talk to something else. The doctors too: telling him to wait, to be a *patient* patient. They spoke of rugby football, tobacco supplies.

His face... his face was not what it had been, was not *how* it had been. That much he could tell. When he put his fingers to it it seemed like someone else's. There were valleys, ridges – *places* – that he could not recall.

In time he left his bed and circulated among the other men. He watched as, also without mirrors, those who chose to, lathered one another's faces with brushes and soap, then shaved each other, negotiating more often than not crusts of scar tissue, which they did with great care, even tenderness.

Many were without limbs and thudded the wards on crutches, pushed themselves, or were pushed, in chairs. He thought of them as cats born of the same litter, looking out for one another, licking each other's wounds. They had brought the war home on their bodies: its craters and trenches, its wire, its mud.

When he spoke to the others he studied their eyes – for signs... reactions... intelligence... about his face, how he looked. But they said nothing... betrayed nothing. No one ever did. Stiff upper lips, for those who still had them. That was the drill.

At night the nurses drew wooden shutters across the tall windows so that the men might not see their reflections, by chance or design, in the glow of a candle or a beam of the moon. And then he would lie awake. Not woozily, as in that French field, but alive, alert, touching himself, trying to make sense of what he'd been given: the mosaic, with its coarse tiles and irregular valleys, that had been laid imperfectly to the mysterious object that was his head. He ran his fingers over it, feeling it, interpreting it, in the way that, with their hands on the faces of others, he had seen blind men do.

As August surrendered to September she and Tom, come evening, stood in the yard and watched *their* bats, as they thought of them, soar and swoop beneath moons that were huge and lazy and low. Only in the autumn proper, long after the swallows and swifts had flown, did the first discordant note sound.

The day was cool, still, echoey. Tom had been trying to change the plugs on one of their elderly tractors which, for its part, had been refusing to let them go. The wrench flew back in his face and fell to the floor. She heard him cursing, and she rushed into the yard. Blood ran from his nose over his lips and dripped from his chin. She tried to comfort him, but he brushed her away. He went into the kitchen, threw water on his face in the big, butter-yellow sink. She stood over him as the tap spattered, watched him as he cupped water to the nape of his neck, noticed – in a way that she hadn't noticed before, or at least not for a long time – his soft, white, draughtsman's hands. When he was done and *still* wouldn't speak she walked out into the yard. He towelled himself, staring after her as the water, clouded red, whirled away.

In London they'd bicycled everywhere. Their bikes had been part of their 'pitch' for business. No... part of *Tom's* pitch. For her it had always been genuine: a signal of her wish to escape. Either way, what their riding said about them went down well with clients and, important to Tom at least, it gave them an *edge*.

Now she slung on a jacket, stuffed gloves in the pockets, crossed the yard to the sheds. She saddled-up on the silver mountain bike that he'd given her as a birthday present (on one of her 'big' ones). She pretended not to look as she left, saw him in the kitchen window – staring back, drying himself.

At the end of their track she joined the mountain road and climbed. It was the first time she'd ridden in months. She seemed fit and was pleased.

In time the road's metalled surface ended in a circle of unmade stones. She slowed, stopped, stood over the bike. She looked to the horizon, made out the smudges of towns. Much nearer lay the reservoirs. They glinted as they were caught by the sun, dulled as it became hidden by cloud.

Then, quite suddenly, it revealed itself: seeking her attention, so it seemed to her, like a peacock (was how she thought of it later) with its fan. And all the while so peculiarly close, as if it had been hiding and only now wished to conjure itself: the house... the hospital... *Y Diwedd*... The End.

He walked. They allowed him to walk. Encouraged him, in fact. He went out most days, always alone, sometimes in the woods, more often on the hills. At first the silence unnerved him, particularly when something cut through it unexpectedly: crows cawing above or behind him, the bleating of sheep hidden in mist. One day he just stood on the mountain and screamed.

In the hazy mid-summer, strolling aimlessly, swishing at heather, he discovered a grouse... almost trod on her: the bird suddenly there, on a nest, at his feet. She eyed him as he bent. She didn't move from her eggs, knew, somehow, that she wasn't in danger... not from him.

Come August there was shooting on the mountain, parties after the birds. He ran up there, ran amok, arms waving, shouting, defending the grouse. A complaint was made to *Y Diwedd*. One of the doctors summoned him, read out the letter. If *the lunatic* repeated his conduct he might well find himself being shot. It would be in his interests to desist.

This, at least, made him laugh. 'And where shall they send me next?'

The doctor smiled. 'Just be careful,' he said.

The house lay in a clearing that resembled a stage. Yet somehow its stonework, its stillness, together with the colours and contours of the mountain, combined to conceal it. Quite a trick of the eye given its scale. It was a shell now, of course: all of the windows gone, saplings on what remained of the roof, fallen trees and thick, wet grass in what must have been the park. Yet it was handsome, still.

Her breath hung around her in shrouds. She considered the light, decided the day held just enough, pushed her bike down a marshy track. In time she cleared its pools and tussocks, entered an avenue of trees, rode on towards the house.

Rooks reared above her as she came, bumpily, into the park. She dismounted, wheeled her bike. Her feet crunched over a border of gravel which had kept the foliage of the park raggedly at bay. In places the small stones had been pierced by tall weeds and thistles, some of which were the size of scarecrows. For all of their insurgent efforts they were black, slimed, dying now.

At the porch she propped her bike against a pillar, worried for a moment about her lack of a lock, half-smiled at her lingering city self, remembered where she was.

There was no need for her to knock or push at the front door... because there was no door. She walked inside. The first hall led to a second that was larger and like an auditorium. Plaster that had sheared from the high ceiling littered its wide tiled floor. A staircase, dilapidated but still grand, rose to the rest of the house.

She wandered the rooms. In many of these water seeped in fine, spindling falls through stained and splintered ceilings. Fractured friezes and cracked cornices – one badly-damaged depiction of doves, in particular, and a second, of cherubs issuing a clarion call – seemed close to collapse. Forests of fungi with caps in colours of rust and slate marched across walls, some bare, some hung with huge curtains of rotting red and green paper which slumped and sagged like abandoned banners, bedraggled sails. Ferns forced themselves thickly between floor and skirting boards that were wet and soft, while in high corners birds' nests clung above panels streaked and bleached with thousands of droppings that had accumulated in stiff, cake-like waves. In places, she found feathers, clumps of fur, small animal bones. In one room, what seemed to be croquet hoops were stacked in a pile and – incongruous now, given the state of the grass – a roller for the lawns. Strung across another, a tennis net that ivy had entwined. It swayed in a breeze that blew through the house.

To the rear were the kitchens. A black range long as a railway platform covered one of the powdery brick walls. She pulled on an oven door that was slightly ajar. Inside lay a nest of some kind: dry leaves, grass, tiny and deft. On a partition hung the servants' bells. She tipped one with her fingers: a ring, of sorts.

Back in the hall she began to climb the stairs. She wondered about the sense of it, but carried on.

From the landing she saw them. First through the doorway to one small room and then almost everywhere: beds... dozens of them... in rows... in rooms – wards they would have been, she supposed. Not beds with mattresses, blankets, linen. Just the frames, the springs: dormitory-style, heads against the walls. Forty, maybe fifty, she thought. Beside them, here and there, wooden chairs, empty lockers. She put her hand on the cold metal frame at the foot of one of them and looked out over the park through a window that still possessed its pane. The sodden grass resembled a sea. The light was failing, a mist was moving out of the trees, across the park. It made her think of gas.

She retraced her steps, found her way back to the porch. Outside, she took hold of her bike, began to push it over the gravel towards the avenue of chestnuts. For a moment she thought she saw something... some*body*. Too fast, too fleeting, for her to be sure. But a person, perhaps... in blue... there... at the side of the house. She stopped and looked, but saw only some shrubbery gone wild. She began to pedal, made her way back to the road.

Autumn brought fierce fronts of rain which, on his walks, gave his coat the weight of a wounded man and plastered his hair to his head. A gale demolished a large glasshouse in the kitchen garden, causing it to crash in on itself on a night when winds harried *Y Diwedd* with mournful, harmonica moans. The sound and, next day, the sight of the wreckage distressed many of the men. Waterfalls on the mountain and streams in the woods that had been no more than trickles for months now surged and boiled. Ravens that had coasted effortlessly all summer found themselves thrown about the steel sky like rags. Often the staff refused to let him out. This detention once lasted for more than a week. Finally, on a day that dawned crisp and clear, he stormed off in his greatcoat, vowing he would be a prisoner no longer.

He marched up the mountain. The hollows between the heather were now wide pools of water. On a plateau below the peak he knelt beside one of them, and saw his face.

She freewheeled down to the farm. As the mossed banks of the mountain road swept past her she wondered why Tom had never taken her to *Y Diwedd*. She again thought about how she'd almost missed it. She remembered something Elwyn, Tom's father, had said. About how the mountain was *constant*, while everything else on it changed: the people, the machines. And how the mountain, when it desired, could conceal, for good or ill, that which was its own. A fox might grow a grey and even a blue coat to survive in its folds. The mountain had secrets, and it knew how to keep them.

It was dark when she entered the yard. The dogs on their chains barked till she calmed them.

He wandered in shock and fever. Hurried, stumbled and hurried again. He pulled at his nose, tugged at his ears, slapped at his chin: wondering if the person in this... *mask*... could really be him. He rolled in the wet heather, moaned, sobbed. The day – the horrifically clear day on which there was no comforting fog, no fret in which he might mercifully become lost – died slowly, painfully, around him, till the wounding sun was an ember on the ridge at last.

And now his coat flapped about him, like canvas caught on a wire, as he looked down on the fading form of *Y Diwedd*, down on the darkening shadowlands of the valley... and he rocked, on his heels, on the high, lichened ledge, wind whipping and whipping at what passed for his face.

Tom's mood improved. She asked him at supper about *Y Diwedd*. She said she'd seen it from a distance on her bike.

He said it had been for soldiers who'd come back badly wounded from Flanders and France. That had been the point of them being up there, at the top of the valley, where no one might see them and (Heaven forbid) be startled. As far as the authorities were concerned it was all about *morale*.

Tom repeated to her what his father – having heard the stories from his own father – had told him: how local people had known all about the hospital, how some of the more able soldiers had worked on the farms, how the farmers had been glad of the extra hands, though in fact a number of the men had worn claws or hooks on their stumps. Those maimed the worst sat on benches in the park at *Y Diwedd* that had been painted red. Clergy, worthies and very occasionally, due to its remoteness, members of the men's families would call. In summer there'd be a fete, tea on the lawn. The red benches were a flag to warn people of the men's physical state.

'They had uniforms,' said Tom.

'Blue?' she asked.

He looked at her.

'Educated guess,' she said.

The autumn was long and jealous. It held the valley in its skirts for weeks. Even by late November frost had barely blanched the land. But winter was coming, she knew. And, although she didn't want Tom to see it, she was anxious about how they would cope, about how things would *be*.

She worked hard. She picked all of the fruit she could, then made pies and preserves. She painted the Moonlight's doors, window frames and bargeboards. She also took her turns checking on the sheep, as well as collecting eggs and tending their vegetable patch. She did the laundry and pegged it out on a line at the back of the house where it dripped and swayed. When she found suitable fallen boughs in the woods she dragged them back into the yard where she cut them and then stored the logs. Among many other things, she ordered diesel for their generators, fixed roof slates, soldered leaks and wormed the dogs. She also wrung the necks of half a dozen of their older birds which she then plucked and dressed. In the evenings she darned socks and jumpers, and sewed patches on sleeves. And, all the while, she looked out for snow.

By their fire she read the diaries of Francis Kilvert, the Victorian cleric, smiling at his foibles, nodding inwardly at his comments about the joys of walking alone in the Welsh borderlands, shuddering at his accounts of icy baths in his wintry parsonage home.

She still walked, of course, sometimes taking one or more of the dogs. And she met him, more than once, on the mountain: Blue.

Met would actually be the wrong word. For she caught sight of him, passed him at best. Almost always he'd be on a different path, wrapped in his greatcoat, higher or lower than her, scattering sheep, in a world of his own. Sometimes it wasn't even that. Sometimes she just sensed him, knew that he was there.

He wondered who she was... why she didn't speak... why she didn't acknowledge him, at least. They'd passed so close... there... on the ridge... more than once. Yet nothing. Not even a nod. It was as if he didn't exist.

There was no sign of her that day. Wind drove at the mountain. The sky was the colour of a Zeppelin and heavy with snow. He knew the look from France. He lifted the collar of his coat, his fingers catching something as he did so: a crag of scar tissue on his neck. He remembered, walked on.

Winter came to the top of the valley with the bite of a mantrap. The snow cut them off and locked them in. The first fall lasted three days and nights. She had known nothing like it. Tom, for his part, moaned, fiddled with his phone. He walked around the house talking about his lost teens, his formative years... ruined by snow. He declared – loudly and repeatedly – that he now knew why he'd left.

After lunch on the third day he shut himself in what they called their office and went through papers for old projects: things they'd abandoned in order to move to the Moonlight, schemes and ideas that she'd forgotten, but he had not. When she tried to open the door to talk to him he grabbed the handle on his side and turned the key in the lock. She went outside, wiped snow from the window. She watched him take papers from a tube, roll them out on the desk. She knocked on the glass. He drew down the blind.

When he first hit her – till then they'd each been guilty of pushes and shoves – it was five days in from the initial fall. She'd asked – through the door – if he was ever coming out of the office, from which he'd barely strayed. When he didn't answer, she asked him what he thought he was *playing* at.

At this, the door flew open and he swung at her, caught the side of her face with his fist.

'*I* am working. FUCKING WORKING!' he yelled. 'Doing what I was trained to do... doing what I'm *supposed* to do. How about you? What have you been *playing* at?'

She held her ground. Didn't move.

'And the farm?' she asked.

'What about it? You wanted it. *You* fucking farm it. Be my guest!'

He went back inside, slammed the door.

She stood there, felt her face.

The yard was darkening as she crossed it to the sheds. The dogs whimpered on their chains. She hushed them, took out her bike, left.

The house blazed with light. As she neared it she heard music: men's voices, carols. A lusty performance of *Good King Wenceslas* was followed by a melancholy tenor solo of *Silent Night*, the singing carrying over the still, blue-white park of *Y Diwedd*. The snow had frozen. It cracked under her as she stepped through the avenue of trees. A red-berried wreath rested on the front door. It opened before she could knock.

Her coat was taken by a nurse. A doctor, she presumed, greeted her in the great entrance hall. At the foot of the staircase stood a beautifully-decorated fir tree. A crystal chandelier lit the scene. The doctor gave her his arm and, together, they walked into the drawing room where the men who minutes earlier had been singing were gathered and waiting.

They were quiet now and received her with shy nods and smiles. Those who had been seated (and were able to do so) rose to their feet. The room was so hushed that, above the ticking of a clock, she could hear the log fire hiss and spit. Some of the men looked away: glad that she was there but nervous of her gaze.

The doctor broke the silence with a call for music. At the piano, a sightless soldier, the sockets of his eyes stitched in a way that suggested oak leaves, sounded a chord. He played the first bars of *We Wish You a Merry Christmas*, paused for a moment, then all of the men joined in. At its conclusion came cheers, laughter, conversation, tobacco smoke. A glass, its ruby contents pleasingly warm, was pressed into her hand. As she sipped she caught sight of herself in a mirror: long, cream dress, pearls, gloves. She wondered how she'd come by them, liked her look.

Next there were calls for dancing. Doors opened to a ballroom. It radiated light. It seemed familiar to her, but in another guise. A memory passed through her: leaves, the tennis net, a dead robin (light as a matchstick) on its side on a ledge (though perhaps that had been in another room, somewhere else in the house).

And now she saw him, the one she'd seen walking the mountain:

Blue. Except that, rather than being in a world of his own, he was walking towards her, across the room. In no time they were dancing, touching, close enough to feel one another's breath. And the other soldiers were dancing, too, seriously, studiously... with each other... waltzing, leading, being led.

In time the room darkened. Moonlight fell through the windows on the manoeuvres of those within, their shadows moving solemnly on the high, pale walls. The logs in the great fireplace burned slowly till all that remained was feathery ash. For a while the music continued albeit faltering and fading, as if one by one its players were taking their leave. Finally, it stopped.

The room was cold now. No one else danced but her and Blue. Their breath rose in white clouds above them. Their shoes moved softly through the leaves at their feet. Each of them chill as porcelain... their hands, their waists, their cheeks.

For several nights she and Tom slept apart. Then, on Christmas Eve, he threw himself at her feet. He begged her forgiveness, and, as he wept, she comforted him. She reached in her jacket pocket for a tissue. As she drew it out a small object fell to the floor. It rolled and became caught in the valley between two flagstones. A button. Tom picked it up, looked.

'A soldier's,' he said.

He held it between his thumb and forefinger, peered at the crest.

'Old... from a tunic.'

He looked at her, his eyes red.

'I found it,' she said.

On Christmas morning Tom brought down the first lamb. He carried it from the mountain, over the snow-covered fields at the back of the Moonlight, boots splashing through the slush of the yard. He stood at the doorstep, holding it.

Tom shook, sobbed, cradled the lamb: throat ripped out, pink bib to its small breast.

She took it from him. Held it

After that there were other lambs. All of them dead.   She   stopped counting. He stopped bringing them down, said that from now on he'd be leaving them up there, on the mountain: blood and guts... *bait*. That's what he wanted, he said. To turn it all red.

She lost track of the days.

'Truce over!' he told her one morning between Christmas and New Year. He marched out into the yard, went up the mountain, took Elwyn's old gun.

All day she heard him firing... on the slopes, on the ridge, near the peak. He kept up his bombardment even as the sky grew black: the dying of the light, if anything, seeming to spur him.

Then he stopped, just as suddenly as he'd begun. And all was quiet and still again, and the mountain disappeared into the dark.

She heard the pick-up rake the grid at the top of their track, its wheels scudding across the brown slush of the yard. A door opened, slammed. Next he was in the kitchen, by the stove, stamping, warming himself.

'I've shot the fox. Killed it,' he said.

Now he was at the sink, grinning, soaping his hands.

'Bluecoat,' he said. 'A bloody bluecoat.'

And at that moment what she wanted, more than anything, was to see those hands of his that he was turning under the noisy, streaming tap... have him take them from under there and hold them up to her... so that she might see and know that they were still white, still soft, still supple... *still* a draughtsman's hands.

And yet she did not want to ask, or look.

The latch hadn't caught and the kitchen door swung open. Light threw itself on the yard. It was sleeting. She saw the vague shape of the pick-up, something over one side of it, like a sack.

His voice came after her as she stepped into the slush.

'Been up there for years, I expect. Four cartridges,' Tom called out. 'Wouldn't lie down. But I got him. I got him in the end. Big, ugly bitch.'

She was crossing the yard now.

Through the sleet she could see the line of the pick-up, the heap over one side at the back.

The Press

The sky is the steel blue of my fertiliser sacks and he is all birdcage ribs, shoulder blades sharp-cut, a wind chime of bones, brown as dried blood, bobbing on the piebald's bare back.

They follow in legion – horses, cars, caravans – out of the white sun. Their convoy streams, jangling and glinting, snaking between stone walls that are slipping and splattered with scrambled egg lichen.

I am rattling the plough in thin Top Field, spitting out stones, ripping at roots, cursing for the sake of cursing. I cut the engine. The tractor shudders and stops. I unhook the door of the cab. It swing-scrapes open and hangs useless on the hill.

Now they are clattering through my yard – medieval army on the move – between the barns and the back of the house. The dog is there, fretful and fierce, on his chain by the tap. They ignore him. Their own dogs don't even bark. The boy on the piebald waits as two of their number drag open the gate to the fields. The piebald steps sideways, and back. The boy kicks the horse on and leads them into and out of the hoof-pitted hollow (where my cows meet in the mornings before milking). The same men pull the gate shut, loop the orange twine over the post that is green, rotting and finned with fungus. They walk to re-join the rest. In Cliff Field the boy pulls the piebald to a halt and they stop, all of them, and settle.

Come the cool dark I watch them from my windows: shapes

moving around fires that wave and crack. I have kept the cattle in their stalls in the shed. Without seeing them I know how they are standing: still, listening, eyes to the wall.

In the morning the people come knocking for water, which they are already taking from the tap in the yard. It splutters into buckets and bottles and pans. I ask the men how long they shall be here and why they have come. They tell me to speak to The Boy. The women nod as they pass, but say nothing.

I did not buy this runt of a farm. I inherited it. Twenty-two acres of nettled cwms, gorsed ridges, thorned copses, ten cows, two tractors (barely amounting to one) and a single roll of barbed wire snagged with yellow wool. It was the 'gift' of my Uncle Rhys – my great uncle, in fact – who scratched a living here, mouldering to his last in this mausoleum of stopped clocks, spent matches, dead flies and dust.

My parents first brought me here when I was young. As a small boy I was drawn to the heavy black range in the kitchen (that I was forbidden to touch). To me it was a train: inexplicably lodged in the walls of the house, yet of the kind an old man like Rhys would surely catch. We always left before dark. *Yr Hollt* (to use the Welsh; The Cleft in English) had only candles and oil lamps. It still does.

When they have finished taking water from the yard I leave the house to milk the cows. After this I walk the herd to the middle meadow. The cows move slowly. Empty of milk, they are full of thought. I stand among them and look down at the camp. Children run between caravans. Thick-set men organise scrap on a flatbed truck. A generator chugs, stutters, chugs again. Women gather at a washing line. Behind them is the sea, like smashed glass. The women are bare-armed. They see me watching. I walk back to the house.

Afternoon. I take the tractor to Top Field, start on the far part.

The plough snags on a spine of rock. I jump from the cab, try to loosen the share. It cuts my left arm where my sleeve is rolled-up. I finish and go down to the house. I run cold water over the cut, strip and wash myself at the sink. I bind my arm with a towel, and say that I shall live.

Evening. Kitchen table. I unscrew my flower press and take from it the orchid I placed inside it two nights before: a pink pyramidal that I found – stem-snapped – out on the dunes. I have only candlelight, but see details that I did not notice before: small tears and abrasions that trouble and disappoint me. I wonder if these happened during my pressing or were already there. I open the album and place the orchid between clean pages. I write notes on one on the pages about how I found it. Below these I add some facts that I take from a book that can only have belonged to Rhys. I discovered it when I moved here: under the stairs, in a box, with his pencil. The book is disbound. The dry, disordered leaves have diagrams, Latin names in italics, lines from poets. Scattered out of sequence are a dozen watercolour plates, among them illustrations of cowslips, wood anemones, poppies and daffodils.

I turn the leaves of my album gently, conscious of the fragility of the flowers that lie inside. The pyramidal rests between a bee orchid 'found ragged after rains' and a twayblade 'recovered during a spring storm that shifted whole dunes'. The cluster pleases me. I pause for a moment over its incidental symmetry.

I place in the press a broken white vetch I found while coming down to the house from the cows. The pyramidal has left small, dark smears on the papers inside. I position the vetch carefully, making sure its petals are away from the marks. I spread its flowers and leaves with the tips of my fingers. I lay the other piece of paper on top of it (having first turned this so that its virgin side shall bear down on the vetch). That the press belonged to Rhys I have no doubt. I found it under an eave. The boards are carved with lilies, their grooved outlines painted black. They wreathe a Bible verse.

**Grass withers and flowers fall, but
The Word of Our God endures forever.**

Isaiah 40:8

I screw down the corners. The boards are chipped and chafed. The screws and nuts are a jumble, but they work. I think again of Rhys's albums: the ones he must have had. Before now I have spent days – weeks – searching for them. Occasionally I have felt close to them. At other times I have imagined the tindery flowers igniting in blooms of flames... Rhys's pages curling to ash on the coals of the kitchen range.

I draw down the board – tight – on the vetch. I sit and look at my arm. My rituals have made me forget the cut, which is deep but clean. A scar shall come, I know. I carry my candle upstairs. Night enfolds the farm.

In the morning, after milking, I find myself inspecting the apple trees: black-barked hunchbacks that cling to the patch behind the house. Their ugly fruit, when it resentfully comes, will, I know, be hard and sour. I wonder if it was ever sweet. Passing the low barn, opposite the cowshed, I catch sight of the millstone. In another age a horse drove it in circle after crushing circle over whatever it was that filled its trough. The stone stands cold in the barn's grey gloom: time-frozen, a kind of menhir now.

In the afternoon I interfere with Tractor Number One, wrenching from it parts for Tractor Number Two (though all the time doubting the usefulness of my actions). Jenkins, my neighbour from *Y Goedlan,* comes and makes a fool of himself. He glares at me in the yard as he drives past me to the camp, his dog lunging and barking beside him. I run after them. He stops near the caravans, hits his horn. Some children who were playing stand still and look at him. Their parents, and others, come to their doors. Jenkins jumps onto the back of his pick-up, like some pumped-up preacher – only he's waving a shotgun, not a Bible or hymnal.

He shouts that dogs from the camp have killed his sheep (though I know he has none and farms only six mothed hens at a place even poorer than mine). He tells them that if they don't leave he'll come back and kill them... and their dogs... every last one. They stare at Jenkins. No one says a word. The generator chugs as if ridiculing him. He gets down from the pick-up and back in its cab. He reverses and then arcs around in the field. Alongside me he puts down his window. His beard is flecked with spit. He snarls, 'Dylech wybod yn well' (that *I* should know better), stabs his finger at me. Then he drives off, as he came, dog barking and jumping, its breath on the glass. I look towards the camp. The people look at me. I say that the gun wasn't loaded and that Jenkins has problems and that he will do them no harm. I say that I am sorry, and I turn and walk back to the house.

Later one of the men I spoke with comes again for water from the tap. I tell him I need to talk to someone from the camp. He says he'll speak to The Boy, and lugs away a drum.

Evening. I set the press down on the table, undoing in stages the nuts that fasten its corners. I orchestrate their removal so that the pressure on the flower inside is at all times consistent. Rough handling now will crease stems and tendrils and even tear petals apart. I lift the top board and place it on the table next to my album. Slowly, I separate the papers that shroud the white vetch that I inserted the night before. I stare at it. Its small blooms lie flat but the stem and tendrils are now more black than green. I wonder if my pressing was too hasty, too harsh. The bruising, I hope, shall pass. I lift out the blue paper, cupping it, then tilting it so that the vetch slides into my album, which is already open and waiting. I write notes. 'Poisonous to ruminants if eaten plentifully,' Rhys's book warns of certain strains. My guilt at the flower's likely felling by one of my cows subsides somewhat.

Having curated the vetch I realise I have no other flowers to press. I contemplate a walk in the morning to some scrub where the saltmarsh dissipates to sand. Yellow flag irises favour its dune slack. I could go further: to the reed beds where marsh orchids rear themselves at the mouth of the *nant*. On my side of the stream the dunes are home to horsetail, wintergreen and, swears my neighbour Martha James, widow of *Ty Gwyn*, fen orchid (if you know where to look). I have yet to see its lemon-white flowers, and could never pick them if I did. Should the air be heavy, as it has been of late, I may take to the cliffs. Before now I have found whitlow, a Mediterranean wanderer, and sea lavenders of a kind not recorded in Rhys's book. Perhaps the woods, haunt of herb paris, purple gromwell and ramsons, shall have me... drowsy and still.

Morning, and I am on the cliffs. Above me ravens ride in lazy circles. I see squill, golden samphire, restharrow, gentian and aster. Sea thrift speckles the sward in pink and white shoals. From the bluff above *Cildraeth Glas* I see Jenkins. He's stretched-out, on his back, on the pebbled shore below. Even from my height I can see the crack in his skull. Waves fall on his boots. The tide already has his dog. I watch for a while to see if Jenkins moves. His eyes stare at the sky. I walk back to the house, quickly, between the gorse.

At the camp I look for The Boy. I see his piebald, tethered. I knock doors and windows. I shout for The Boy. I shout for him to come to the house. I go there, and wait.

When he comes I do not hear him. He seats himself at the kitchen table. A candle burns between us.

'You have to leave,' I say. 'You can't stay.'

The Boy says nothing.

'Why *here*?' I ask.

He is as calm as I am anxious. 'We go where we are called. What's *your* reason?'

'God knows!' I say.

Rain spots the window above the sink.

'You keep a book,' he says, '... like your uncle.'

'Rhys?' I say, wondering how he can know.

'Cemeteries of flowers. Both of you.'

'What of it?' I say.

'We can help you,' he tells me.

'Help?' I say (my voice barely a whisper). 'How?'

'This place is barren... dead. My sister has... gifts. She will heal it, *if* we stay.'

'Gifts?'

'She is blessed.'

'How long will you stay?' I ask.

'Till the apples fall. That's all.'

Two days later and I'm milking the cows. The warm milk streams from them: twice the normal yield. I pat their sides. My arm is no longer sore. I twist it and see that the cut from the share has closed. A dry scab runs its length.

Summer unfolds: the most bountiful I have known. The fields brim with fat red loam. A month of drought does nothing to lessen the lushness of The Cleft. Crops that have only ever grown small or riddled rise strong and clean. Even an apple I take early from one of the trees is unscarred and sweet. I speak to one of the men. I ask him which of the young women is The Boy's sister. He points to her... and my desire is sown.

All summer my longing scalds. It is as if the brambles and nettles that have withered on the land now grow back... inside me... thorning my throat, stinging my eyes, strangling my organs and veins.

On an evening of starred, slate darkness she stands at my door, and steps into my candlelight.

The bed's counterpane is cold. She tells me to lie back, while she undresses. I am already unclothed. We hear sounds from the camp: laughter, singing, then clapping in rhythm with the singing. My windows have no curtains. Fire from the camp flickers in the glazing of one of Rhys's Bible verses, framed on the wall.

The one who comes to me I will certainly not cast out

John 6:37

She climbs onto me. We shiver with our touching. Red flames writhe in Rhys's sun-paled text. We grow warm till we are burning, raging and, finally, in my hot, wet fever I am garlanded with all of those stems and blooms that, in my entrancement, rise to reveal themselves from Rhys's found albums of flowers. Lady of the night, wild honeysuckle, goldilocks, virgin-bower, lords-and-ladies, shepherd's delight, beard tongue, cockscomb, sea stork's bill. *Reaping*. Devil's horsewhip, butcher's broom, goat's beard, viper's bugloss, buckhorn plantain, dog-rose, dog-violet, adder's tongue, snake's head. *Pressing*.

Morning, and she is gone. On the bedsheets there is blood. I look at my arm. The wound from the share has re-opened. I take the sheets to the kitchen and soak them in the sink. I wring them and throw them over the apple trees. They are like something from war-time, parachutes of pilots baled out.

Autumn. The days dawn with oxblood skies. Apples I've neglected fall in the patch at the back of the house and are picked over by wasps. The yield from the cows has ebbed. More often than not fog cloaks The Cleft. Rain drills at the house and land, sometimes for days. The dunes that defend my bottom fields are being sucked into the sea by high tides.

In wintry light I take the dog along the bridle path that borders the farm. The grass is matted and soaked. Cow parsley rots in the banks. Blackberries bleed in my fingers and are sickly in my mouth. As we walk back to the house I beat at thistles with a stick. The day dies before it has begun.

Evening. I search again for Rhys's albums: running my hands inside chimney breasts, through dust on the tops of beams and wardrobes. I pace landings and bedrooms, listening for creaks that are different or new. Darkness forces me to stop.

I wake to the sound of hooves in the yard. I roll naked from my bed and stand by the window. The Boy, stripped to the waist, is on the piebald's bare back. He reins the horse to a stop and looks up at me.

Men enter my bedroom and force me downstairs. One is the man I've spoken to. Others are waiting in the yard.

The Boy kicks the piebald on.

In the thin light we follow him. Hands shove at my shoulders as we cross the yard. My feet splash through slurry. The Boy halts the piebald by the cowshed. He nods to the barn opposite, and I'm pushed inside. I see the millstone.

My first screams come as I'm bundled into its trough.

Women I recognise from the camp hold down my legs. They drag my feet, left and right, over the rough sides of the stone's valley. Men pinion my arms and shoulders. Behind them other men lower a harness over the piebald. This agitates the horse and it moves forwards and backwards, jerking its head. The men comfort it with words and pats and strokes. It steadies.

Next they heave a beam into, then through, the hole in the millstone, and fix the end of the timber behind the horse. The Boy puts blinkers on the piebald, whispers to it and gets on its back. I have no hope of moving for all of the hands that are holding me down.

Petals fall on my face and chest: vetch, gentian, violets. Through their tumbling shower I see The Girl. She is among the women, scattering me, anointing me. They smile and nod as the perfumed petals fall.

Driftwood

'Say that again,' Davies said.

'What?' his wife said.

'About Brynley Baines, and the beach.'

'Have you even *been* listening to me?' Susan said.

'Of course. I was just... distracted, for a moment.'

'*Distracted*?' She shut the fridge door, sighed, slumped her shoulders, tilted her head, and spoke in a tone which made plain her exasperation.

'He's been going *down*, to the *beach* and just *sitting* on this log. For hours.'

'How d'you mean *sitting*?' Davies said.

'I mean *sitting*,' she said, 'legs astride, you know... as if he were on a horse or something.'

'Is that so strange?' Davies said.

'At night, Stu? In the nude?'

'Nude?' Davies said. 'I never heard you mention that.'

'Do you *ever* listen to me?'

'All the time,' Davies said.

She poured herself a second juice. He bit on some toast, wondered when it was he'd last seen Baines, thought of him – paunchily naked – on this log of his. The latter wasn't something he particularly *wanted* to picture, but he was curious nonetheless.

'So what does Carys say?' he asked.

'She wants us to go over. Have a chat, you know. Old times. Bring Brynley out of his shell.'

'Old times?'

'School, uni.'

'That was thirty years ago,' said Davies. He chewed some toast. 'Maybe he should see a doctor.'

'He *is* a doctor,' Susan said.

'Oh yeah. I was forgetting,' Davies said. 'Are they still on the bay?'

'Still there... over the cove. They're so lucky. I'd love to live in a house like that.'

'And he's walking down there to the beach at night... naked?'

'Exactly.'

'Why ever's he doing that?'

'He's like a zombie when he's down there. That's what Carys says. Their dog comes in and tugs her. That's how she knows Brynley's down there... on his log. It's an Irish setter.'

'Clever dog,' Davies said.

Susan loaded some dishes into the washer. 'Isn't he president of the Rotary or something? I'm sure we read it in the *Star*. It had his photograph, with Carys,' she said.

'Past-president, I should think... by now,' Davies said.

They sipped coffee.

'So, anyway, it happened again last night. She wants you to have a word.'

'A word?'

'Yeah, you know. Man-to-man. She's worried that if this carries on he'll get arrested, or a patient's going to see him and he'll get struck off or sectioned. I said we'll go on Saturday.'

'Saturday?'

'For lunch. After we get the leaf vac from Johnny Williams.'

'What am I going to say?' Davies said. 'I mean, how do you raise a thing like that? Being on a log? In the dark? Nude?'

'Well, if I were you I'd take him aside and begin with some old uni stuff... you know: did he know Mike Wallis was a minister now, how Mike's a good listener by all accounts, had he seen Clem Pritchard lately...'

'Clem Pritchard? Brynley Baines hated Clem Pritchard. Clem Pritchard held his head in the toilet at school and flushed it while half the class laughed.'

'Okay, forget Clem, but then just get into this log business. Gently,' Susan said.

'Get into it,' Davies repeated, 'gently.'

Davies drummed the steering wheel. Susan was full of the leaf vac: how Johnny Williams had discounted her ten per cent without her even asking, how she clearly still had a nice backside, how she couldn't wait to get to work on those leaves. This matter of the leaves was something they talked about a lot every autumn. Half of the leaves were from the Jarretts' horse chestnut next door, and, as Davies often pointed out, weren't even rightfully theirs to sweep. There was also, he said, something unnatural about blowing and sucking things, out of doors, at least with a machine. His wife, however, invariably won out in such matters and the vac was now stowed in their boot. Her eyes gleamed. Davies pictured himself blowing Edgar Jarrett's leaves, in the way that he knew he would be later, as Jarrett held back his lounge curtain and watched.

'Well, look!' said Carys, scampering towards them over the lawn. She wore white trousers and a blue-and-white kimono-type garment that, to Davies, looked a little light for the time of year. 'Bryn!' she called without looking back. She kissed them and then turned to the house behind her. 'Brynley! Where are you?' she called.

Baines bowled out goofily from the porch like some gameshow host from the studio wings.

'Howdie pardners!' he said, all grins.

The setter was with him, barking and twirling.

Carys called out 'Lady! Settle down!' The setter ignored her.

They went into the house. As they did so Davies's eyes fell on Carys's toenails, which were bright pink. He wondered why it was that some women, like Carys, painted their toenails and others, like Susan, lusted for a leaf vac.

After lunch Carys said to Baines, 'Bryn, why don't you and Stu take Lady on the beach while I clean-up with Susan?'

Susan gave Davies a look that told him this was his cue and said, 'Yeah, you guys get out from under our feet so that we girls can have a good catch-up.'

Baines put Lady on one of those retractable leads that can both grant a dog slack and rein it in. He showed Davies how it worked as they walked down the drive. They followed a path between some bushes of gorse, then cut through the grass-tufted dunes at the bottom and came onto the beach. Baines did his thing with the lead and Lady zigzagged over the sand.

'Great dog,' Davies said.

'Irish setter,' said Baines. He reined her in a little. The lead whirred. 'Got a dog, Stu?'

'No,' Davies said. 'Susan has her cats.'

'Cat woman, hey?' said Baines, eyes fixed on Lady.

'Twenty-six years,' Davies said.

'Hell, Stu,' Baines said, turning. 'Has it been that long?'

The beach was empty. Some gulls wheeled and shrieked over the falling waves. The air had a chill and the sky a determined whiteness that Davies knew heralded winter. He zipped his fleece, stuck his hands in the pockets.

'Still teaching at the uni?' asked Baines as they walked.

'They haven't rumbled me yet,' said Davies.

'And writing? You're still doing that?'

'Trying to.'

Baines stopped. 'Tell me you're doing another Harry Hawkwind. He's our favourite. You know that, don't you Stu? The Tomahawk Tec,' said Baines. His tone was bitter-sweet.

'I killed him off, Bryn,' said Davies. 'Blaze of glory. You must know that.'

'I know, I know,' Baines said. 'But look at Conan Doyle... Sherlock Holmes. I mean, Stu, a guy like Harry Hawkwind... he should never die.'

'Ten slugs in the chest, Bryn. Burial according to ancient Comanche rights. Hard to bring a fella back from any of that – even Harry.'

They continued walking.

'You're right,' said Baines. 'Still, I expect he was good to you. In his prime.'

'Oh yeah. Harry was good to me,' Davies said. 'The TV rights have helped.'

Baines stopped. 'TV rights? What's happening? A series? A film? Carys will love this. You've always been too modest, Stu. Kept things to yourself. That's your problem.'

'Nothing's happening, Bryn,' Davies said. 'My agent just sold the rights to a company in the States, that's all. They won't do anything with them. They just buy them to stop anyone else having them. Shove them in a safe.'

'Are you serious?' Baines said.

'That's how it is, Bryn,' said Davies.

'Jesus!' said Baines. 'Whatever happened to... what do they call it?... the American Dream? I mean... that's *criminal*, Stu.'

'Way of the world,' said Davies.

'So this company, or whoever... they've got Harry, and he's *theirs*?'

'Bang to rights.'

'Jesus!' Baines said again. He continued walking, as if in a daze.

Ahead of them Lady was barking.

Davies looked along the beach and saw what he felt sure could be only one thing: Brynley Baines's log.

Davies's first thought was that 'log' – as in something you threw on a fire – was most certainly the wrong word. For a start, the thing was massive, an entire tree, more or less. By the look of things it had been hefted ashore and dumped by an unusually high tide. Its base pointed seaward, the roots clawing at the air as if somehow trying to right the stricken monster or drag it back to the water that fell teasingly out of reach. Those of its branches which weren't snapped or smashed dug into the sand on either side of the trunk, as if also part of this attempted propulsion. The 'log' seemed to Davies more like some kind of shore-dwelling dinosaur than anything else. He pictured Baines, naked on its back, holding onto its roots, as if they were horns or tusks.

Davies looked down as they approached it, wondered how to begin. Baines's tasselled loafers sank and slipped as he struggled through the sand. Davies wondered why he didn't have more appropriate footwear, given how close he and Carys lived to the beach.

It was then that Davies remembered how as a boy Baines had worn callipers to school, at least to begin with, because of something that was wrong with his legs. How, more than once, Clem Pritchard had tried to take them off. How, more than once, he – Davies – had also been there, behind Pritchard. One time Pritchard succeeded. He waved the rods and clamps around before flinging them into some nettles while Baines watched and wept. Baines hadn't worn them to school after that.

Davies remembered his mission.

'That's some lump of wood,' he began. 'What is it Bryn? Elm? Oak? How long's it been there?'

Baines didn't answer. He made a show of trying to rein-in Lady, whose leash had become snagged on some of the roots.

Baines's display convinced Davies that this was his timber.

Davies touched the tree. The bark had been stripped and the bole bleached to a honey-ish blend of grey and fawn. It was pocked here and there with big, dark knots that were like eyes. It was taut and smooth and cool under his fingers.

Baines finished fussing with Lady and came alongside.

'Wonder where it's come from... where it's going,' Davies said.

'Oh I don't think it's going anywhere,' said Baines. 'I mean, look at it.'

'Tide'll have it sooner or later,' said Davies. 'You'll probably come here one day, find it gone.'

'You think?' said Baines.

'Force of Nature, Bryn. Power of the ocean. Next stop Ireland. America even. I think its days are done here. Don't you?'

'We'd better get back,' said Baines. 'The girls will be wondering.'

Baines turned, let Lady whir out on the leash.

'So how's work, Bryn?' Davies asked. 'A practice as popular as yours... must be stressful at times.'

'Oh, it's fine, Stu, fine. There's the odd thing now and again, but... Oh damn!' said Baines.

They looked down the beach at Lady. Her back was arched in a way that indicated only one thing.

'And I didn't bring a bag,' said Baines.

Lady skittered off as they walked towards her. Baines scuffed sand over her poop with his loafers. He scanned the houses over the cove.

'Could've happened to anyone, Bryn. Tide'll take care of it,' said Davies.

They walked on. At the foot of the dunes Davies stopped.

'Bryn, there's something I've been meaning to say,' he said.

Baines made a clicking sound with the leash. A look that was part surprised, part serious came over his face.

'About those things that went on when we were in school,' Davies continued. 'Well, the fact is... I'm sorry.'

Baines nodded in a doctorly way, as if listening to a patient outlining their symptoms.

Davies went on, 'Mike Wallis is a minister now, and a very good listener, by all accounts.'

A silence fell between them. Lady barked.

'Mike Wallis?' said Baines. 'Who'd've thought? I haven't seen Mike for years.'

He and Davies stood there looking back at the water.

'I just—' began Davies.

'You're not still worrying about school, are you, Stu? Look, all of that was a long time ago. Maybe you should give Mike a call. Who's your doctor? Which surgery? If you like, you can transfer to me.'

'No, I'm fine, Bryn... thanks... honestly,' Davies said.

'Sure?'

'Yes... really.'

They climbed one of the dunes back towards the path, struggled for breath at its peak.

'So how was he?' Susan began in the car on their way home.

'Lucid enough,' Davies said.

'*Lucid*?' she said, stopping for a moment and then beginning again to fiddle with a scarf inside the collar of her fleece. 'Did you talk?'

'We talked.'

'What about?' she said (turning up the heater).

'Lots of things,' Davies said. 'Harry Hawkwind—'

'Harry Hawkwind?' she said. 'What's Harry Hawkwind got to do with any of this?'

'Brynley brought him up. He's a fan.'

'You were supposed to be talking about the log. That's what

we went there for,' Susan said. She reached and snapped down the heater a notch.

'We talked about the log,' Davies said.

'Hail Mary to that,' said Susan.

'I saw it,' he said.

'The log?' She turned to him. 'What's it like?'

'Big,' he said. 'Smooth. More of a tree than a log.'

'Did he... own up to anything?'

'Not really.'

'Just as long as you talked about it.'

'I said we did, didn't I?'

Davies turned down the heater a notch.

'He had this idea of bringing Harry back,' Davies said.

'I told you what to say, Stu,' Susan said, shoving her hands in the front pockets of her fleece. 'Resurrecting Harry Hawkwind wasn't one of them.'

'I know. Can we drop this?'

'I think we'd better,' she said.

She turned up the heater.

Davies was deep in a dream in which he was blowing leaves over a hedge and onto Edgar Jarrett's lawn with the aid of their new vac. The sound of various *Oh Noes* and *We'll Come Right Aways* caused him, reluctantly, to wake. Susan put down the phone. 'That was Carys,' she said, skipping out of bed and turning on the lights. 'We've got to get over there.'

'It's... ten past three,' said Davies, looking at the clock on the table on her side of the bed. 'What's happened?'

'Never mind that now. Just get yourself dressed,' she said. 'Second thoughts: don't get dressed. Just put on your dressing gown. I'll grab you a towel.'

'A towel?' said Davies. 'What do I need a towel for?'

A full moon hung over the bay as Susan hurried their Honda along the coast road. Davies asked her what was going on, but also found himself looking at the moon and the etched expanses of its seas. He wondered which of them might be Tranquillity.

When they got down to the beach Carys was already there, sinking in slingbacks on the slope of one of the dunes. Her face was a mess of streaming make-up that had Davies wondering if she'd put it on before or after she called them. The sea was right up to the dunes so that it was sloshing practically at their feet. She raised her arm and let out a horrible moan.

Susan and Davies followed her finger onto the water. The tree that had been on the beach was being taken out by the tide. Silhouetted on its trunk was the seated (and, Davies presumed, naked) form of Brynley Baines (who appeared to have hold of two roots, as if he were at the wheel of some galleon or man-of-war of old).

'I thought you spoke to him?' Susan began.

'I did,' Davies said.

'Well, get in there!' she said, taking his dressing gown from his shoulders.

'Are you serious?' Davies said.

'Give me your pyjamas.'

The water was bitterly cold. Davies broke into a kind of crawl, hoping he wouldn't have a heart attack or stroke on account of Baines's *idiocy*… his *recklessness*.

Davies crashed through the black water. *No wonder Clem Pritchard had held Baines's stupid head down that toilet*, he thought to himself.

He got alongside the tree, trying to avoid its sharp branches. He trod water, called out between gasps. Not *Bryn* or *Brynley* now, but *Baines*. 'Baines!' he shouted. 'For God's sake!'

He reached for Baines's leg. Baines kicked his heel down on him:

first on Davies's arm, then on his head.

Strong, purposeful kicks.

They were getting further from the shore. The swell lifted and dropped them. Carys and Susan's voices came in splinters from the dark beach.

Baines's leg was white and shiny, like the belly of a fish.

Davies reached for it.

Baines kept kicking

and kicking

and kicking...

The Lock

Leaves carpeted the canal almost completely. A narrowboat in drab livery of green and burgundy moved steadily through the water. Alone at the stern stood Bevan, hand on the tiller-bar. Staring at the trail of gold and rust ahead, and partially-hypnotised by the boat's pumping rhythm, he found himself thinking of an optician he'd visited years previously... in the city: an old-style practice with a brass name-plate in a side street, a wood-panelled examining room and a ticking clock. The optician – suited, calm, deferential – had shown him a series of cards. Not in a game, but to assess whether he might be colour-blind. On them were numbers, shapes, concealed to a degree by their pigment. The man turned over the cards methodically, noting quietly Bevan's response. 'And this one?' he whispered, going through the pack. Among them, Bevan remembered, had been a ship (in outline) and also, he seemed to think, an anchor. Later there had been a waterway of some kind that he had taken to be a river.

The narrowboat sent a low, syrupy wake to the banks. In places this broke the film of leaves, giving the covering the look of some holed and ripped garment. After a few moments these wounds closed so that, behind the beating boat, there was no evidence of its journey, no sign that its heavy, black hull had ever been there.

Bevan went over what the woman in the office at the terminus had said.

– He'd be on his own out there. Now. At this time. There'd be no one else.

   – That would be fine.

   – And the water might freeze. It wasn't unknown.

   – He'd cope.

   – Did he know anything... about the canal... where it went?

   – He knew the valley, and the hills: three summers as a boy on his aunt and uncle's farm. It would come back (the lie of the land), soon enough. He wanted to remind himself. One last trip. (For this he used the Welsh.)

The woman seemed not to listen. She wore a stained navy-blue body-warmer. Broken veins littered her face. The filthy shack stank of paraffin and dog. Ancient pamphlets curled in a window whose glass was beaded with damp. What looked to Bevan to be some kind of quiz played out its pantomime on a muted TV.

   – Days were short now, nights long, the woman continued (now also in Welsh).

He took out his wallet, showed her the money.

She threw the hawser to the deck from the wharf, walked off without waiting. He steered the boat – smokily – from its mooring. *The Keeper's Queen* read peeling white letters on one side of her, the same in Welsh on the other.

'Old queen...' thought Bevan. '... Queen Mother.' But she would do.

What light there had been drained from the sky quickly. The boat pumped through the water, passing skeletal trees. Bevan gripped the tiller-bar tightly, as if he had hold – in his pale, cold fingers – of the faintly pulsing heart of the whole, freezing, blackening land.

In the morning he woke confused by his surroundings: the chill cabin, the sun spearing the thin curtains opposite his bunk. In a cupboard in the galley he found a tin of beans, a box of damp teabags and some powdered milk that had dried to a crust. As he ate and drank he let the rings of the gas stove burn on for warmth. Afterwards he went on deck and steered the boat from under the canopy of hazel where he'd moored the night before. The vessel soon acquired the rhythm of the previous day. The sun fell upon her in the breaks between the trees. Bevan felt its glow on his face and hands.

About mid-day the boat entered a gorge. On each side rock-faces rose in moss-cankered cliffs. The sight of them – saplings groping from crevices, lichen blistering the steepling stone – caused Bevan to remember... two Regency terraces on a once prosperous street: in their day grand, high-end townhouses, and, even in their decline, still worthy of 'listing', preservation: iron railings, porticoed frontages, facings of Portland stone that had remained gracious in spite of graffiti and grime. The shifts of city life had trapped them in a suburb-gone-to-seed... a slum, in fact. His people had pulled them down – swift action was always the thing... before questions could be asked. And then he'd waited. In time the district was fashionable once more. Four high-rise blocks went up in their place. Each with a gymnasium, private parking, concierge and, above all, leases that favoured the landlord: him. Progress – it had to be made. Bevan let the boat beat on.

The vessel moved through the water in a way that seemed to say it had no need of his hand on her. Entering a curve, Bevan glanced down at the tiller-bar. The slightly twisted fingers and leathery skin that met his eyes surprised him. He thought at first he'd caught sight of someone else's limb – an old and breathless man's – then realised it was his.

He stopped for a lunch of scraps scavenged from the galley. From his mooring he studied the empty countryside: neatly hedged fields in the lowlands lifting to hills more grey than green. The land was completely still.

In the afternoon he entered a tunnel. Moisture from the bricked ceiling dripped onto his head. In the half-light a boat approached from the opposite end. The noise from their engines swelled to a roar as the boats neared. As the other passed, Bevan nodded and waved. The man and woman aboard made no response, fixated, so it seemed, on their vessel's safe passage. He noticed their dress: the man in a cap, neckerchief, and dark dungarees; the woman shawled and heavy-skirted. Bevan turned as their boat pulled into the eyelet of light at the end of the gloom, smoke clouding the vague shape of the vessel's stern. At his end, meanwhile, *The Keeper's Queen* emerged into a wash of pink light from the collapsing sun.

Bevan looked for somewhere to moor. He found a wharf behind which rose an embankment that seemed part of a railway: a signal and telegraph posts visible along the top. This puzzled him because he had no knowledge of a line in the valley. As a boy he'd caught two (or had it been three?) buses and then walked the last mile and a half to *Y Groes* (The Cross), his aunt and uncle's farm. He tied the narrowboat alongside.

That night, in the yellow light of the cabin, he went over his plans. Fifty lodges in the woods to begin with. Five times that number eventually, when the watercourses had been diverted and the lake finished and filled. The golf course to be nine holes initially, rolling out to eighteen. On the site, a clubhouse (licensed), gym, spa, café and shops. Off it, to catch the spending of those who might stray, a filling station, pub-restaurant and something wholesome, *nut-cutlety*, in a prettied-up mill or barn.

Later, as he slept, he dreamed of *Y Groes*. He saw plainly the thick, whitewashed stone of the farmhouse, the slate roof, the low barns and the rough orchard at the back. Suddenly his uncle was striding over its yard, hand around the neck of a dead, swinging fox. Next he was dabbing blood on Bevan's nose and cheeks. 'Red in tooth and claw, boy,' he was saying as he did so, though Bevan, looking at the animal (its brush and hind legs on the floor of the yard) could see nothing of his uncle save his boiler-suit trousers and boots. These turned and pounded off, the arse and legs of the fox sliding through slurry: its eyes, so it seemed to him, beaded on Bevan.

A scream woke him in his bunk. He sat up in the dark. The scream rang out again: a vixen, he presumed, on the hills. He remembered the call from his childhood: nights in a curtainless bedroom at *Y Groes*, moonlight moving on the chill walls through the branches of the trees at the top of the apple orchard. Bevan went on deck, pissed into the canal, his urine drumming loudly. He zipped himself and turned. As he did so a movement caught his eye... a figure... moving nimbly, busily, stepping along the boat, up to the bow. On the towpath a moonbeam illuminated the form of a harnessed horse. Suddenly the silver light was extinguished by cloud. In the darkness Bevan thought he heard a muffled whinny. When the moonlight returned both horse and man were gone.

Come daybreak Bevan lay on his bunk and wondered about the night before. Eventually he breakfasted and went on deck. A hoar frost coated the boat and bank with its white crystals. In the cold air his breath hung around him like smoke. Ice pressed against the hull in a thin sheet impregnated with leaves. It splintered as he fired the boat up and swung her out.

From the stern he scanned the land. *He should have seen it by now*, he told himself. *A farm couldn't move, couldn't hide... could it?*

And then he caught sight of it, in its cleft, on the hillside, where it had always been: *Y Groes*.

Mooring the boat, he cut over fields, crossed stiles, climbed gates. All the while he kept his eyes on the nearing farm, somehow feeling that to remove them might allow it to escape. He was surprised at the vigour with which he advanced. It was as if the farm, which he hadn't visited for sixty years, was in some way infusing him with youth, with light, with... life.

Even before he entered it he heard the hoofs of a heavy horse on the stones of the yard. Edging boyishly around a barn he caught sight of his uncle leading the animal by its halter. Next he saw his aunt, standing on the step of the house. Neither seemed to notice him. Their presence was impossible, Bevan knew. Yet there they were... in front of him. Some hens scattered noisily at his feet as he walked on. His uncle turned, and looked right through him. Bevan began to walk to the back of the house. Two sheepdogs he recognised but whose names he could not remember barked, spun and whined in their chains. He found the orchard, and wandered among its bare trees. As he did so, he looked up at the rear of the white farmhouse. There, in a window, *his* window, the one of his room, stood a boy he recognised as his ten-year-old self. Unlike his aunt and uncle, the boy *saw* Bevan. And not only saw him but – and this Bevan understood – *knew* him, too. The boy stared, then drew back from the glass.

Shaken by these apparitions, particularly that of his boyhood self, Bevan hurried as best he could back to the canal. Not striding and vaulting as earlier, but stumbling, struggling now. The stiles and gates he'd crossed and climbed were no longer there. Thick briar hedges and rough stone walls rose and extended in their place. Thorns ripped at his cheeks, the ridges of rocks slashed at his palms as he pushed and dragged himself through and over them. The hard, frozen ground smashed at his knees as, more than once, he fell, before hauling himself up and staggering on.

All the while he had the sense that the farm, having somehow gathered itself from the earth, was moving after him – its stone, slate and beams, its fetid beast-house, its wretched orchard, its miserable acres, its gate-posts and bed-posts, its boulderous Bible, its heavy black range, its straw bales and zinc bath, its barbed wire, its bread knife, sharp scythes, hammers, staples, nails and hooks curved and hateful – all of it, pounding and pitchforking, after him – Bevan – over the angry, jealous land. He looked back over his shoulder as he fled. Each time *Y Groes* sat there, as before, on the hillside, but he careered and, ultimately, crawled on, even so. On the boat he bolted the cabin door, and barricaded himself in.

In time, Bevan calmed himself, telling himself that what he'd seen had been ghosts, tricks of the light, and perhaps not even that: he was tired, that was it... so many projects... bound to take their toll, even on a man like him. When he got back home, he'd take a break, a *proper* break: go on a cruise, or charter a yacht, *buy* a damned yacht *and* a crew... make a proper job of things, instead of messing around on this old tub: the queen of whatever. Money would pour in from the resort soon enough. That's what his people had told him.

In the last of the light he drew back a curtain in the cabin. The trees of the bank seemed closer than before. It was as if they had stepped forward in the gloom.

Come daybreak Bevan went on deck, and shivered. Looking around he realised the boat was moored somewhere other than where he'd put in. On the bank, in a wilderness of bracken, were the ruins of a cottage. There was no sign of *Y Groes*. Somehow, in the night, the boat had moved.

Bevan struck up the engine: not afraid now, but angry. He swung out the boat in a pall of grey smoke. As he did so he remembered the basin – its calm, mud-brown water, barges parked-up, flotillas of ducks. He'd been there as a boy. Journey's end: he was near it, he knew. He would get there, he told himself, moor the... no, *abandon* the boat... find a phone with a signal and call a cab from somewhere... anywhere.

'Right, bitch!' he yelled, hand clamping the tiller. 'You're taking me home!'

Bevan worked the vessel hard, churning the water so that it foamed at the bow and boiled white at the stern.

In the fading light of the afternoon, amid the rhythm of the fast-beating boat, Bevan remembered something that, through his will, his ability to conquer, his hunger to win, he had, till that point, believed he'd not merely forgotten but eradicated from his mind. *Before* the basin – he now recollected – stood the lock. He remembered, specifically, how, as a child, his aunt had taken him there, to its great gates, its huge, black beams, its deep, dripping dungeon. He'd committed some misdemeanour: he remembered a bed-wetting in the cold, back room of *Y Groes*. And she had taken him there – dragged him there – to the lock... held him at the very edge of the smooth, grey stones. He remembered looking down at the black water... her tight, bitter mouth – in it the odour of damp, fungal *Y Groes* – whispering in his ear. 'Keep away, Will. Keep away.'

In the gloom Bevan gripped the tiller-bar tightly. He would manage, he told himself, even on his own. That was what he'd always done: managed, beaten. Dragged himself up, hadn't he? No father that he knew... and packed off as a mere boy by his mother to the hillbilly sticks whenever she felt like carrying on with whoever at Christ knew what. And look what he'd made of himself, look what he'd become. No, he'd be all right, he'd get through... and then... *away*... for good.

There were others on the banks, but the first he recognised, as the boat passed between them, was the woman who – however many days earlier it had been: he'd lost count – had hired him the boat and cast him off. Like the rest of them, she held a flaming torch aloft in the darkness. 'Do you know where it leads?' she hissed, as the light from the flames danced on her face. Beyond her, he recognised, from all those years earlier, the optician who, in the hushed examining room, had shown him the cards. Except the man was not *mousily* respectful now, but in the guise of a rat, which, leering and rearing, shuffled and fanned in its claws its shining, teasing pack. Its tail snaked into the flame-dappled water and tugged the narrowboat on. 'And this one?' the man-rat mocked, holding up a card. Bevan withdrew his hand from the tiller, as if it were some poisonous thing, but the boat kept its course. Finally, at the end of the chain of figures, he saw them: his uncle and aunt, and, between them, a small boy who leaned forward and looked at him while holding their hands. 'Keep away, Will. Keep away,' his aunt whispered across the black water. 'Red in tooth and claw, boy,' his uncle said after her. 'Red in tooth and claw.'

Bevan did not see the lock gates open. His enclosure only dawned on him when, looking back at the figures and their beacons, the great gates drew themselves closed. He stumbled from the stern to the bow of *The Keeper's Queen*. The walls of the chamber loomed around him. Standing at the very front of the boat, he held up his arms, as if in supplication. 'My people!' he screamed. 'Where are you?' And then the gates ahead of him opened. Not to lift him up to the quiet basin that he remembered from his childhood, but to unleash a monstrous broth brimming with wrecking-ball rubble, torn-down trees and the mulched remains of countless grubbed meadows, that had been swelling, there, for fifty years, in a giant, steaming cauldron, as witness to the progress of one man.

In his watery dungeon Bevan's pleas petered to nothing.

For a moment, in the darkness, all was quiet and still.

Then the flood thundered in.

Queen Bee

When he installed himself and his hives on the flower-rich grasslands of the peninsula Owen Roberts had the overwhelming feeling that he and his bees had found the perfect home. He detected what seemed a special contentment in the way the insects hummed, harvesting pollen in the warm sunshine while below them waves fell and dragged in the sandy bays and pebbled coves. As he set about his tasks on his newly-acquired property – replacing slates, fixing fence posts, brightening woodwork with fresh coats of paint – he noticed that he, too, seemed often to be whistling or humming in a way that mirrored the happiness of his bees.

The arrival of Roberts on that part of the coast caused no great murmur among the longer-standing locals accustomed as they were to the coming and, more often than not, the eventual going, of those who'd chosen it as the setting for some faintly eccentric attempt at *escape*. Among their number snail farmers, poets, sculptors, ukulele-makers and those with an interest in herbs of various kinds. One drifter, a teacher who'd lost his licence, or so it was said, built – and sank – his own submarine.

One whose interest was definitely stung, however, was Hywel Rhydderch whose home and – more importantly – whose hives were on the other side of the estuary from the holding taken by young Roberts.

A bluff, even somewhat wild-looking figure, Rhydderch had long been the pre-eminent beekeeper in that part of the country. In fact he was seen by some, not least himself, as something of a legend in the world of bees. The likes of the Archbishop and even the Prince of Wales were among those to whom he sent his most select of jars. Occasionally a flunkey would respond with a letter of thanks, which Rhydderch would read with satisfaction and then carefully file.

When Rhydderch arrived unannounced at Roberts's holding Roberts was startled and delighted, unaware that the celebrated beekeeper lived quite so near. For several years the younger man had read Rhydderch's articles in *Drone* and *The Hive* with something akin to awe. One piece, 'Plant Diversity Central To Yields', had been a major factor in Roberts's relocation. Roberts had also been a keen follower of Rhydderch's somewhat stony column *View From The West* – noting, with concern, how it now seemed to appear in *The Hive* less frequently: a photo-strip feature showing Tricia Kent, the TV presenter, seemingly taking its place (above the bee-themed crossword).

As Roberts showed Rhydderch around, Rhydderch responded with great interest in the new man's operation. Anyone observing the men that day might well have taken them for master and pupil. Even father and son, in terms of their manner, though very definitely not in terms of their looks. Roberts cut a slight if determined figure. Rhydderch, on the other hand, was a big, burly man who was said by some, rather cruelly, to be the beekeeper who'd put the ape into apiarist.

After the tour Roberts asked Rhydderch to join him in his farmhouse. There, in the kitchen, Roberts removed the lid from a jar of honey, which he described as his 'prototype'. He had produced it, he explained, in what he called a 'crude' set-up in the garden of his mother's house in England prior to his move back to their native Wales. Roberts said he would be honoured if Rhydderch would be kind enough to take a small taste. He held out a spoon. This, somewhat to the younger's man surprise, Rhydderch immediately disregarded. Instead, taking hold of the jar, Rhydderch lifted it to the light of the kitchen window. The honey possessed the mahogany hue of fine whisky aged in old oak casks. Rhydderch tilted the jar a little so that the honey inside slid heavily. He then drew the jar under his nose, flaring his nostrils so that their silver hairs switched and shifted as, with eyes shut, he inhaled the sweet scent. Only then, with the solemnity of a robed druid at some grave and highly-important ceremony, did he accept Roberts's spoon, pointing, at the same time, to a tea towel hanging from the stove. This he used to rub the spoon's bowl between his large right thumb and forefinger till its chill was replaced with a detectable warmth. Then, and only then, did Rhydderch lower the spoon to the jar and penetrate the surface (as if a surgeon with a scalpel).

'At last!' thought the watching Roberts, his knuckles, white as goose feathers, clasping the back of a chair.

Yet *still* Rhydderch was not done. For next he twirled the spoon vertically this way, and then that, so that the rich, heavy honey was taken with what – after his worship, after his science – now seemed its own luxuriant, almost *magical*, eddy. While this spinning whirl took hold of the honey something even more astonishing occurred. From Rhydderch's mouth the largest, widest tongue that Roberts had ever seen uncurled. And now it hung there, swaying from side to side, like some horrible pendulum.

Finally, digging deep into the jar, as if raising a mighty oak tree by its roots, Rhydderch scooped a glistening hillock of honey. As he raised it to his cavernous mouth sunlight fell through the window giving the spooned sample a glorious golden glow. As the spoon climbed, Rhydderch reeled-in his enormous tongue and, at the same time, began to lower the portcullis of his grey and gap-toothed upper jaw. His mouth slammed shut on the neck of the spoon; those fine strands of honey that had trailed after it falling against and sticking on his broad and bristled chin.

Now Rhydderch closed his eyes and stood stock-still, the spoon firmly fixed, so it appeared, in the centre of his mouth. There, he and it remained, for what seemed to the watching Roberts to be one, two, three... four minutes, if not longer. (The ticking of a mantel clock sounded through the parlour's open door.) Then Roberts watched in near-disbelief as, with his arms and hands to his sides, the spoon (that part which was visible, at least) began to twist in Rhydderch's still shut mouth, so that it turned like a key, its shank seemingly independent of any means of propulsion (though, in fact, powered, Roberts realised, by the concealed force of Rhydderch's monstrous tongue).

First the spoon turned over on itself. Next Roberts watched as the handle repeatedly rose and fell in a way that indicated Rhydderch was directing its dome against the roof of his mouth almost in the manner of some mechanical press. The younger man looked on in continuing astonishment as, after that, the utensil rolled first to the left-most corner of Rhydderch's mouth, and then to the very right – all whilst Rhydderch's eyes were shut and, as has been said, his arms and hands lay by his sides. Throughout he uttered not one word and betrayed not the slightest emotion.

What ran through Rhydderch, however, (*surged* in actual fact) was a feeling whose nature was such that, notwithstanding his apparent transcendental state, it was all he could do not to choke. For the honey, Roberts's honey, the honey of this callow novice of a beekeeper, was the finest that he, Rhydderch, master apiarist, lifelong bee-man, had ever had. Its gorgeousness filled his every atom and fibre, slipping into him, warming him, transporting him, like the most stunning sunset... liquefied. As far as Rhydderch was concerned it was like nothing he had ever tasted. It was the nectar of the gods.

Finally, after what must have been six or seven minutes of ecstasy, Rhydderch opened his eyes, raised a hairy hand to his mouth and withdrew the spoon. He attempted (and, so he thought, brought off) a look of unconcern.

'Not bad...' he said, handing the utensil back to Roberts, who

158

accepted it as if receiving a holy relic '... for a first attempt.'

Roberts beamed.

On seeing this, Rhydderch added that the tasting had been 'far from scientific' and many things should have been done differently for the opinion to be 'authoritative'. To which Roberts nodded respectfully.

Still, said Rhydderch, he'd tasted worse.

On leaving, Rhydderch invited the younger man to visit his own holding on the other side of the estuary. Roberts expressed delight and voiced the hope that they would enjoy a relationship of fruitful co-operation and friendship. He asked Rhydderch to accept the jar of honey as a gift. No sooner had Roberts screwed its lid shut than Rhydderch's hand was on it, depositing it in the pocket of his coat.

As he left the farmhouse Rhydderch heard the soft hum of Roberts's bees behind him. The sound had, at least to his ears, a satisfaction which irked him. As he shut the last gate, and turned, the tone of this hum altered in such a way that Rhydderch felt the bees were mocking him. Rather than quieten as he stepped into the lane, the noise rose so that, as he walked away, it occupied his ears to the exclusion of all else.

What no one could have seen that day, what physically no one would *ever* have been able to see, was that beneath Rhydderch's rough-hewn exterior and brusque air lurked something dangerous: a very thin skin. Exactly how this had come to hang itself on the broad bones of someone who in all other respects looked as if they ought to have the hoariest of hides was speculated upon occasionally by those who weren't exactly his friends – of these he seemed to not really have any – but those in the bee world who knew him (to that limited extent that he let anyone *know* him). Part of his insecurity (and, strangely, also his sense of superiority) stemmed, so it seemed to them, from the fact that his knowledge had been garnered in the field – holding bees, watching bees, breathing bees, *living* bees, as he put it – while that of many of his *rival* experts (as he saw them) had been gained in the laboratory through the lenses of microscopes. On one occasion a bee man from the English side of the border had been in a cubicle in the men's cloakrooms during a conference at a hotel. He heard a heavy figure swill at a tap and growl to himself about *bloody BSzees*. 'Rhydderch!' those who were told the story unanimously agreed.

All that night, after his visit to Roberts, Rhydderch considered how he might best destroy him. For without swift and decisive action *he* would be destroyed, Rhydderch told himself. He lay awake tormented by the day's events. Had anyone in the entire history of bees created such glorious honey as he had tasted that afternoon? The ousting of his column from *The Hive* was one thing. But *this*... this was something else. In his restless state he saw his hives, his certificates, his cups, his books, fuelling a bonfire whose flames split open wedges of oozing comb that ran over his fields and into his house like channels of molten lava. His whole world was engulfed. Above all of this his bees raged in a terrible whine till every last one of them fell to earth like those fat splats of rain that precede a great storm.

Having barely slept, Rhydderch rose with the dawn and went down to his kitchen. There he took from the table the jar Roberts had given him, and hurled it to the floor.

Still, though, he could find no peace. Unable to resist, he crouched his great and naked bulk over the flagstones and began licking, hungrily, at the pool of delicious honey, scooping between the shards of broken glass with his big, grey tongue.

All that week Rhydderch's fever grew, to the point that, one afternoon, he felt sure he could see Roberts's hives marching towards him over the sward of the opposite cliff. Not only that, but that he could hear the murmur of the other man's bees in the salt air, and even see their specks in the low, white cloud, like a squadron of Spitfires.

When Roberts arrived at Rhydderch's holding, on the visit that the two men had previously agreed, Rhydderch had still not settled on a way of 'dealing' with him. In fact, the older man felt weak... sick. It was, he felt, as if the young pretender was taking his crown – and without so much as a blow. They each put on hats and veils, drew gloves with gauntlets over their hands and wrists.

The light that morning had a hard brightness to it which meant that when they moved they saw themselves as little more than black shapes, the sun strobing at their flanks and shoulders. A slight breeze apart, Roberts was struck by the overwhelming stillness. The few bees that could be heard seemed languid, even listless, as if they, too, were wilting from whatever it was that was leaching the life out of the day. Rhydderch eyed the younger man hatefully through his veil's dark tulle while outwardly guiding him cheerfully through his ranks of white hives.

After going through some inspections of a routine nature Rhydderch took Roberts to an outpost of hives he'd established on a clifftop away from the coastal path. Waves fell and the seawater dragged on the pebbled beach some five hundred feet below. Rhydderch explained that he'd created the colony to take advantage of the many wild flowers, such as gentian, whitlow and aster, that grew there. Others such as petalworts, wild orchids and samphire also flourished in the locality thanks to the calcium deposited via the fragments of broken shells that blew in from the beaches. Roberts listened and nodded. Whilst speaking Rhydderch's mind drifted to the faintly audible roll of the larger, weightier pebbles on the shore. He sensed something moist at the corner of his mouth and realised that it was his tongue... hanging. He drew it in. The flowers of the cliffs, Rhydderch continued, brought special qualities to his honey in terms of its texture and bouquet. He ushered Roberts to the furthest most hives so that the younger man stood within mere feet of the drop. Rhydderch watched as the sea breeze tugged at the tulle of Roberts's veil. He imagined the *crack* of his body hitting the stony shore. All that was needed was one good push. In fact, given their difference in physique, he could probably pick up the young fool and throw him off: legs kicking, arms flailing, as he went. Yet Rhydderch felt weak, so weak. His fever had sapped his strength: it was all that he could do to stand. Roberts came away from the edge, and the opportunity was gone.

The two men went back to Rhydderch's cottage. When Rhydderch removed his hat his hair was soaking. Sweat ran in rivulets down his jaw and dripped from his chin. Roberts noticed but said nothing. Rhydderch saw that he had noticed, and this was one more thing that irked him.

In the kitchen Rhydderch presented Roberts with an already opened jar of what he considered to be his finest honey – a sample of which would soon be dispatched, with a toadying note, to the First Minister, at Cardiff Bay.

'Only one of my ordinary ones, I'm afraid,' Rhydderch said as Roberts took a spoonful.

Roberts placed the spoon in his mouth, found the honey heavy, bitter.

Rhydderch turned away, determined to signal that this was a matter of mere politeness on his part: that the response of Roberts would be nothing to him. But in fact he followed the younger man's face keenly: registered the slight wince, the pursing at the corners of Roberts's funny little mouth.

'Very nice,' said Roberts.

Rhydderch pretended not to hear. Inwardly he fumed. 'Nice? Nice!?!' Forty years of expertise had gone into the cultivation of that jar. Not to mention the efforts of the finest bees in Wales. And this damned upstart had the impertinence to stand there – in *his* kitchen – and call his honey *nice*. The little bastard!

'Yes,' said Rhydderch, as casually as he could. 'As I said: not one of my special ones.'

He screwed the lid back on and took the jar into a pantry of the traditional, walk-in kind. Roberts watched as Rhydderch turned a key in the lock, drew it out – a heavy, iron, long-shanked thing – and placed it in the right pocket of his trouser where his thick, muscular leg pressed its shape against the brown moleskin cloth.

'So,' said Rhydderch, 'did you find the tour instructive?'

'Very. Thank you,' said Roberts. 'But...' He paused.

'Yes?' asked Rhydderch.

'Well,' began Roberts, '... and please don't take this the wrong way – *you* are the expert here, after all. But I couldn't help notice that your bees were... quiet.'

'Quiet?' said Rhydderch.

'Yes,' said Roberts. 'Subdued.' He paused for a moment, then asked, 'Are they... all right?'

No sooner had the words left his lips than Roberts realised he had said the wrong thing. *Utterly* the wrong thing. Rhydderch, who, with his burliness and his hairy, mutton-chop sideburns, had struck him as rather bee-like at their first meeting, now seemed to swell before him, like some great, bristling bumblebee. Visibly struggling for words by way of response, the older man seemed to emit a kind of furious hum

'I think you'd better leave,' Rhydderch said at last.

He marched Roberts to the front door.

'There is NOTHING wrong with my bees!' he called out as the rattled Roberts skittered down the path.

When Rhydderch was sure Roberts had gone he went out to look at his hives. And, much as he did not want to, he found himself agreeing with Roberts. For, lifting lids and drawing out frames, it was indeed the case that his bees were somehow *lethargic*.

'Bzzz,' said Rhydderch as, not even bothering to wear his veil, he leant his whiskered cheeks to the hidden world of his hives and their walls of comb. 'Bzzz,' he said again and again (this being his longstanding way of greeting his bees and encouraging their endeavours).

Rhydderch hurried his heavy bulk from hive to hive in mounting panic.

'Bzzz... Bzzz... Bzzz.'

Finally he approached a hive that seemed particularly quiet. With a deep sense of dread he lifted its lid. As he did so not a single bee flew out. He bent to the hive.

Like a deserted city, the interior was entirely still and silent. He lifted out the frames: steadily at first, but with gathering speed so that, by the end, he was practically ripping them from the hive. The last he simply flung over his shoulder. And then he looked inside and saw it, on the floor of the hive: the thick, dark carpet of dead bees.

Three days later Rhydderch called on Roberts. He greeted the younger man warmly, which, after the acrimonious end to their previous meeting, took Roberts by surprise. Rhydderch apologised for what he called his 'testiness', attributing this to his hermitic existence remote from any real neighbours let alone the companionship of other keepers.

'I bring you not an olive branch, but this,' Rhydderch said, finally.

He placed a small box on the table in Roberts's kitchen.

Roberts wiped his hands in a towel, moved to the table and opened it.

Inside reposed the intensely regal form of a beautiful queen bee: huge eyes, glistening wings, vast tigerish abdomen arcing to her distinctive bullet-shaped tail.

'Gwenllian,' said Rhydderch.

'She's gorgeous,' said Roberts.

'One of my best,' said Rhydderch.

'I couldn't possibly take her,' said the younger man.

'Oh, but you must,' Rhydderch replied.

Roberts closed the box gently.

The two men stood without speaking for a moment. The mantel clock ticked in the parlour. From beyond Roberts's cottage – in what sounded to the ears of Rhydderch in his inner turmoil like a warning to the younger man – came the whisper of the sea.

'Wait!' said Roberts suddenly, and he walked out of the house.

Rhydderch went to the window. He watched as Roberts moved through some of his hives. Despite their difference in physique the sight reminded Rhydderch of his younger self. Oh the boy was good, he thought, a natural: far better than he had been at that age... better than he was now. Which meant that he was dangerous. Lethal. Rhydderch saw him coming back, stepped from the window.

'Here,' said Roberts, placing a small box of his own on the kitchen table. 'One of mine.'

Rhydderch, who had been haunted so severely by the wonderful honey Roberts had given him, stiffened his trembling fingers behind his broad back. Then, with as much indifference as he could muster, he opened the small treasury that had been set before him. He studied the compact, lustrous queen that rested within as if she were in her bedchamber... and he felt himself salivate.

'Alys,' said Roberts. 'Not as big as Gwenllian, of course. But, as they say, size isn't everything.'

At that moment Rhydderch felt as if he held in his calloused and lumpen hands not only the keys to the gates of El Dorado, but the cool and dazzling wonder of the Koh-i-Noor diamond, the inexplicable genius of Amadeus Mozart, the meaning of Life itself. His brawny legs were suddenly jelly. He fought to find something to say. He remembered those words Roberts had uttered in his kitchen. Those stinging, cruel words that had slipped so casually, so woundingly, from the younger man's lips.

'Very... nice,' Rhydderch said, at last.

To Rhydderch's confusion Roberts then launched into an account of medieval chivalry: a field he indicated he had studied at university. Rhydderch barely listened as Roberts spoke, his thoughts instead being firmly on his own hives and the queen that was now his.

'A queen for a queen,' said Roberts, finally.

The words caused Rhydderch to come to.

'As in a game of chess,' Rhydderch said.

'Quite,' said Roberts.

As Rhydderch left he closed his eyes for a moment whilst dropping the latch on the gate to Roberts's yard. He listened to his host's bees. Yes, there was a pleasing shrillness in their hum. Faint, but it was there – as if they knew what was coming.

'Sod *chi*,' (you) he said, using the Welsh, and went.

Rhydderch enthroned his new sovereign in a hive isolated from all of his others. Then he set fire to the rest. As they blazed he strode between them in his hat and, unusually for him, his full white suit, anticipating how, at this moment of their incineration, his previously torpid charges would rise – as they now did – in fury against him.

The hives cracked and hissed and snapped as the flames took hold. A horrible whine filled the air.

Rhydderch worried that Roberts might see the smoke from his side of the estuary. But the grey light of the late afternoon concealed him. In the falling darkness Rhydderch's figure moved among the smoking hives like that of a ghost. He poked and prodded till nothing remained of the hives but ash, his bees – in their hundreds and thousands – exterminated. Every last one.

A week later Rhydderch received a telephone call from Roberts. The younger man reported that his bees were sick and a number dead. He begged Rhydderch to visit.

Rhydderch refused.

The risk of contamination to his own hives, if he stepped anywhere near Roberts's, meant it was out of the question, Rhydderch said. He was sorry, but there was nothing he could do.

What action should he take? Roberts asked.

Destroy, said Rhydderch. Destroy the whole lot, and then leave... try something else. Had he thought of goats, or llamas, or bananas?

Bees were such fickle things. There were places where land was cheap now after all of the burnings, all of the pyres. Mad cows, infected pigs, scabied sheep, influenza-riddled flocks... death, disease: the countryside was full of it. Safer to find something else, better to go back to the town.

Rhydderch put down his phone. And as he did so he neither buzzed nor hummed, but purred.

In the coming weeks Rhydderch indulged the queen that Roberts had given him with every treat he could think of. He brought fresh hives and new bees to his holding from all over Wales. His enterprise grew to three... four times the size of what it had been. And, thanks to the presence of Roberts's queen, whose influence was somehow felt in all of Rhydderch's hives, the honey they produced was of the same heavenly kind that he had tasted that day in Roberts's kitchen. Rhydderch's bees laboured with such machine-like intensity that he felt as if all of the pollen of Wales were his, as if he were amassing vaults of pure gold, a Rockefeller among men, a Midas among keepers.

Roberts, meanwhile, burned his hives and his bees, and left.

A few villagers who had got to know him said the experience had broken him.

Some while later there was talk that he had taken his life.

Rhydderch ignored all of this, telling himself he didn't have time for such distractions. Besides, *that* was how life could be in the countryside: harsh.

In fact, Rhydderch's mind became so pre-occupied with his bees that, in his reveries, he found himself *entering* their hives so that his head rose up between their frames and the bees coated not these but the contours of his face – his eyelids, his cheeks, his lips, his ears – with their heavy, luxuriant comb.

As the year wore on Rhydderch's supply of honey became so great that he engaged a boatyard to build him a vast new vat. This was installed in one of his old barns (only just squeezing through the building's double doors). There, under the slate roof and oak beams, it became a huge, golden lagoon. At night, in Rhydderch's dreams, this vat grew even bigger, assuming the dimensions of an ocean which he sailed upon in a yacht. Occasionally, in these visions, the face of Roberts would surface, the rest of him clinging to the wreckage of a shattered hive. The younger man would call out to Rhydderch who would turn the yacht's wheel so that it set sail away from him in that slow and glutinous sea.

One night, at the very end of that summer, Rhydderch's sleep was disturbed by a buzzing. He woke to find a bee hovering above his face. He reached to swat it. The bee, a slight, determined specimen, evaded him and continued to buzz in the moonlight that fell over Rhydderch's bed. Annoyed, Rhydderch threw back his bedclothes and pursued the insect about his bedroom. The bee dodged and wove in an impish way that Rhydderch found impudent. After some minutes of this the insect glided, with the utmost dexterity, through the peephole-like aperture left by a small knot missing from the wood of the bedroom door. Rhydderch, who was naked (always sleeping that way: his copious body hair and layers of fat more than a match for any chill) followed the bee first onto the landing and then down the stairs.

The bee veered into the kitchen through an open door. In the silver light that shone into the cottage Rhydderch chased it around the kitchen table, swiping and flailing. During the third or fourth lap he stubbed his toes on a chair and let out a furious yell. As he bent his big frame to take hold of his hurting foot, the cheeky bee landed on the end of his nose. Then, as he screamed and waved in disbelief, off it once again flew.

Next they were in the hall where, avoiding the swings of the broom with which Rhydderch had armed himself, the bee dived into, and tunnelled through, the keyhole in the front door. The enraged Rhydderch flung the door open and, never minding his nakedness, went after it down the path.

Now man and bee were crossing the still and shadowed yard beneath the moon and stars. Courtesy of a gap between its old stones, the bee flew next into the barn that housed the lagoon. Fearful of thieves, Rhydderch kept its big double doors chained and locked. One door, however, had a smaller door set into it, and, after snatching its key from a little crevice, he stepped through this Judas gate.

Shafts of moonlight entered the barn through the holes between its stones and its slipped and missing slates: these moonbeams criss-crossing like searchlights above the honey in its still and golden lake.

For several moments Rhydderch heard nothing, just his own breath and his heavily beating heart. But then the buzzing began. Looking up, above the vat, he saw the dark dot of the bee flitting in the silvery beams that lanced the gloom above the lake. Rhydderch started to climb the steps that rose against the vat to the platform he'd had made specially for the purpose of glorying over his harvest. Now that it had his attention the bee seemed to taunt him with a display of aerial acrobatics that included corkscrews, swallow-dives and tailspins above the lake. Rhydderch stood there naked on his podium, looking out over the great expanse of honey at the antics of the infuriating bee. He knew, though, that to swing at it now would not only be foolish but dangerous, and he stepped away from the edge of the vat.

It was at that moment of Rhydderch's retreat that the bee abandoned its performance above the honey and, with a speed that Rhydderch had never before seen in his lifetime of apiary, advanced on and stung him in a particularly personal place.

As a beekeeper Rhydderch had, of course, been stung countless times. But he had never been stung *there*. He rocked, then staggered, then spun with the searing pain. Before he knew it he had lost both his balance and his footing, and he was falling, head-first, into the lake.

The lake's thickness was such that it received Rhydderch with no more than a small *gloop*.

The pale soles of his platter-sized feet were the last that a mother owl and her brood of owlets saw of him as, with the coming of the dawn, the honey closed over his gradually sinking form. Such was the honey's clotting density that it took seven full days for his body to reach the bottom of the tank.

Only the curiosity of the postwoman who wondered why she had not encountered Rhydderch for several weeks led to a search by the police. They pierced and drained his huge vat – itself a process that took nearly a week, the honey flowing from it slowly, like sap from a tree.

Rhydderch's corpse finally emerged.

The apiarist's appearance, sealed from top to toe in the honey's golden glue, caused one detective, of a bookish mind, to utter a line about the Duke of Clarence and malmsey wine. Others thought of wasps drowned in sugary summery traps: honeytraps, no less.

Beneath their coating Rhydderch's eyes were open and fixed in the horrified glare that had possessed them before he was immersed. What intrigued the officers, though, was something else. Not, you may think, his swollen member. (The healing power of the honey had safely taken the sting out of that.) No, what fascinated them was Rhydderch's enormous tongue. This hung – glazed like the rest of him – from his mouth in such a way that the tip possessed a slight, but distinct, upward curl... as if he had tried to eat his way out.

Smothered like a toffee apple, his corpse was almost perfectly preserved. It was the sweetest cadaver he'd come across – and all that he could do *not* to take a nibble – the pathologist who cut him told friends at dinner parties. Maddeningly good!

But what, I hear you ask, reader, of that single, teasing creature whose sting precipitated the downfall of this Queen Bee of the West?

The answer to that is that in ending the reign of Rhydderch it extinguished its own life also, so that it simply lay there, expired, on that same ladder to the vat that Rhydderch had come to regard as his private stairway to heaven.

In time, a passing officer's boot ground it into the step, where it came to resemble nothing so much as an old and crushed hop.

As someone once observed: country life can indeed be harsh.

The Griffin

I first found myself in *The Griffin* when it was on Glyndwr Street. When I say that *it* was on Glyndwr Street, rather than *I* was on Glyndwr Street, that's because, when it came to *The Griffin*, that's how it was. You see, weird as it sounds, *The Griffin* was a pub that got around. The whole place, I mean: bricks, mortar, pickled eggs in the jar on the bar, spongy dartboard, crusty towel on the wonky wooden roller in the gents that had hung there for years. You've doubtless heard of flying doctors, flying fish, *The Flying Scotsman*. Well, *The Griffin*, in its way, was a flying pub: a place that had the habit of taking off, winging it, then landing   soft chink of its glasses, small cloud of dust – more or less wherever it felt like making its nest. Which meant that you – well, *I* – could never be quite sure *where* in Cardiff I'd find it: the back streets of Splott one week, the leafy avenues of Pontcanna the next; Roath one lunch-time, Grangetown come supper.

Now, as I tell you this story, there are two things you need to keep in mind about *The Griffin*. First: it was very definitely a pub from another era. Second: during the whole of the time that I probably counted as one of its regulars it was never because *I* was able to go find *The Griffin*; it was always a case of *The Griffin*, somehow, finding me.

On its tendency to take flight, I should tell you that sometimes the place disappeared for weeks. It was as if it crept away into a crack in the walls of Cardiff Castle, or slipped through the grille of a storm drain into the waters of the Taff, maybe even snuck itself into a fallen pine cone in some corner of Bute Park. But, even then, in its physical absence, I still somehow sensed its presence. Not as if it was hunting or stalking me exactly, but as if, quite definitely, it was there, *watching*, if you like – *at*, sometimes even *on*, my young and vaguely innocent shoulder.

Our first encounter was in freshers' week. I got off my bus late or maybe it was early. Either way, it wasn't my stop. I found myself in a maze of back streets that all looked the same. What's more it was getting dark. I thought I'd call a cab, but the screen on my phone was blank. I wandered for ten minutes, maybe more. The terraced streets were deserted, and it was starting to rain.

Suddenly, halfway down what looked like a dead end, the glow of *The Griffin* greeted me. Its frosted windows, grimy bricks and squeaking sign (of a strange-looking lion-cum-bird) didn't seem as if they were meant for a student like me. But I told myself I'd only be going in for a Coke and to ask for the use of their phone.

And so I went in.

Inside, the place was something else. Okay, so my experience of pubs was limited to my village local: the haunt of moody in-breds still feuding over some fence post erected by one or other of their tribes three hundred years earlier.

But even so... *The Griffin*...

First thing that hit me was the smoke, clouds of it, heavy in the air, like a sea fog, rising from the mouths and funnelling from the nostrils of its patrons, who swirled and drifted in and out of it in a way that made them spectral.

Eyes watering, I headed to the bar.

I asked for a Coke.

The barmaid stuck a bottle, to my surprise made of glass, on the counter. She clamped a scarlet-nailed fist around it and – with one jerk on an opener – took off the top. She pushed the bottle towards me and drew her hand down it... slowly. Next she produced a glass, looked me in the eye and asked if I wanted anything else.

My life up to then had, if I'm honest, been sheltered. Never mind that she was clearly a fair bit older than my mother, I looked at her large bosom in her low-cut, leopard-print top, and was quickly – and firmly – of the mind that, yes, there was – very definitely – something else that I wanted. And it wasn't a phone. Or a taxi. At least, not yet.

Before I could say a word the jukebox butted in. Not a band from my own era, but something I knew my grandfather had on vinyl (scratched to bits) which he stuck on his old player, cussing the needle, when he'd had a few back home: Max Boyce, Live at Treorchy, *Hymns and Arias* (from some time back in the last century).

The barmaid asked what seemed a stupidly cheap price for the Coke, then disappeared to serve someone else.

In that sizeable part of Wales left vacant by her bosom I could now see a bunch of rugby photos, pinned to the back of the bar. A standard enough sight in a no-frills Welsh boozer. Except that the boys looking back at me seemed to be from my dad's time… maybe even *his* dad's. I'm talking Benny, Gareth, Merv, J.J. and J.P.R. – side-burned, red-shirted, fresh as daisies the lot of them, as if they'd just been snapped.

When Max finished on the jukebox, Mary Hopkin took over (*Those Were the Days*) and, after her, Tom Jones (*It's Not Unusual*). Finally, Tina Charles trilled-in (*I Love to Love*). During this one the barmaid's huge, heaving bosom surrounded me, so it seemed, panoramically, as I nursed my Coke.

The ringing of a bell, like that on an old ship, signalled the night's end.

I fell out of *The Griffin's* fog and into the wet street. In drizzling rain and breaking light I eventually found my way back to my hall.

At uni I mentioned *The Griffin* to a couple of students who were in the year above me. They said they'd never heard of it. I kept the particulars of my night to myself. That following weekend I went back to Glyndwr Street, but *The Griffin* had gone. Where it had stood –

or at least where I thought it had stood – was a gap: a weed and rubbish-covered lot that looked as if it had been empty for years.

The next time I found it – well, that *it* found me – was two months later, down at the bay. I'd been thinking of quitting my hall, and had gone to view a small studio-flat. I couldn't find the right block: there were so many that seemed the same.

I was about to give up and go find a bus when I heard singing – which I recognised as Mary Hopkin at *The Griffin* from those weeks before. And there, suddenly, it was – as if it had just landed – on a building site where the contractors had gone home: the brine in its jar of eggs, I imagined, still sloshing as the pub's bricks and mortar settled into place.

I pushed open its doors. It was quieter this time. The barmaid asked where I'd been.

She introduced herself as Bev.

I told her I was Dan.

I asked for a Coke. Feeling some sort of need to prove myself, I told her to stick in a rum.

'Stiff one, is it?' she said, raising a glass to the optic. 'Could do with one of those myself.'

She winked at a little old guy who was standing at the bar.

He set down a pint glass of beer, wiped froth from his lips, sniggered.

'Did I give you too much head, Albert?' she asked him.

'No, fine, Bev – fine, girl,' said the old boy. 'Beautiful pint. You've always known how to pull one. I'll say that for you,' he tittered.

Bev looked at me. Her jaws worked slowly on a piece of gum.

Desperate as I was to supply the stiffener to which she'd alluded, I knew that one drink was nowhere near enough. Not for a greenhorn like me, with a woman of the world like her. And I had lectures, I told myself, lots of lectures.

I made my excuses and left.

'I'll be back,' I said, putting down my glass.

'I know,' said Bev.

I was a pretty conscientious student. I worked hard and, in the post-Christmas exams, acquitted myself well. When the results were out some of my course-mates asked me to join them for a night on the town.

We were having a reasonable time of it in the bars and clubs around St Mary Street when, somehow, I got separated from the rest. I found myself in a gloomy backstreet: a chilly breeze blowing chip papers, sending tin cans rolling. No one else was around.

Suddenly, as if with the throw of a switch, *The Griffin* (between a boarded-up shop and the shell of an old cinema) came blazing to life.

Strangely though, while every bulb in the place seemed to be burning at maximum watts, the building was oddly silent, as if no one was at home. The moment I walked in, however, the place— well, it erupted.

Half of the regulars seated on one side of the bar (which was decorated with streamers and all sorts of party paraphernalia) struck up Shirley Bassey's anthem *Big Spender*.

Those on the other side chorused-in - louder - through a smog of smoke.

I walked between them - maybe a tad unsteadily, I concede - as Bassey, Tiger Bay's finest, belted out her song on the jukebox, with the backing of *The Griffin's* rasping, gasping, kippered-lunged choir.

Getting to the bar seemed to take me an age. Behind it I could see Bev, black blouse open at the collar, three... no four – the number seemed to grow the closer I got to her – of its buttons undone.

She was rouging her lips and staring right at me.

I reached her as Shirley's brass boys were bringing down the house with their tumultuous, screaming, helter-skeltering last bars.

I leant there, weirdly exhausted, as if I'd done ten rounds with Jim Driscoll, Jimmy Wilde or one of the other famous fighting sons of Wales (who may also have been named Jim or Jimmy) that my grandfather went on about when pissed. I propped myself on the ropes.

'Congratulations on your results,' said Bev, bringing down her bullet of lipstick and snapping its shell-like tube tight shut.

'Now...' her hand pinned my wrist to the counter '...forget your books, Danny boy, and come up and spend some time with me.'

She opened the bar, pulled me through.

The pub went wild as she took me upstairs.

I'll spare you the details of what unfolded in Bev's private quarters that night. Let's just say my performance was virginal rather than vintage. If you really want to visualise it just bring to mind a bottle of milk stout – the kind favoured by certain of the oldsters at *The Griffin* – highly-shaken and with its top torn off. Afterwards we lay on Bev's bed and listened to Bonnie Tyler singing *Lost in France*, the music rising from the jukebox in the bar below. I rested my head against her big breasts. She said that, while in terms of performance I still had plenty to learn, my graduation, as far as she was concerned, was official. I was no longer a boy, but a man.

For the best part of the next two years I had virtually nothing to do with 'normal' student life. As I've said, *The Griffin* didn't always come calling and sometimes it went away for quite a while. But when it *was* there its card and dominoes nights, singalongs, comics and drag-acts knocked the spots off discussions about current affairs with my student colleagues or the dreary alternatives of games on my laptop, fiddling with my phone and TV soaps. I even got a taste for its drinks, once asking on a rare night out with my course-mates for a pint of mild at a 'rave' someplace – much to the mockery of my peers.

Most of my nights at *The Griffin* ended in Bev's bed. It wasn't just the sex, which, under her tutelage, got better on my part. It was the lying there... afterwards... the warmth... my sweet surrender to the intoxicating nerve gas that was her perfume... the way she played with my hair.

As time went on she said that soon I'd be leaving her. I denied this. But she made it sound inevitable. 'The time will come, Danny boy,' she said.

And Bev was right. For what seemed like a stack of logical reasons I began to tell myself I'd have to give up *The Griffin*. One being that my parents had declared themselves keen to meet the girl I said I was dating. I couldn't see Bev's bust, boots and beehive going down a bundle with my mum. And so I started going out with Megan, a girl my own age, who was also at uni, albeit not on my course.

To begin with things weren't too bad. Meg took me to workshops, poetry readings and similar stuff, to get me out of what she called my 'shell'.

Once, we went to London to join a march. I can't remember the cause.

We had sex, of course, and when this happened it wasn't unpleasant. Yet, after Bev and her curves and her spilling folds, being with Meg felt so different. There could only ever be one Bev. Remembering our first night, to the strains of Bonnie Tyler, I came to think of her, wistfully, as like a ripe Camembert cheese.

Still, I stuck it out. One night I even shunned *The Griffin* to its face. It appeared to me across the road from some dingy venue I'd gone to with Meg. I was outside, getting some air, when it landed on a garage forecourt opposite.

As soon as it settled I could hear that in *The Griffin* – at least – the night was banging.

I pictured Bev behind the bar, admiral of her ship, asking some old boy if he was all right for nuts. Spencer Davis was on the jukebox... *Keep On Running*. His band fired out the number as if aiming it at me.

Behind me, in the community hall or whatever it was, fiddles scraped and tambourines shook at the folk night I'd gone to with

Meg. I went back inside and re-joined her. When we came out later *The Griffin* had gone.

Not long after that, I did as Spencer said, and ran.

Out of consideration for Megan I wrote her a letter trowelling-on my shittinesss so that she'd think the worst and feel well rid of me. I told her I'd always been involved in 'something that went back'. When we next crossed paths at uni she was holding hands with a pale and serious-looking guy who had a picture of Fidel Castro on his T-shirt.

Meanwhile I searched Cardiff for *The Griffin*, re-visiting improbable places where it had appeared to me previously: the steps to the museum, the island in Roath Park lake where Jimi Hendrix once passed a night, platform six of the central station, the ice rink. I also checked the natural history section in the library, the gents beneath the precinct at the Hayes, a pelican crossing in Cathedral Road and the *Dream Clean* 24-hour launderette in East Ely (where, puzzlingly, they demanded money for what they claimed was an unpaid bill). All with no joy.

Eventually, as was its way, *The Griffin* found me, appearing from nowhere one morning, as the light brightened after a rainstorm, on the wharf of one of the deep docks, near the water's edge.

I ran to its doors, pushed against them, my heart pounding. They were locked. I went to the frosted windows. Inside, the curtains – since when had *The Griffin* had curtains? – were drawn tightly closed. I rapped the glass, went back and hammered the doors.

Despite this commotion I became aware of a step behind me, and with it a voice.

'Steady! That's enough!'

I turned to see a policeman. Not one of the modern paramilitary type, but a copper of the old school: woodentop helmet, cape.

'Don't you know what time it is?' he asked. 'They're hardly going to be open now.'

'I need to get in!' I told him.

'I think *you* need to slow down,' he said.

'It's urgent!' I said.

'Not for them by the looks of it,' he replied. 'Besides, they know the law. And you do, too, I don't doubt. Haven't you got a watch? It's barely half past ten.'

'Well, *why*'s it come then?' I said, switching from the doors to the windows.

'Now...' he said, his voice assuming a graver tone, '... my advice to you is to move along quietly. If not, you'll be coming with me.'

I wanted to keep hammering, but the copper looked as if he meant it. I did as he said... and walked.

After a bit I looked back. Both he and *The Griffin* were gone.

In time, I completed my studies and graduated. A petro-chemical company recruited me as a research biologist working mainly, as we call it, *in the field*. I've had a couple of promotions since, but, essentially, I still check out sites to see what's there from an ecological point of view: anything that might prove 'problematic' for us before we set to work.

Recently, in Wales, not that far, in fact, from where I grew up, our ground crews found something on a site exploration that required me to fly in (from Venezuela, as it happens). They'd come upon a series of ancient fossils of a strange avian hybrid, which, on account of the site being in Wales they'd labelled 'the dragon'.

When I studied the rocks, however, my thoughts turned to something else, something I hadn't thought about for nearly fifteen years... but which I'd also never really, fully, forgotten.

After visiting the site I drove down to Cardiff and checked into a hotel. That evening I went for a stroll, thinking about my old haunts... and one in particular. I knew I wouldn't find it if I went looking for it, but wondered, all the same, whether it might find me.

The city had changed massively. It had blocks and towers that were almost skyscrapers now. I was running my eyes up two of these – one all smoked glass, its neighbour a mix of steel rods and grey stone – when I dropped my gaze to street level and saw it, stuck between them, squatting, like a toadstool... *The Griffin*.

And, of course, I went in.

My heart beat heavily as I made my way to the bar. My head spun with so many memories that my eyes absorbed almost nothing.

It was only when I was standing there, being asked by the young barmaid what I wanted, that my senses seemed to snap back to work.

How different it was.

So clean, for one thing. Not so much as a wisp of smoke.

And the clientele... oh how suited and booted... and white-wined and red-wined and all pilsnered-up they were. Not a single milk stout to be seen.

A piece of jazzy piano tinkled in the background.

I looked back to the barmaid, glanced past her. The rugby photos... Gareth and Co... at least *they* were still there. Except that, when I looked carefully, they were old men now: still in bright red shirts with silver feathers, but with hair gone grey, even white, gone completely from some of them... mortal, every one.

Seated proprietorially on a stool at the end of the bar, surveying proceedings, taking everything in, was a figure that could only be... Bev.

After fifteen years she was somewhat slacker of bosom and, on what looked to be her spray-tanned neck, creases and wrinkles cut and wove in a way I didn't remember... but she was regal, immaculate, nonetheless.

An eyelid heavy with mauve mascara dropped a wink.

Not at me (it transpired) but at some young guy in a pencil tie, prissy beard, sharp suit. He walked over. She let him kiss her cheek. They began talking. She took his hand.

The girl behind the bar asked me again what I wanted.

'Nothing,' I said, and left.

My *Griffin* had flown.

The Comfort

A foot.

On the tips of its toes.

A woman's foot, by the look of it.

Painted. On the wall.

Sideways-on. Sole slightly arched.

Harris put down the knife he'd been using. He bent, studied what he'd exposed. Above him, paper curled from the plaster.

He straightened, stepped back.

Harris thought for a moment, struggled for a word, something to describe how the foot... looked.

Balletic.

Wasn't that the word?

Yes, *balletic*... that was it.

He'd heard or read that somewhere. A dancer's foot. That was how it looked – *this* foot – painted on the plaster, on the wall.

Around it the wall was washed with a kind of wine colour that had gouges and lumps of glue and torn paper which were pale and looked, in spite of their irregularity, not completely unlike falling flakes of snow.

What struck Harris most was how the foot resembled a wing, as if it were, in fact, one half of a pair of wings. The whiteness of it wasn't swan-like though. It was more chalky than that.

Harris turned to the room's curtainless window, looked out, saw the snow that had settled on the village. His eyes detected no horizon because of the way the grey countryside blurred in the distance with the equally grey sky.

Harris turned back to the wall. He stepped forward, bent (lower this time), took off his glove and laid his left hand against the foot: his palm partly on the ankle, partly on the sole.

The wall was cold (which did not surprise him because the day was cold). His breath had hung round him like a beard as he'd traipsed through the house. What surprised him was that a woman's foot should be painted on this wall – *his* wall. He drew his hand back and stood up, slowly. His knees cracked.

Harris remembered a tree he'd seen in a drift while out walking some days before. How a branch had poked from the snow. How the tree had been practically buried, right to its top.

He put the glove back on. He wore gloves not because of this job he was doing but because of how cold it was even *inside* the house. The benefit was questionable. The gloves were sawn-offs and the tips of his fingers were hard and bloodless. It was almost as if they weren't really *his* past the knuckles and had, in fact, been carved out of wood.

He picked up the knife from the floor and went back to stripping the wall. He was... *curious*... about this foot, and glad that, at his not insignificant age, this was something he still could be.

It wasn't much of a community. At least not now: a strip of black and weathered properties that tombstoned a frequently fogged and rain-soaked ridge, like a row of rotten teeth.

Once, almost unimaginably, the place had boomed. Miners struck gold. People swarmed there from all over. Churches, chapels and a railway were built. But the seams were thin; so fine, in fact, that many of those who rushed there wondered if the gold had ever existed. Most drifted back to their valleys and towns. Those who stayed cut not gold but slate: great grey slabs of the stuff, of which there was plenty. And as they did so they came to believe that the slate was the real reason that, like fools, they'd been lured there. In time the slate's dust heaped itself inside them, silting their lungs. Meanwhile its spoil grew to surround their village – enclosing the lives of those who lived there – with hills that were like a herd of so many whales.

On its own hillock, away from the other properties, sat Harris's house. Compared with the others in the village it was big and looked as if at one time it must have belonged to someone of standing: a minister, doctor, or manager at one of the quarries. Double-fronted and having a façade a shade blacker than the rest, it stood at the top of steps that were slippery with slime. An iron knocker, stiff with rust, hung in a crescent from a front door whose few remaining flakes of paint suggested that it had worn a coat of scarlet... once. Harris had never been able to open it for want of the key. He came and went through the scullery at the back. The garden had gone wild: a forest of rhododendrons at the front, an infestation of brambles and berryless hollies at the rear. In their midst stood the throttled forms of hideous trees that had the look of creatures half-risen from a swamp. Thorny sloe hedges made a ragged border to the plot. The chimneys of the house splayed as if about to fall. Any guttering that hadn't already given way sagged with fat deposits of moss and, now, snow. The wood in the window frames was so rotten that no more than fingers were needed to pick the wet pieces apart. It was hard to see how or why anyone would have bought the place. But Harris had. His reasons were, firstly, that it was cheap – the price reflecting the property's near derelict state. Secondly, and more importantly, it represented the chance for him to be somewhere that, on the whole, other people weren't.

Harris had found it on the internet through a site called *Godforsaken*, a gazetteer, only part-joking, of bleak and remote settlements which contributors – typically pipeline workers, soldiers and ex-prisoners – deemed so awful that it was only decent to warn the rest of humanity about them. Among the locations listed were bomb-blasted parts of the Middle East, bandit-controlled territories in South America, and parched corners of the world visited by nothing but sun and the occasional (lost) lizard. *The Greyest Place on Earth* was how one contributor summed up the village. As soon as Harris saw it he knew that it was for him.

Harris's search had been prompted by an incident at the all-night supermarket where, despite his advanced age, he'd taken a job. He stacked shelves on the night shift, thinking it a way of keeping active in retirement, killing those small hours of the morning when he'd almost always been unable to sleep. Before the supermarket he'd been a porter at his local general hospital. It was one of those split-shift week of days / week of nights jobs that turn people into zombies. In twenty-five years he'd never got used to it. Working at the hospital had made him ill, in fact.

The *incident* at the supermarket involved a woman who was drunk and who wanted to buy more drink. Although the store had a 24-hour licence the booze aisle closed at night on account of past troubles. The woman, however, had moved aside the cordon and was clattering up and down in high heels, tossing gaudily-labelled bottles into a wire trolley. Maureen, the night supervisor, had followed the woman and was asking her to stop. Harris had sight of this from his nearby station in 'Snacks' where he was stacking 'multi-flavour' crisps in 'party packs'. When Maureen tried to stop her the woman grabbed Maureen by her hair. At this, Harris – forgetting how old he was and all of the *protocols* he'd received in a red ring-binder at an induction meeting along with his official store trousers, shirt and belt – hurried over and took hold of the woman around her waist. The woman reacted by driving her elbows into him and stamped with her heels on his feet. The two of them fell against a display of canned ciders, trays of which now crashed to the floor. One of the woman's heels pierced one of the cans so that it clung to the underside of her shoe. Another burst and spun around in the aisle, spraying madly, like a fire extinguisher on a hotel landing that some clown had let off.

The woman was screaming and cursing now. Harris didn't know what to do. Maureen was running away... to get help, he hoped. The back of the woman's jacket pressed against Harris's face as she fought this way then that. For a moment all Harris could think of was a stall where an Asian guy sold leather goods in a precinct where it almost always rained.

Harris became aware of the absurdity of his position in the aisle: how, in some respects, it looked – if you could only have turned off her noise – as if he and the woman were dancing: that he was lifting her in some ballroom routine for which each of them ought really to have been grinning maniacally in mascara, spray tans and sequins. Except, of course, that she was screaming, swearing and kicking (never mind any judges' votes). Harris could hear the *La Bamba* song on the speaker system and wondered why the supermarket played the music that it did in the middle of the night when the customers – at least those of them who were sober – were sleep-deprived shift workers, or people who were lonely or disturbed, who bought things that, by the looks of them they didn't really need to buy, like bird seed, frozen scampi and pressure washers for patios, without knowing why they did. Perhaps *that* was the reason for the music, Harris mused: a comfort.

And now Maureen was running back. Thank God for that, thought Harris, catching sight of her around the side of the woman, who he was still holding and whose blouse had come loose so that it was now riding up over the rolled, white, yogurty fat at her waist to her bra which was tight and patterned and black. But then, *Not* Thank God, thought Harris as a guy came bowling around the corner after Maureen, a guy who was big – not *athletic* big, but *fat* big – but, still, fundamentally, *big*, who was now pushing Maureen aside. And all of this as the woman Harris was holding was screaming – seemingly louder now than before – and the guitarist in the *La Bamba* song was flying with his fingers and thumbs at the fancy fast part while the cider can on the floor was still rocking and spewing its contents albeit less fervently than had been the case. And then, before Harris knew it, the big guy was punching him in the face so that he went over and the woman went over with him onto the blue-grey tiles of the aisle. Then, as Harris lay there dazed, the woman rolled off him, pulled herself up and began kicking him, in concert with the man. Eventually the man stopped her and said that was enough. At which point almost all of the night staff ran into the aisle, including several guys from the warehouse who finally saw the man and woman off the premises, the two of them shouting back and giving the finger as they went.

Maureen sat Harris down at a checkout that she chained off, and fetched tissues for his bleeding nose. An hour later two police officers arrived. They asked Harris what he wanted to do. Nothing, he said. He just wanted to go home.

The air outside was cool and damp. It revived Harris a little as Maureen helped him to his car.

'Matt Monroe,' he told her. 'There was a guy who could carry a tune.'

Harris let his car engine run and waited for the screen to de-mist. One of his teeth – a right-side molar – seemed loose. He fiddled with it for a bit, pressed against it with his tongue. He thought of Mrs Koolahmari, who'd been exposing herself to him through her kitchen window at their flats. He wondered if Mr Emmanuel, the warden, had made good on his promise to *intervene*.

As Harris pulled onto the main road the car made a horrible metal-on-metal sound. The stick by his knee jumped out of gear. He pushed the stick in again, found second. His small car stammered away into the dark.

Next day Harris found the website. Others had tempted him. *Dump Towns* and *Hell's Graveyards* being two. But *Godforsaken* was the one that Harris sensed would serve him best. He scrolled through its contents while drinking a powder and boiled water soup that claimed on its packet to be oxtail. This, on account of his heavily swollen face, he sucked through a straw.

Harris reached an entry that said 'Godforsaken: removed *The Original*'. Next to it beamed the website's gold rating: five dead cats (in black silhouette, on their backs, legs skyward). A banner proclaimed, 'Wales's Number One', the nation's red dragon flag rippling proudly in some geek-induced breeze.

'You'd have to be mad to move here,' said the reviewer, March Hare. Beside the comment was a picture of a white rabbit puffing a cigar and wearing a top hat. Thanks to some small piece of wizardry the image turned repeatedly from side to side in its box on a clip of film that made it seem alive, all of which Harris found strangely hypnotic. March Hare had posted a video. Harris clicked on it. After an advertisement for a penis enlarger that Harris wasn't sure was a spoof or not – it featured a stick of seaside rock with the logo 'For *Rhyl* Men' – the clip began.

The film opened with rain. The village, initially a blur behind a curtain of water, gradually came into focus in its tombstone line on the ridge. The film looked to have been shot from inside a car. The picture wobbled. A pirated soundtrack, *Riders On The Storm* by The Doors, began as the car climbed its way upwards in the wet murk.

As the car closed in on the settlement the camera panned across the crescent of slate and quarry spoil that reared over it. Rain spotted the vehicle's windows, which became fogged. A wipe with some fingers restored the view (albeit one that was smeared). Harris noted a charm of some kind – it looked like a rabbit's foot – dangling from the rear-view mirror.

The driver – March Hare, presumed Harris – paused outside the boarded-up municipal hall, the camera fixing on a clump of weeds rooted in a ledge. The car then moved slowly past a café and what seemed to be the only shop. Both had signs in their windows that said *Closed*. A mongrelly dog – there were no people – crossed the street and slunk down a back lane where there were nettles and black bags. Water streamed sheds whose corrugated iron sheets were coloured mud-brown. The car drove on, leaving the place behind. The soundtrack changed to another Doors song: *The End*. In a final flourish *not*, Harris suspected, authorised by Warner Brothers, Bugs Bunny flashed up to proclaim, 'That's all Folks!' Then the film went dead.

Harris had always quite liked the idea of retirement: a static caravan somewhere on the coast, portable television, microwaved meals. It had crossed his mind on many a shift at the hospital as he pushed trolleys along corridors, wheeled chairs between wards. But, now, moving his mouse and landing on links, he was studying properties *not* with a view of hundreds of other caravans and occasional slivers of grey-green sea. Instead he was in the reaches of this perversely compelling DO NOT ENTER place where, declared March Hare, no one in their right mind would want to go... let alone live.

Next Harris was scrolling through the portfolios of estate agents, noting particulars, weighing-up properties: terraced cottages, pebbledash bungalows, a former telephone exchange with a tree in its roof. All dull admittedly, yet not *too* grim: several quite liveable, in actual fact, thought Harris. And then he found it... peeping over the rough thicket of rhododendrons that largely obscured its front: Y Cysur (*The Comfort* in English), the home, the elusive object (if he had only ever slept well enough to know it) of his distant and wandering dreams.

All of which meant that now, instead of pushing a hospital trolley, instead of stacking packets of crisps, instead of watching TV in a caravan sandwiched amid scores of other, similar caravans, Harris was unpeeling the wallpaper – or attempting to – in a room at that mysterious house of his heart's desiring: a bedroom it once had been, in fact – not that anyone now would have recognised it as that.

Harris's pre-occupation with the wallpaper made no strategic sense given the state of the rest of *The Comfort.* But unpeeling the paper was what Harris *felt* like doing and, at his age, why not? So he chipped and he picked and he prised. The paper looked about ten layers deep. The uppermost covering was tangerine, patterned with lanterns of a slightly deeper shade. Black speckles of mildew and furry white spores that had the look of dandelions gone-to-seed climbed the walls.

Soon Harris found there was more to the foot than just the foot. A calf was attached to it. Then, as he tooled and dug upwards, Harris found that beyond the calf was... a knee.

A raucous chatter erupted above Harris. Suddenly a large accumulation of twigs – a nest or the greater part of one – crashed down into the room's empty fireplace. Soot and dust blew from the grate. Harris looked at the thick and intricate nest. Its architecture impressed him. He'd seen the crows – whose work he took it to be – circling the house and strutting on the roof. They seemed to have selected sticks of exactly the right size so that the components of the nest thatched together geometrically. And yet, it had fallen, crashed. Harris put a match to it. The nest flared and crackled. Harris warmed his hands, heard the agitation of the birds on the chimney above him, heard them go quiet, sensed them fly off.

Harris looked out of the window and saw the greyness deepening. He knew that very soon it would be dark. He went downstairs and lit some candles. The house had gaslight once. No longer. There was a debt – something *historic* – he was told when he called the company from the phone box with ferns in it by the municipal hall. (His mobile had no signal, which didn't bother him because he didn't really know how to use it or anyone who might call.) A woman at the gas company had told him to hold. He kept the phone to his ear for what seemed like an age, until the line went dead.

Now, in the kitchen, Harris lit damp coal in the range. He blew on it, then half-filled a kettle, which he stuck on the sputtering fire. He watched as the kettle worked up a weak whistle in the chill gloom.

Later, on his camp bed, Harris observed his breath. It rose to the ceiling in ghostly draughts as moonlight fell on it through the kitchen window. He lay there in his sleeping bag: balaclava helmet, fully-clothed, only his boots removed from his feet. Outside, brambles chafed the panes. Occasionally Harris heard snow slipping from the roof. Beyond that... nothing.

As he lay there his thoughts turned to the village, how it must have been: the prospectors who'd flocked there with foolish, fevered dreams of gold, who'd died there with lungs full of dust after lives in caverns and quarries in servitude to slate. In his head Harris saw a rainbow. It rose from a lush lowland valley. As it arched, its bright colours bleached. Finally, it sank – in bitter greys and bituminous blacks – on that bleak, tombstoned ridge.

Harris heard something: a strange, *short* but intense sound: a harsh snap, like a whip crack. It lasted no more than an instant but unsettled him nonetheless. He unzipped his sleeping bag and rolled quietly out. Finding his matches, he lit a candle as noiselessly as he could. Then he shuffled, in his socks, into the hall.

A pink blush wandered the walls as Harris moved with his small flame over the cold, clay-tile floor. At the foot of the stairs he paused – then he began to climb. Halfway up he heard the noise again. It was like the sound of a blind flying up followed by a *rocking* that had an awkward, scraping aspect. It faded as he neared the landing.

At the top of the stairs Harris pushed open the door to a bedroom. The room was black and still. Next he gently undid the handle to the bathroom. The white suite lay there with a strange, animal quality, like livestock in a barn. The cold-water tap of the bath, which could not be turned off fully, whistled softly as it dribbled in the dark. Harris drew back, continued along the landing. Suddenly the flame of his candle pulled towards him in a small and noisy pennant of light. The sound made him think of the time when as a boy he'd held a moth whose tawny wings had beaten furiously in the cupped palms of his hands. He now raised his left hand and placed it in front of the flame, which settled, part-illuminating the landing with a thin and moving glow.

Now Harris was at the door of the bedroom where he'd been that afternoon. Beyond the door he heard the same rocking and scraping sounds as before. He put his free hand to the brass knob. It was buttery-smooth. His palm slipped. He gripped it again. This time he undid the door, and pushed it open wide.

In the morning Harris kept from the house. Pointless as the task might have appeared to many, he hacked at the brambles that rolled in barbed and seemingly infinite coils down the bank at the back of the property. Snow shook from them, hissing as it collapsed through the dense and ugly canes.

When he had worked all day and the fruits of his labours were such that it seemed as if he'd done almost no work at all, Harris stopped and went inside. He lit the fire in the kitchen range and warmed the kettle. He poured tepid water into a mug with a teabag in it and ate corned beef from a tin, standing in front of the range, digging with a fork at the corned beef.

That night, on his camp bed, Harris slept on his side and kept his eyes from the ceiling. The brambles, now cut back from the window, no longer tapped on its glass. But Harris's sleep was shallow and fitful at best.

The next day also he kept from the house, taking his chopper to the rhododendron bushes at the front. Untended for years, the bushes had ballooned. They squatted in front of the house like huge plum duffs, roots lifting the tiled path and dislodging the stone steps. The bushes rose much higher than Harris. As a young man he'd stood at more than six feet, but had shrunk in his senior years, he knew.

A covey of pigeons took off noisily as he began. He plunged the chopper into the branches and trunks. Sometimes it stuck there and he needed both hands to pull it out. At times he was right inside the bushes, the snow that layered them showering him in cool, sugary falls. More than once it found its way inside his collar, dripping down his back and chest. The branches did not come apart with precise, dry cracks and splits. Instead Harris had to put down his chopper and pull the boughs asunder with his own gloved hands. This he did in moist, ragged rips and tears that broke open the black, scaly bark and revealed the orange and yellow – almost fleshy – wood that was concealed within.

Harris worked without rest, the sound of his hacking and chopping carrying from the tump on which the house stood not only to the village but across the surrounding land which was silent and still save for the occasional movements of lorries transporting slate from the one quarry in the area that was still worked. In time, Harris's throat grew dry, his arms and legs feathery-weak.

Come mid-afternoon the greyness of both the sky and the land seemed to close in on Harris strangely. Although he knew *The Comfort* was near – no more than a few steps, in fact – he was unable to reach its black stones and mortar. As darkness fell he became lost in one of the bushes, its branches wrapping around him in the manner of an orchid that opens to the sun and folds in on itself come night.

No one heard him cry out.

When Harris awoke all was blackness and silence. And yet he had a sense of where he was: on his camp bed in the kitchen of *The Comfort*, though it... he... seemed *different*. For one thing, he seemed to be looking down on himself. His appearance made him think of a potentate or patriarch, deceased and lying in state. His face... his face was as pale and, so it seemed to him, cold – he touched it, or so he believed, with the tips of his fingers – as the ashes in the grate.

Suddenly Harris heard a sound that – after all of the rawness, all of the numbness – was warm and honey-sweet: piano music – a melody no less. The tune made its way through the house like a spring thaw. Harris rose. And not to the cracking of his joints as was usually the case, but now surprisingly nimble, as if he were... young.

Harris had no need of a candle to navigate the hallway to the stairs. For the house was now suffused with gaslight. How it glowed! A hubbub issued from the drawing room. But this Harris passed, beginning to climb instead. The stairs were thickly carpeted. The banister felt different, too: no longer worn and loose, but stiff and smooth. It seemed almost like marble under his fingers and palm. The wall of the staircase was similarly transformed: red, velvety paper now covered the pitted plaster that had been there. But what Harris noticed most, as he rose to the top, was his own nakedness. This confronted him in the glass of a mirror framed with bevelled gilt. And he saw not the young, energised man he'd felt himself to be as he rolled from his camp bed to pursue the piano chords, but another, who was different entirely: white-haired, yellow-nailed, grey-eyed, thin. One who, to an onlooker, thought Harris, might through vague, passing resemblance have been taken to be the father... or, more probably, the *grandfather*... of that vanished, younger man.

Suddenly Harris felt himself ancient again, and confused. Thoughts tumbled about him like the snow that had scattered from the brambles in the garden. He rested against the wooden ball at the top of the stairs. He was struck by what seemed the pointlessness of his life, its strange dénouement – marooned by his own hand – here, on the ridge, in the Village of Slate. It was as if, all of his life, he'd been carving his own headstone, nothing more; cutting, chipping, tooling, reducing... like the slatemen, in their whiskers and waistcoats, who'd gone before.

The lights on the staircase, and in the hallway below, dimmed and went out. At the same time, the chatter in the drawing room muted and ceased. Only the piano music – albeit fainter than before – remained. Harris's breath hung thinly in the air, like smoke from a candle snuffed out. His limbs acquired a silvery whiteness in the landing's murk. Behind the newel and spindles of the banister he seemed, for a moment, like an old and heavy-antlered stag, disturbed...

hesitant... in woods. But then, never mind the dark that surrounded him, he saw – beckoning him – the sight that he'd found those days earlier when he'd walked with his candle through *The Comfort*. What he'd... laid hands on. What he, Harris, who had never known a woman (in the physical sense), had touched... on the wall... *above the knee*... revealed by that cylinder of curling and uncurling paper, hoisted as it had been, like some stage curtain, that had stirred him from his bed.

Now, in his nakedness, Harris stood there, before that same bedroom door. And it opened.

Harris lay down on the bed between them. And in the lamplight they received him gently, as if washing someone who was very sick. Their fingers ran over his ribs and elsewhere, as if his bones were the keys of the piano which, in Harris's head, was playing melodies of exquisite softness and beauty.

Amid these ministrations and despite his awkwardness about his dusty, sack-of-bones self, and also his sense that, by now, he was no longer the sweetest-smelling bloom in the garden, Harris became... invigorated.

And, as they took him, and as he cupped them, the brass bed started to shudder and its steel springs began to sing. These motions, to Harris, seemed to propel the old bed into flight so that the three of them now were riding together as if on some jingling sleigh, out of the house and into the night. And quite soon they were dancing, turning, whirling, on the mattress as it soared... *above* the tombstone village... *over* the whale-back spoils of slate... rocketing and rocking between the shining planets and the sky of twinkling stars... white sheets waving to all who would see them from down below, beneath their feet... their *balletic* feet... and to, finally, incredibly (Harris holding on, so he felt, for dear life), loop-the-loop in the fabulous silver glow of the magnificent and endless moon.

And now – after his journey to the heavens, his magical flight –

Harris sensed himself back on land, at his house, like, so it seemed to him, a pilot who had breached some impossible barrier. Ecstatic, priapic, he unlocked by means of his still-tumescent member *The Comfort's* sealed scarlet front door. His mind and body firmly in possession, so he felt, not only of the key to *The Comfort* but to the meaning of his life... of *all* life.

He stood there now – vital, erect – at the top of the slimed stone steps where, in the attitude of a conqueror, he surveyed the slaughtered bushes and trees of *The Comfort's* garden. And before him, and his lifted and wand-like organ, the snow rose-up in the moonlight, as far as his eye could see, scattering itself to all four winds, as if ten thousand white rabbits had, at his baton-given command, suddenly found their feet.

And through every empty cavern and in every craterous pit, not only in that sad, mad village on its ridge, but in the whole of the land of Wales, Harris's cries, from that hillock, corkscrewed and pealed.

'Oh Godforsaken! Sweet Godforsaken! What a wonderful place this is!'

Bait Pump

Bait pump.

That's what it's called.

It sounds sort-of sexual.

Has the ring of something rough.

And I suppose it is... disturbing... at the receiving end.

I'm talking about that tool – looks like a bicycle pump – that blokes, they're mostly blokes, in beanie hats, boots and hi-viz, use to suck worms from the flats, spit them out, scoop them up. If you've been on a beach at low tide you'll have seen them – *worming* – though you may have wondered what they were at.

Things were different when I was a kid. Back then guys who fished *dug* for their worms with a fork. And they had to know where to dig, and where not to.

Which, in a way, brings me to Deek.

It was Teg Powell – out on his boat – who found him, though when he set eyes on him Teg's brain couldn't make sense of what it was that he was seeing. Crazy as it sounds, Teg thought Deek was some kind of squid or even a shark – dragged in by the net of the *Madlen* with all the other fish Teg had been trawling for. He'd seen some things at sea in his time but, whether it was the light, or the swell, or the sheer improbability, the truth was that Teg's mind struggled to understand what it was that he'd caught – that the bony white things sticking out from his orange net weren't tentacles or tails but a boy's own arms, and that those arms belonged to Derwyn Keith Davies, my friend Deek, our town's missing kid.

Teg winched in the net, so he later told the police, and opened it on the deck of the *Madlen*, knocking mackerel, bass and whatever else had been in there from off of Deek who also had a starfish clamped on his face and various eels and leeches coiled around or stuck to his arms and his legs. Teg said he'd taken some of these off Deek there on the deck, the remainder he picked off in the hold of the *Madlen* having carried Deek down there on his shoulder and laid him on a bed of ice away from the rest of his catch. Teg was the best of a day out when he turned to port, he said. He ran the *Madlen* hard through the night and into the dawn, a cortege of black-backed gulls shrieking at her stern.

Every so often Teg went and shone a torch into the hold, hoping Deek might somehow be gone. Deek just lay there and stared up from the ice, like a boy-knight on a tomb in a crypt. A couple of times the ice rattled under him and he slid a little, this way and that, as the *Madlen* rose and fell. Before they entered the harbour, said Teg, he put a blanket over Deek 'to give him some dignity'. That was how the police found him – eyes open, on the ice – when they climbed down the ladder into the gloom of the hold.

The coppers (one being Bill John, another being Dai Nelme) interviewed Teg in a room at the police station that had bare walls and an ashtray that filled with fag ends as they spoke. They asked Teg if, when he took Deek out of the water, there were any signs that Deek had been interfered with. Teg said Deek's head had looked really bad, all swollen and bruised, with one horrible gash above his right ear. The police said that wasn't what they meant. What they meant was did it look in any way like Deek had been *interfered with*. Teg said Deek had his trousers on but no top, if that was what they meant. They asked Teg why he and his wife Ionwen had no kids. At this, he got up and asked what the hell was their point in asking him that. They told him to cool it and sit down. After some other questions concerning the *Madlen* they said that he could go, but that he was not to leave town nor take out the *Madlen* until they told him further.

It wasn't till a lot later, when the water was cold and grey, that Teg put to sea again. Small towns are full of nods and winks, and ours was no different. Poison had it that Teg was in some way to blame for the death of Deek. I'm sure part of this was Teg's very act of bringing Deek back. The return of his skinny, blue-lipped corpse went against the town's will, its desire to deny that Deek had ever disappeared. The following June, almost a year to the day after finding him, Teg took out the *Madlen,* smashed a hole in her side and wrapped himself in her chains as she sank. Those who'd smelt a rat, and there were plenty, said Teg's suicide was 'proof', as if proof had ever been needed. But the truth was that Teg Powell had nothing to do with the death of Deek. That, I know, for a fact.

We called it The Fort. It was far out. By which I don't mean Jimi Hendrix *far out*. I mean distance-from-the-shore far out, practically-over-the-horizon far out. It seemed to take us hours to get there, me and Deek. We'd traipse over the sands and then the mud – the town slithering, melting behind us – till we were out there, on the bank, in a blur of our own.

How The Fort got there, God only knows. We had the theory it was something to do with the War, like the buried bombs that occasionally blew sheep to bits on the saltmarsh, and the empty huts at the back of town where men and women who weren't married fumbled and panted in the dark. Physically The Fort consisted of an ugly jumble of cones and cubes made from concrete that resembled dirty porridge. Most of it was plastered with mussels and limpets, or sea weed of the green and slimy kind. Anemones the colour of pig's liver squatted in nooks and crannies. Small crabs skittered in mini waterworlds waiting for the tide to wash them out. Under the concrete was an iron skeleton which held The Fort together. In places chunks of the skin had collapsed to show girders and joints that were rusted and flaking. The whole thing just sat there on the far side of the bank: dripping, rotting, stinking.

That late spring and summer was the only time in my growing-up that The Fort revealed itself. A run of low tides separated our town from the sea in a way no living person could remember. To begin with, Deek and I dug with our hands in the sand and the mud, thinking we might find bullets, or coins, or bones. After a while we just went there and sat and talked. Something I learned then that has stayed with me since is how loud the slightest thing can sometimes sound: the clatter that a single dry leaf can muster as it cartwheels on caked mud, the reach of an oystercatcher's *peep* even above the sea's roar, the wind's teasing way of swelling and silencing the voices of children across empty sands.

The sea's retreat from our town led to a stream of letters to the local press. God, the Moon, the Soviets and the *bowler hat brigade* were variously blamed. Not having the sea cosy up to them panicked people, made them feel cut off. They complained they could no longer *smell* the sea, and they had *always* been able to smell the sea. This parting with the waves was the strangest physical happening in a year that was strange from the start. A Post Office strike – not just in Wales but in England, too – meant we had no mail for what seemed like months. Then the Government changed our money – *decimalisation* was the word – so that, among other things, a ten bob note became a fifty pence piece. More to the point, ordinary people – my nan being one – were convinced the new coinage was worth less than the old. How else to explain the price of small cod and chips from Will the Fish at *Plaice on the Front*? All this and Deek's going missing shook up the town in a way it didn't like. Ministers had more in chapel and church than they'd seen in years.

Bait Pump

The Fort attracted me, I suppose, because no one went there apart from me and Deek. It was a place no one could see us, where no one could disturb us. When Deek went missing I stopped going out there. I wondered if it was safe.

I never knew my father. My mother ran what she said was a boarding house. People in the town called it something else. She wasn't a loose woman exactly, but men came and went. Some gave me money for chips or to go the arcade. Bill John was one who called. As well as being a copper he was a bastard who knocked my mother about (especially if she'd been seeing other men). I asked her once if he was my dad. She went quiet and said no.

When Deek went missing Bill John asked me if I knew anything about it. After Teg found Deek, Bill John came to the house and asked me again. He told my mother to stay in the kitchen. I saw her light a cigarette as he pulled the door to. He spoke to me in the lounge. When I went to sit he told me to stand. He said coppers were coming from away and they wouldn't be messing. So if I had anything to say I had better say it to him now – or those other coppers would have it out of me, and they'd be bastards all right. He said that if I thought he was a bastard then to think again because he was nothing on those other coppers. There was nothing *they* wouldn't do to get their man. Or boy.

I stared at him and he stared back. The fish tank on our sideboard bubbled. The bubbling grew loud in the way sounds did at The Fort. I went over to the tank and raised the lid. I sprinkled some feed that had a salty, fishy smell over the water. Angelfish and rainbows nibbled my fingers as I dipped them in the tank. Bill John and my mother argued in the kitchen.

After what happened to Deek I was wary of other boys. The first time I saw Davy I just watched him: the arcade's red and mauve glows dappling his face as he wandered and hovered near older, bigger boys who slammed at the pinball and cursed. I looked as he put his hands and head against the case of the Derby Day machine where little lead horses and jockeys vibrated on rods down a painted green track. I studied how he slid his body and pulled his fingers along the glass as the horses ran their jerky furlongs. I noted how he spun his head on hearing the *chug-chink-chug* as the bandits paid out, how he scooped his small hands through their troughs for any coins that might have been left. I watched how, above all, he stared at the opening and closing of the claws of the Lucky Dip crane that foraged uselessly above a seabed of sunken treasures – cigarettes, chocolate and glamour girls on playing cards – all of them fading and growing old. When a man I didn't know, with a woman on his arm, dropped a bob on the floor Davy was onto it like a mudlark. The man and woman laughed. Davy saw me looking and went to leave. At the way out he turned for a second, looked back, darted.

When I left it was dark. Gulls skulked under the lamps on the front. The sea was as far out as ever. Waves fell somewhere distant on the flats. The water drew back with a sigh, telling our town to hush.

All next day I thought about the coppers who were coming. I wondered what they'd do if I told them Bill John beat my mother. I went to the huts at the old camp. Glass cracked under my shoes. I imagined Bill John being taken there, tied to a chair, getting smacked about. I found a map on a wall that showed our town. Afterwards I walked to the top of the bryn and looked for the sea. It lay broken in shiny puddles, miles out. Boats were on their hulls on the saltmarsh, their paint peeling in the sun.

That night my mother had a caller. He gave me money and I went to the arcade. I pushed my fifty pence at Nod Roberts. Mari Roberts had wanted her boy to be an architect or a vet. Instead he read horror paperbacks in the booth at *Pleasure Island* where he smoked, wore T-shirts and grew his hair long. Without looking up he slid me some silver for the bandits and some coppers for the cheap slots. He went back to his book. Didn't give a damn. I could have been five years old. That was Nod.

I couldn't see Davy. I half-expected him to show up as I fed the Penny Falls – his hands and head against the glass as a fat jam of coins teetered on the edge, always needing just one more to send them crashing in the *rat-tat-tat* that was music to my ears.

I was on a bandit when Bill John walked in. His hand stopped mine as I was pulling the lever. He said I was under-age and to get home or he'd take me to the station and lock me up. My playing the bandit wasn't the issue, of course. The issue was that I could only have been there if I'd been given money by someone – a man – who, more likely than not, was, at that moment, with my mother... in her bed. Seeing Bill John made Nod put on the noisiest music he could find. Jimi's jewelled fingers jammed into *Purple Haze* as Bill John took my place at the bandit. I walked out, onto the front.

I saw Davy. He was by the sea wall, eating chips from Will's. I leaned against it, a little way from him. We nodded. I rolled closer. I asked him if he was from the caravans on Emlyn Harries's field, and he said that he was. He said he was on holiday with his mam and dad (though he called her his *mum*, as English boys did). He asked me if I wanted a chip. I took a handful. I told him I was Llew and he said that he was Davy. I asked him if he liked our town. Not really, he said. I asked him why. He tilted his head. Well, for one thing, there was no sea and when his dad had talked about it, where they lived, up in England, his dad had said our town was by the sea. But there *was* no sea. Just sand and mud. The sea would come back, I said. I didn't know when, but it would. Soon. When it was ready. I looked at him. He was small and could barely look over the wall to even see the sea that he was so put out about. For all he knew the tide could have been in, washing and frothing against the wall, right there and then.

I struck a match and lit one of my mother's cigarettes. I offered him a drag but he shook his head. I told him I knew somewhere that was special. He said nothing, but he looked at me in a way that told me he was interested. It was a place over the sands, I said, that no one else knew about. It was to do with the War. I could let him come, if he wanted. As a favour. He said he'd think about it. He said he had to get going, back to the caravans. I could always take someone else, I said, if he wasn't interested. There were loads of others. I told him to find me on the front in the morning and that if I wasn't on the front I'd be in the arcade. He turned to go. I caught his shoulder. It was bony, delicate, like he wasn't a boy at all but some small and slender animal – a marten or a cat.

'Don't tell anyone,' I said. 'It's my secret.'

'I have to go. My dad'll kill me,' he said.

His white windcheater disappeared into the dark.

When Davy went missing there was all kind of trouble in our town. People turned on Bill John in the street and asked him what he was doing about it. First Delme Davies's boy, they said, now this lad from England. Too much of a coincidence, Bill John, they said. He came to our house in a fury. I lay in bed. I heard him and my mother quarrelling downstairs, shouting, table legs moving on the kitchen floor. Next morning my mother's face was red. She sent me for ten fags from Morris's on the corner.

Coppers came from all over. Plain clothes from London, too. They drank among themselves in the lounge in the *Mermaid*. The women who served at Will's eyed them nervously from behind the fryers. There was talk Pross Pryce, who was slow with people but good with animals, had been half-blinded in a beating at his place in the woods. Teg Powell was held at the police station for three nights before he was let go. Lewis Milk and Jenkyns Bread stopped delivering to his door. For two Sundays his wife Ionwen had the pew to herself before she told Teg she would go to chapel no more.

And so it went, all summer and autumn, as the skies grew white and the woods above our town turned brown. Coppers in boots, with sticks and dogs, searched them over and over, and every inch of the quarry, too. But Davy was never found. Deek, meanwhile, was laid to rest after a funeral to which the whole town went, save Teg and Ionwen, who everyone shunned. Everyone, that is, apart from my mother who, if ever she saw Ionwen, would make a point of speaking to her and touching her arm so that all might see and hear.

And then the sea came back. Winter tides brought it slapping against the front. Some nights it sloshed over the wall so that Will Fish and others had to sandbag their doors. Even when the tide went out the water hugged the town much closer than before. There was no chance of getting to The Fort now. The early tides sluiced its walls. Those that followed hefted sand against its hollows and cracks. Fat weed swayed in the tunnels to its chambers, which grew silted and dark. Finally, one night, thick, black water closed over it and drowned it for good.

The returning tides soothed the town, calmed it. People stopped thinking so much about Davy and Deek. In time there was talk of things having been accidents, of not being quite what they had appeared. The end of the postal strike, in particular, seemed to break a spell – the falling of mail on hallway floors proof that our town really did exist and was not just a name on a map. A magazine I read at Morris's said Jimi Hendrix really was dead no matter what Nod Roberts claimed in his booth at the arcade. The coppers who had come went back to wherever it was they were from. Bill John went with them. My mother's beatings ended, and no more boys went missing from our town.

Teg Powell killed himself the following summer. 'Boy Riddle

Skipper Sinks With Boat' was the headline in *The Leader*. His suicide stirred up stories about Deek and Davy again for a while, but also brought everything to a close. On the surface, at least.

And how do *I* cope – all these years on? Shell shock. That's what they called it once. Appropriate for a seaside town. Post-traumatic stress disorder is what it's known as now – the disturbance that goes on inside you, the shockwaves that wash and drag. You can get help these days, of course – tell people, have them listen, have them hear it all. Or you can try to get a grip, by yourself, on your own.

Me? I go for the grip. Suck it all up. The whole mad mosaic. Deek, Davy, the town, the past. Spit it all out.

Every hair, every lash, every stare, every touch, every whisper, every kiss, every tear, every wound, every word, every breath.

Every last grain.

Bait pump. That's how it works.

The Dive

Price was at the bottom of the town baths. He was there because his finger was stuck in the grid amid the white tiles on the floor of the main pool. He had never seen it (the grid) before in all of his years of swimming there. All that he knew was that it was there *now*, and that the middle finger of his right hand was stuck in it, at the knuckle.

Seconds earlier he'd been on the edge at the deep end, holding in his stomach (not that it had needed much holding), adjusting his goggles, springing on the balls of his feet, raising his arms above his head. Everything was as normal. Except that *inside* he'd been that bit more aggrieved than usual. And so he'd hit the water harder, steeper, angrier, than he normally did.

His morning hadn't started well. He'd been irked. First by what *The Leader* had announced on its website as he drank his juice. It wasn't the story that had bothered him, but the headline:

HORSE RESCUED FROM RIVER
Fire Crew in Emergency Dash

On reading the account Price had discovered that the horse had climbed out of the water *before* the brigade had even got there. The fact was there – plain as a mare's backside – in paragraph eight. Which meant that no 'rescue', as made out by *The Leader*, had taken place. A photo showed the fire engine parked-up under trees at The

Leap, where families liked to picnic.

The truth of all this Price had intended to bring up later, in the coffee shop, where the other Early Bird Senior Swimmers retreated when the schoolchildren were due. He'd rehearsed his lines as he jogged to the pool through the park, hoping the words would sound man-of-the-world... off-the-cuff. 'Yes, but I can tell you that...' He'd kept losing his rhythm, though. Not his stride, but his speech. It was the fault of the magpies. Nowadays they seemed the only birds in the park. He counted thirteen. Their chatter sounded like laughter.

And then there'd been the Chinaman (as Price called him in his thoughts), who, today, had got there first, and was already in the pool... doing his *thing*. You couldn't call it a stroke. Not what *he* did. Not with his face all scrunched-up like that, blowing bubbles through the water, with that... *hum* of his, as he heaved, sounding like some sort of not very expensive food blender. Still, there he was, on the far side, by the wall – well into his first lap... at least.

Price's last sight above water as he javelined the surface had been the red-shorted arse of Kev, the lifeguard, sloping out for a fag. And then...

Whoosh. Submersion. Hell of a dive. He'd like to see any of the others match *that*. He cut through the blue gloom. A human otter: that's what he was, thought Price, if there could be such a thing.

At such moments, when the water was rushing past him and any sound above the surface had been lost, Time, Price found, stood still. The events of his life would habitually appear before him and assume great clarity in a way that never happened anywhere else. Facts came, were dealt with, and went from his head. Such as how he could have been married, if he had really cared to be. But life had got in the way: national service (RAF), the health farm, his spell as a nude model and then twenty-nine years in his own successful small business. Those early starts on the milk round had kept him trim, jumping on and off the float. And the sights he'd seen: sunrises like fire on Beaufort Hill, the centre of his empire, every house a customer, every doorstep his own; one time, on Rogerstone Road, a river of rain had nearly swept away his float, and then, after it, a rainbow. He'd been right to quit when he did. Everybody was at it towards the end: supermarkets, corner shops, garages. You couldn't move for milk. Knowing when to get in and when to get out: that was the secret of success.

He continued down through the water. Otter Man.

He'd had his eye – metaphorically – on Iris Weaver for a while. Hers, he felt sure, had been on him. She always seemed to be there, removing her cap, throwing back her head, when he showered. He'd caught her watching him as he lathered his hair. When he blow-dried it, over at the mirrors, she was invariably there also: putting on lipstick, doing her eyelashes. Today was the day he'd make his move. 'Let me get that,' he'd say as she opened her purse in the queue at the coffee shop. And in the next breath he'd work in the word *croissant* to the girl on the counter so that Iris Weaver heard his perfect pronunciation.

The penetration of his finger into the grid was doubtless assisted by the ferocity with which Price had propelled himself into the water. He was in the act of rising when he realised he was snagged. At first – when the digit went in – he'd felt only a slight chafe and bumps to the tips of his other fingers as they evaded the neighbouring holes. It was when he tried to move up and away that the small plastic portal (a yellow-edged square) locked – painfully – on his knuckle, and jerked him back. It was as if something predatory had hold of him.

When Price pulled at the finger it seemed to swell so that it lodged there all the more. He brought his free hand down beside the grid. Not agile Otter Man now, but awkwardly, with the ponderous manner of a heavy-suited deep sea diver. He pushed with this hand against the tiles and at the same time pulled hard on the finger in the grid. It wouldn't come.

Price hung there, diagonally, like some streaming piece of weed... and wondered.

He told himself not to panic: any minute now Kev would wake up in his highchair beside the pool and come crashing in, probably with some special cutting gear in his trunks. He – Price – would be taken to the first aid room. An ambulance might well arrive. Price imagined the story on the website of *The Leader*:

OLD FOOL RESCUED FROM POOL
Fire Crew in Emergency Dash

He pictured himself stepping into the back of the ambulance in a blanket in the car park just as Iris Weaver came past: a large bandage on his finger, the boulder-like dressing Kev's handiwork, the presence – or otherwise – of his finger unclear. Price would tell Iris not to worry, that it was all an exercise, that the management had needed a volunteer. And then he remembered: Kev's arse... red shorts... sloping off... fag. Kev's absence actually calmed Price: at least he wouldn't come out of this looking like a clown.

So, Price realised, it was all down to the Chinaman now, ploughing his furrow by the wall. Granted they'd never spoken, but that also meant they'd never had *words*. He would be over soon enough, Price thought. International collaboration: that's what fellows did these days. Space stations, places like that: all handshakes and grins, exchanges of small gifts. He'd seen it on the net.

Above Price, there was a disturbance in the water: chopping, churning, bubbles, clouds. Price wondered if it was Iris or some of the women, gossiping as they liked to while clinging on at either end: they weren't fussy where they talked. But then he thought: surely it was too early? It was only ever him and the Chinaman for the first half hour: duelling, end to end. Maybe that was him... now... *occupying* his (Price's) lane.

Price thought of the horse in the river; how it had been rescued, how it hadn't been rescued, how it had rescued itself. *Fake News*. Wasn't that what they called it?

Suddenly, and for no more than a moment, the animal's dark shape seemed to be upon him: its muscular legs kicking in the chlorinated water of the pool. Although he could not turn to see it, he sensed its shadow, felt its mass: the neck and head jerking above the surface, the snorts, the huge eyes.

For a second Price saw himself on the first day of his round: lifting a crate from his electric float. He remembered Hughes, the old-timer he'd bought out... how Hughes had shown a photo of himself at the reins of a horse-drawn dray.

The disturbance above him stopped. The water stilled.

In the distance, the Chinaman's buzz-cum-hum grew softer, as if somehow he had broken the bounds of the pool and was now doing his *thing* towards a great remoteness where there would be only clear water ahead of him and, above him, the very occasional bird.

And Price was at the bottom of the pool, floating, caught by his finger, as if it were in a dyke, on the seaward side.

Sand Dancer

PERYGL - Hen FAES Tanio
Peidiwch a chyffwrdd ag unrhywddeunydd milwrol
Gallai ffrwydro a'chiladd.Ffoniwch Heddlu DeCymru

DANGER - Former Firing RANGE
Do not touch any Military debris it may explode and
kill you. Telephone South Wales Police 01792 456 999

MOD

Conger eel sky: thick, endless and monger slab-heavy on the shore.

Jobey's detector goes *bleep*.

Not that he notices.

His ignorance – *bleep*... there it goes again – has nothing to do with the crash-and-sigh of the in-coming tide. Nor either the bullying wind that hurls itself looking for something to batter on the long and empty beach. Nor even is it on account of any failure of his headphones (which are of the muffed kind that clamp his ears like the shells of scallops).

No. The reason Jobey hears nothing is because he is dancing... waltzing (after a fashion)... on the sand.

He cuts a bizarre sight (not that there are many who go down to the sea there, particularly at that time of day and year)... dancing solo, in his yellow oilskins, with his metal detector.

Yet, far from being alone, Jobey, as far as *he* is concerned, is with Rita... *Hayworth*, that is. And, tonight, he is really sweeping her off her feet.

Sometimes his detector is Ava (Gardner), Elizabeth (*never* 'Liz') Taylor, even a young and shy Lauren Bacall; at other times the rubber-handled stick and disc becomes Marilyn (no surname necessary); Vivien Leigh, if an evening calls for an English rose; Bette Davis, when he needs to be bossed. Always a star... a screen goddess... from Hollywood's Golden Age. And tonight it's Rita that he waltzes with.

And... my... *what* a woman! Yes, he'd been nervous... dry-throated... a tremble in his voice when he'd asked if she'd do him the honour. But how they were moving now... *gliding*... just the two of them... eye to eye... arms around one another... on the shell-studded sand... to the shrieked symphonies of gulls that watched and wheeled.

The detector bleeps again, and *this* time, thanks to some fiddling back home in his shed – souping-up the sound for those moments when his mind wandered – he hears the call. Suddenly the alloy and circuitry in his hands is again just that: his detector (albeit a *Quantum Strike-Gold XRB*). And Rita disappears, as if into some sea mist, blowing him a kiss.

Jobey stops, takes his spade from his backpack, digs.

It's almost dark when he connects with the source of the signal that had pulsed through Rita.

Down in his hole, Jobey worries the tide might wash over him. He kneels and sweeps at the dark metal beneath him which now bears only the faintest layer of sand.

Steel... and heavy-duty, Jobey thinks. *The tip of a very big iceberg. Not a bomb or a mine, though. Too big... wrong shape.*

Jobey brings down his spade on it – once, with a clang – then listens (albeit that he doesn't know what for).

Water spills into the hole, a pool foams at his feet. Jobey hauls himself out, heaves slurrying sand on top of his find. As he does this, something strange occurs. From down in the hole, a clang, so it seems, comes back.

The weather is turning tricky now: what Jobey judges *a proper strop*. He gathers his gear, and bustles from the beach. Sand swirls after him. In the dunes the wind bends the marram, beats the thistles. On the track and then the lane, Jobey has a job to keep his moped upright. He veers from one side of the road to the other, Rita in his lap. Rain starts to spit.

Boiling the kettle in his kitchen, Jobey decides the first thing he must do is say nothing to no one. Everybody knew the sands were off-limits... banned: that, though they'd quit now, the Army had fired bullets and bombs there for donkey's years. But if *he* Jobey stepped on a mine... well, that was *his* lookout and nobody else's. What he certainly wasn't going to do was tell Morgan, Praggy or any of the others who took the mick in the bar at *The Ship*. He remembers how he told them once a whale had risen in the bay to watch him on the beach. How it had very probably – this whale – been four hundred years old and therefore a *contemporary* – yes, that was the word – of Oliver Cromwell, Florence Nightingale and Sitting Bull. Praggy had spouted-out beer, the rest almost choked as they laughed. Another time they'd announced him as 'Indiana Jones and Olive Oil' as he walked in with his kit, albeit that *that* evening it was Italian bombshell Gina Lollobrigida with whom he'd tripped the light fantastic (though her name, he knew, would have meant nothing to them).

On his sofa, in the gloom of his front room, Jobey ponders the hunk of steel. Headlamps of passing cars cut through the blinds on his window, running slatted beams over the trophies on his walls: the mudguard of a Fordson Major tractor – date unknown, but certainly 'early' – centre-stage above the gas fire on the chimney breast.

That what he has found is a German submarine or U-boat (very probably War-era), Jobey has little doubt. All that puzzles him, to use the terminology, is its 'type'.

The following afternoon Jobey goes back to the beach, digs. Four feet down he finds the tower and, with it, the hatch. He hits it with the back of his spade, twice. After a moment, a double-knock comes back. Jobey hits again: this time just once. A single strike returns.

A stiff *unscrewing* sound emanates from the tower. The lid pops up. Jobey peers in.

On a ladder, a few feet below him, stands the figure of what

Jobey presumes to be a German officer. At the bottom of the ladder Jobey makes out the faces of the U-boat's crew, which possess a papery paleness in the gloom.

'*Guten tag*... I mean, good afternoon,' says the officer (seemingly the captain), correcting himself and blinking at the light while seeming to look for the sun. 'It *is* afternoon, I presume.' He has fair hair, blue eyes (beneath the right is a small scar that reminds Jobey of the fossil of a trilobite he once found) and a pointy, silvering beard. He wears a thick, white sweater.

'Good afternoon,' says Jobey.

'A splendid day... by the looks of it.'

'Not bad.'

'It's very good to meet you,' says the captain, who seems to Jobey to be excited, but also anxious. 'I was wondering if you might be able to assist us,' continues the captain. 'We were looking for some water.'

'Water?' says Jobey.

'Yes,' says the officer. 'Drinking water... for my men. Our situation... it is rather like Samuel Taylor Coleridge and his *Ancient Mariner*: water, water everywhere and not a drop to drink...

'My name is Captain Trautmann.'

'Jobey Jones,' says Jobey.

The man rises a step. Jobey moves back, puts his hand on his spade. *In case things turn nasty*, thinks Jobey. The captain seems to notice, stays where he is.

'What are you doing here?' asks Jobey.

'Seeking only water, as I have said,' the officer replies. 'Will you help us?'

Jobey thinks: consorting with the enemy... people had been strung up for that; women tarred and feathered. And there was family, too. The war was over... seventy years... but what about Great Uncle Jack... and Auntie Bopa?

'You killed my Uncle Jack,' says Jobey.

'What?' the captain replies. A murmur ripples among the men in the boat's dim interior. 'Where?' the captain asks. 'When?'

'El Alamein, North Africa,' says Jobey. '1942. Ruined my auntie's life, you did. That's what my *mamgu* said.'

'Oh, but that wasn't us. Ours is a submarine. El Alamein was nothing but a sea of... sand.'

A shower of grains falls in through the hatch. The captain draws his hand from the ladder, runs it over his face, looks back up at Jobey.

'So why are you here then?' asks Jobey. 'This is Wales.'

'Following orders: surveilling your coast. We put into your bay because we needed fresh water. I was going to send a party ashore, but a storm blew up and grounded us... buried us, in fact. We've been here ever since.'

Jobey eyes him... the men at his feet.

'I myself am old, I admit,' the captain begins again, 'but look at these men – they are... *young*... boys most of them... recruited long after the war was begun.'

'You know you lost, don't you?' Jobey says.

The men below the captain stir, say things to each other in German.

'No, we did not know,' the captain replies. 'We've had no communications – with our fleet, Berlin... anyone... for years. But I suspected as much.'

The two say nothing for a moment, hear the waves falling on the shore. A gull flies over Jobey. The sight of it and the sound of the waves seem to cause the officer's face to brighten.

'So, will you help us?' he asks again. 'Water and, perhaps some other assistance... so that we might... get from here?'

'You won't be getting anywhere. I can tell you that,' says Jobey. 'There's mines and bombs all over this beach. You're surrounded.'

At that moment the tidewater begins to fall into the hole. Jobey sees the officer's eyes light up as the water sloshes at the rim of the hatch. The men in the boat bunch close to the ladder. Jobey slams the lid shut, begins burying it with sand.

'What are you doing?' the captain calls from inside the hatch.

'Putting you back,' says Jobey, '... for now.'

'Will you help us? Please!'

'I'll think about it,' Jobey says.

That night Jobey goes to *The Ship*. He drinks ginger beer in a corner. He sees Praggy, Morgan and Rhys sniggering at the bar. He thinks about the U-boat, the men on board her: how no one would believe him if he told them; how they would say that Jobey Jones had gone completely mad. He thinks about the captain and his lips, which had been dry and cracked, his calls for water, the way the men had looked up. He thinks about the smell which had risen through the hatch... connects it with a shed on a farm he'd been taken to when he was very small. A pig had been killed and was hanging by its feet. Its snout was caked with dried blood.

Outside the pub Jobey sees the tyres on his moped have been let down.

In the morning Jobey chases his pigeons from their loft. He takes his trophies from the parlour and hurls them over the loft, into the back lane. Then he goes to the *Spar* and buys ten big bottles of water which he puts in his panniers. Then he sets off for the beach.

Some way before the dunes he comes upon PC Tal Prothero who is blocking the road with his patrol car.

All I need, Jobey thinks to himself as he stops his moped.

'What's up, Proth?' asks Jobey, lifting the visor on his helmet.

'Bomb on the beach,' says Prothero. 'Big one an' all. You are not going down there, I hope.'

'Course not,' says Jobey. 'Off-limits. We all know that. Who's down there then?'

'Bomb disposal – the lot,' says Prothero. 'Going to send it up, I think. No one's allowed near.'

'Duw!' says Jobey. 'I'll be on my way then. Good job I've got my helmet! Cheers, Proth.'

He swings his moped around, back towards the village. As soon as he knows he's out of Prothero's sight he turns off and cuts over the fields, bouncing on the seat as the moped traverses the dips and rises.

Soon he's in the foothills of the dunes. He parks his moped, then strides between them, spade in his backpack, panniers with the bottles of water across his shoulders, helmet still on. He looks part-prospector, part-astronaut.

Away from the lanes the coast is fenced off. Jobey crawls under one line of barbed wire and then another; at the second, he plants his hand on a thistle as he works himself clear. He manages to stifle a yell.

From the brow of a dune he surveys the beach. He sees the Army team clearly, working in the area where the bomb has been found – test-fired years before, he doesn't doubt, and now exposed by the tide or a sandstorm. Red flags that have been planted by the soldiers are tugged by a breeze.

He scans the shore, calculates the U-boat is no more than a quarter of a mile from the hotspot. There's no way he can attempt anything till dark. And if, before then, the Army boys detonate their discovery, it'll mean, Jobey reckons, one thing only for that sub and her crew. Boom! Goodnight Berlin.

Jobey hides in some scrub, waits.

As the sun drops, Jobey wonders what the crew on the boat might be doing – singing songs sung by Germans when they've the beer in them, *or* sitting there holding their breath: all ears for the excavations, the barked orders, the hammering of flag posts by the soldiers on the beach... thinking that he, Jobey, has betrayed them.

When he judges it dark enough he moves quickly over the sand. The Army team have erected floodlights to continue their operation. The buried boat, Jobey calculates, is just outside their arc. He starts to dig, in a way that he has never dug before... as if his life depends on it.

Having found the tower, he works his way – with a good, deep trench – along one side of the sub and then the other, loosening the sand similarly at its nose and propeller. The sun has set now and the moon is climbing and casting a silver path across the bay. Jobey is grateful when clouds close over it. He digs faster and faster, frightened that at any moment the rising silhouette of the submarine will be seen. The voices of the soldiers echo from their worksite. The generator for their floodlights hums.

Finally, with dawn almost on him, he taps the hatch with his spade.

No sound comes from inside the sub. Jobey taps again.

Eventually, he hears the hatch being opened... *gradually*, *carefully*. The lid lifts.

Jobey looks inside. A pistol pokes out. Below it is the figure of Captain Trautmann.

'So... you have elected to betray us,' he says.

'No!' says Jobey. 'I have not.'

At that moment, whistles sound along the beach: first one and then another... then more... in a horrible, high-pitched scream.

Jobey sees Trautmann's pale finger pull on the trigger: the pistol is point blank in his face.

Suddenly the boat rocks as the night tide – which has been advancing all the while (as if in secret) under cover of all of the other movement and din – sweeps into Jobey's trenches.

A bullet flies from Trautmann's gun. Jobey feels sure he actually sees it: whizzing past his ear.

'We are moving,' says Trautmann.

'I know,' says Jobey, 'and I've got the bloody blisters to prove it!'

He holds up his hands.

'Quickly!' says the skipper. 'I misjudged you! I'm sorry! Get in!'

As Jobey pulls down the hatch a blast of incredible proportions shakes the shoreline. Its enormity is such that cottages, farms, livestock, even *The Ship Inn* back in the village, are showered with sand, shells, seaweed and trees. The flash of light can be seen (so people say afterwards) from one end of Wales to the other, and the *crump* of the blast heard just as far.

One consequence of the apocalyptic explosion is that it helps a certain very old submarine finally put to sea.

The vessel sails out into the bay under the breaking light of morning. Jobey stands among the young men as they laugh and sing and dance. He then watches as they grow old before him: their hair receding, their faces creasing, their frames withering, in front of his very eyes.

'Thank you, Mr Jones,' says the captain, putting his hand in Jobey's. 'We are at sea now, and can find our peace.' He pauses, looks Jobey in the eye. 'And you, Mr Jones? Are *you* ready?'

'Yes,' says Jobey. 'I'm ready.'

With that, the captain's palm and fingers collapse and slip through Jobey's, like so many ashes. And the boat begins its descent into the cold, grey depths. It creaks and it moans around the solitary figure of Jobey as it falls in its downward drift.

The Word

A MOST DESIRABLE

SMALL DAIRY FARM

OVER 28 ACRES

including well watered Dairying Pastures : valuable Growing Timber :
comfortable House and exceptionally well built block of Farm Buildings.

To be offered for Sale by Auction by

FRANK LLOYD & SONS

AT THE WYNNSTAY ARMS HOTEL, WREXHAM,

ON

THURSDAY JUNE 3rd, at 3·15 p.m.

Auctioneer's Offices - Wrexham, Crewe, Chester, Whitchurch, Etc.

I
blame
THE LLEWELLYNS.
Them and their place.
Y Gair.
That's Welsh if you didn't already know it.
Second part sounds like liar.
In English it means
The Word.
Welsh and bleak.
Go visit.
See for yourself.
But there again
DON'T.
Read this instead.
Read all of it.
It's better like that.
Trust me.
Think of me as your open book.

It was late February, Saturday tea-time, when Old Man Llewellyn called. I was emptying a van round the back of Unwin and Trent's in Chelsea; stuff I'd picked up on a run through Suffolk, on which the margin was looking good. At first I didn't have a clue who he was. He sounded like someone who seldom used the phone. All pauses, whiny phrases that rose at their end. The verbal equivalent of a dog sniffing at something, backing off, coming back. It was as if the guy, wherever he was, wasn't sure his sentences had reached London, that he could really be heard.

He told me I'd been out to his place six months before. It sounded like a gripe: money, damage, some other complaint. I gradually remembered it: dead end track, grid, yard full of scrap, stone house in a hollow, the shitty land all slopes and scars. The name *Y Gair* in cheap, hardware store letters on an oval of cracked wood. Plastic windmills, the sort played with by kids, whirling in a line on a fence. Their spinning the only sound. The whole place cold and in shadow at the top of a valley which had otherwise been in sun.

Why I really remembered it was this: it was the only place on that tour where we *hadn't* got in. Not even Cat, my girlfriend of the time and a door-stepper *par excellence*, had managed to talk her way in. Our card was taken, and that was it. I remembered Cat coming back, shaking her head, me turning the truck in the yard. At the front door the young woman who'd denied us watched as we left. I'd been in the game ten years and our dismissal told me this. The Word was a place where treasure was to be had. All the way back to London I wondered what we'd missed.

Old Man Llewellyn got to his point at last. He wanted to know when I'd be back. Not for a while, I told him, half-teasing. As far as I remembered, they had nothing to sell. The situation had changed, he said; he'd be grateful if I could call. Difficult, I said. I was due in Norfolk and, after that, up North. The line went quiet. Then a scuffing sound as if he was consulting someone at his end. He came back on. He was really looking for something quite soon, he said. How much was he looking to dispose of? I asked. 'Everything,' he said – his voice having a puzzled ring, as if my question made no sense. Two days later I pulled into the yard. Rain swept the screen as I brought the lorry to a stop.

Llewellyn stood at the door of the farmhouse. His wife appeared at his side. Think of the painting American Gothic – the farm couple and their fork – and that was them, more or less. Except the Llewellyns were thinner, older, greyer: more worn-out, and Welsh.

They let me in without a word, Mr Llewellyn guiding me through rooms that were still and dark. Small windows and the low-slung pitch of the place kept what little light there was at bay. The house smelt of cave, and had the coolness to match. But I had no interest in any of that. It was treasure that I sought, and my eyes fell on plenty. I was casual, of course, non-committal, unimpressed. I wandered. Llewellyn watched. The parlour felt as if no one had entered it in fifty years. I looked – but only for a moment – at an oil painting over the empty fireplace. Shepherd and sheep, snow-covered trees (nineteenth century) beneath what seemed like one hundred years of dust.

Upstairs, a four-poster bed whose mattress looked as hard as stone. I wondered how the couple slept. Perhaps they didn't.

Mrs Llewellyn handed me tea: the cup and saucer Nantgarw, I felt sure. On the saucer a spoon too bulky by far – a pleasingly agricultural touch. Silver. I pressed my thumb to the mark. The sword and wheatsheaves of Chester. My party trick. Mrs Llewellyn snapped Welsh at her husband then left. He cleared his throat. 'We just want it *gone*,' he said with finality. '*All* of it,' like he was expelling a ball of phlegm.

We set to work. For the next five hours, he and I virtually cleared the place: the old man more than matching my keenness. Between us we carried out an oak dresser and all of its crockery, an ancient organ with ranks of dusty, painted pipes, a fine circular mahogany dining table and chairs which appeared to have never been used, three carved chests from the hall and the bedrooms (the black wood of which I felt sure was Jacobean), a rosewood dressing table and stool, and, finally, for that first wave, a sturdy Edwardian bureau. I went through its chambers and drawers in the lorry while Llewellyn rested on the edge of an old enamel bath in the yard. I took out a red leather-bound volume that had *Y Gair* in gilt to the front. It recorded the history of the farm's cattle in a kind of family tree. A second volume, similarly bound, was inscribed *Y Flock*. This listed the farm's sheep – births, sales and purchases – across more than two hundred years. The copperplate writing in both was the work – in all of that time – of just four hands. I felt I had the title deeds to The Word right there in my palms. In a small upper drawer I found a medal which was, I learned later, from Queen Victoria's Zulu War. With it a pocketbook containing sketches of South African scenes – tribesmen, a village, British soldiers – and notes in pencil. All in Welsh.

I returned to the house, found Llewellyn in the kitchen. We went back to work. Next we took out half-a-dozen paintings including an oil that showed the farm and, in front of it, a group of fat, black cattle. When done with those, Llewellyn stopped two longcase clocks even as they ticked. He removed their heavy iron weights and passed them to me with his firm, cold hands. I thought of dead lambs and babies stillborn.

All afternoon I splashed back and forth, arms laden: horse brasses, candlesticks, mantel clocks, books that spoke of Livingstone and Stanley as if they still lived, silver-backed brushes, pewter plates, prettily-painted china, stuffed songbirds under glass, the masks of foxes and badgers, love spoons, Davy lamps and lace. Still later: meat dishes, inkwells, pens, tea chests, copper kettles, samplers, stern ebony-framed Bible texts, rugs, tapestries, a radiogram and, with Llewellyn helping me, the most glorious harp. The wind drew a faint sound from its strings as we carried it over the yard. It let out a moan as we set it down in the truck.

After that, and between us again, a large corner cabinet crammed with collectables. These I removed and either boxed or wrapped in the lorry one by one: bulls of various breeds (which meant nothing to a city boy like me), a woman in Welsh costume at a spinning wheel, thimbles by the dozen and mementoes of castles and cathedrals in the shape of condiment sets and cloches for butter and cheese.

On one of these crossings I nodded to the farm's name on the crummy, dried-out sign and asked Llewellyn what it meant. He told me it translated as The Word. I asked him where the name came from. He said the farm had *always* been The Word, from the time of his grandfather's grandfather, as if my question about its *coming* was absurd.

Last came the greatest prize of all, which, if I'd been doing my job properly – I cite excitement as my excuse – I ought to have moved first.

The kitchen table.

Table though was hardly the word. It lay – no, make that *occupied* – the kitchen (and therefore the house) heavy as history, dark as beef gravy, bigger than a boat. As if it had been there *before* The Word. As if the stone walls of the house had been built around it. As if, without its presence, the roof and the heavens themselves would fall in.

I'd seen tables like it fly into five figures at auction. I stared at it, wondering what it might make.

Two big, almost black, knots seemed to stare back at me, like the eyes of an elephant.

'Ready?' said Llewellyn, putting his fingers under one end. He looked as if its disposal were the most logical thing in the world.

We moved it a few steps at a time – which was all that we could. Carried it then stopped. Carried it then stopped again. Now that I had my hands on it I was prepared to spend all night, inch by inch if need be, lumbering this monster from its lair, dragging this dreadnought from the deep. I feared it might prove too much for the old man. But he persevered: the table's removal seeming to mean even more to him than it did to me.

I studied him for a moment during one of our breaks. He was old but had a rangy toughness and still stood straight. Far from weakening him, the tasks seemed to have lifted him, given him strength. I wondered if, when young, he'd ploughed his land by hand.

Mrs Llewellyn, in a pink pinafore, barked bits of Welsh – that I took to be directions – as we heaved the table over the flagstone floor. Once in the hall we made it to the big front door.

After many more stops and starts in the yard we finally reached the lorry. The tail-lift took one end up as the two of us got under the other. Together we shunted the table inside, exhausted.

Llewellyn returned to the house. I lit a cigarette, smoked it in the yard, remembered something about boulders being rolled from Wales to Stonehenge. It was cold, near dark. Job done, I thought, at last.

Through all of this I'd made a point of *not* asking about the young woman who'd turned Cat and me away those six months before. Their daughter, obviously. During my fetching and carrying I'd moved a photograph which showed her with them, put it safe by a window. Now that I'd loaded I was keen to be gone. I was worried she might show up, ask her parents what was going on.

I went back into the house, a bundle of notes on my thigh. I wondered how much lighter it would be when I left. Farmers could be tough. There were few tougher when they fancied a fight. The couple faced me in the kitchen, their backs to the stove.

'We've no need of your money,' Llewellyn said. 'She's dead, you see.' He moved awkwardly across the kitchen, as if wrong-footed by its emptiness. He reached for the big, black Bible that I'd put by the sink. I'd moved it there from its place on the table before we'd set about shifting the great wooden slab.

'Take it,' he said, placing it in my palms.

I laid it on the seat next to me in the lorry, thinking the Llewellyns would appreciate this show of respect.

I backed the truck up then brought it around in an arc in the yard.

The headlamps swung over The Word like searchlights. The glare seized them for a second, side-by-side, in the frame of their front door: the two of them rigid, like statues of saints over a cathedral porch.

When I shifted round in the cab to catch sight of them again, the door was shut.

They were gone.

My life and times, in so far as they're relevant.

I've always hung with a certain set. My father had casinos. One in Mayfair (well... on the edge) and another that he ran without a licence on the South Coast. They were the kind where the girls who worked for him had to squeeze into outfits that were too tight. When I was thirteen I lost my virginity to Anna who was Polish, pretty and lonely. She worked for my dad in the London club. We'd lie on her sofa in a dingy bedsit in Balham, listening to the traffic, saying nothing much. One day I found out she was pregnant: one of the other girls let it slip. I was scared but went round to her place anyway. The neighbours said my dad had already slung her out. No one knew where she'd gone. Soon after, he sent me to a boarding school run by Benedictine priests. Not that he had anything to do with Roman Catholicism. His parents were Romanian Jews. My mother had long gone, living in Spain, as far as I knew. I left school at sixteen. No exams, but reasonable manners, prettyish looks.

Dad set me to work under Lenny Hartmann: Heartless Lenny as he was known. A modern-day Fagin when it came to antiques. Shameless in parting folk from their gems; peerless in trading-up bodge jobs and tat. Lenny was camper than a Soho drag queen, and had all the mercy of Genghis Khan. He wore a boot-black wig, fly-away cravats and rings that clacked on his fingers like castanets. Twice he tried to rape me. Once in his lock-up with a Hermes scarf. The other while swinging a halberd on a clearance at a baronial hall. 'I'll screw you if it's the last thing I do, you stuck-up little tart.' Lenny was adored by all, even those – and there were many – that he robbed.

Things cooled between us when he found out about Ruby, my first proper girlfriend. They turned glacial when I set up in business on my own. Basically I replicated Lenny's act. Except I pushed harder, drove further, pried deeper. His customers came over to me. That's business. Lenny bowed out, spitting and hissing, to a flat in Brighton. The queen was dead... long live the king.

The really *big* difference between me and Lenny – apart from my not being gay – was this. I had women on the team. And by that I don't mean girls whose job it was to answer the phone. I mean girls who were my scouts, patrolling: 'at point', as I think it's called. And, if not scouting, then riding shotgun at least. That's not to say they were Amazons or banshees (though they did their share of the scalping, that was true). They were mostly small, ordinary and, arguably, on the plain side of pretty. Ruby was the first.

Our target territories were places like the borders of Wales, the Somerset Levels, the moors of the North and the East Anglian fens: districts and counties where, to some extent, Time had stood still. Places where people and, more importantly, possessions had stayed put, sometimes for hundreds of years. Potholed tracks, rotten gateposts, sheepdogs on chains, wary-eyed natives who accepted only cash... that's what we looked for, that's where we went.

The hunt was getting harder though. With every passing year, genuine locals were being forced out, getting scarcer on the ground. Media types, bankers and well-off liberal wankers: they led the siege. The kind who, if it had been happening anywhere else in the world, would have been monstering the UN, bleating non-stop on the BBC. All of them buying up farms and cottages – not even as their actual homes – thanks to their city salaries, pensions from Joe Public and the sale of some shoebox in the South East.

Pubs where farmers once drank in boots at the bar now served *goujons* of this and medallions of that. Village shops, those that remained, had shelves full of pasta, poncy 'craft' beer and fair trade fucking tea. A new four-wheel drive in the yard flagged the fall of each fresh castle. Another drawbridge pulled up on the likes of my girls and me.

Career-wise my big and maybe last notable break came in my very first summer. I was working the Welsh border in my transit with Ruby – upland farms, backwater cottages, old halls and schools. We pulled-in at some shack that looked like it had been there since Offa dug his Dyke. Something told me we'd get nothing but buckshot at best.

I was about to turn when Ruby said, 'Stop. *You* stay here. *I'll* go and see.' Ten minutes later she was calling me over to settle a price on a Civil War musket that some old coot was surrendering with a toothless grin. The experience taught me this. That when it came to getting *into* a place a woman always knew best. Rubes eventually left me to set up as some kind of therapist in Slough. But those who came after her were just as adept. And Cat – my latest – is... was... the cream. *Oh no madam / guv*, has always been my line if asked. *I'm just the piano shifter. If you're looking for the player, she's the boss... over there.*

I'd been back from The Word for no more than a week when I read about the shit that had gone down. The first jolt was a photo in the newspaper. I was outside a café I used in Hampstead, catching some sun. I set down my cup. The faces looking back at me in the photo were the Llewellyns': ten years younger, but definitely them – on a seafront... smiling... daughter between them – pretty – clutching an ice-cream cone. Beneath the photo the word *Massacre*. And, below that, a report of how *every living thing* on *a remote farm in Wales* had been found SHOT DEAD. The farmer, his wife *slain* inside the house. Dogs, cattle, sheep... even hens... *slaughtered* all over the shop. *Shocked* neighbours said the couple's daughter had died from cancer *some months before*. Police wanted to hear from anyone who'd seen the *chapel-going couple* or had visited the farm *recently*. There was a number to call. I looked back at the photo. For a moment I wondered who'd taken it. A passer-by to whom they'd handed the camera? Or maybe the daughter had a friend? I wondered if she'd died a virgin. Up there. On that shithouse hill.

My heart beat hard. I thought about calling Lenny, then thought the better of it. Surely the cops could see it was some kind of suicide pact? That the old man had gone mad? That's what happened at places like that. Hadn't I met enough head-bangers in my time on the road? Anyway, there was nothing to connect me. Except... my card – the one the daughter had taken from Cat. That's how he'd rung. All the police had to do was check their phone. What if there were questions? About all the stuff that had gone? When I left it the place was a shell. My number would be there. Right there. In – doubtless – their big, clumping bitch of a phone, with a dial on the front and some old school ringtone. Quite possibly it would be the *only* number. I remembered Llewellyn's voice. His answer to my question about what exactly he wanted to get rid of. 'Everything,' had been his reply. 'Everything.'

I folded the paper. Against my thigh I felt the bundle – the one I always carried – bigger than normal. I finished my coffee and left.

When I got back to *Bella*, my houseboat at Camden, there was a note from Cat. She was tired of *fleecing hillbillies*, and was off to Bali instead.

That evening – possibly from shock – I found myself studying the Llewellyns' Bible, the one item of theirs that, for whatever reason, I had not sought to sell. It was like a boulder. If nothing else, I thought, it would be useful ballast for the boat.

It was entirely in Welsh. I ran my fingers over the pages, mining memories from school, trying to work out what the verses meant.

My eye was caught by what seemed some kind of doodle or cartoon. I went past it, leafed back. It seemed to have gone. But then – at the foot of a page – I found it: a serpent. Small, rust-coloured and, by the look of it, drawn maybe a hundred or more years before. I ran my finger over it... forked tongue... slit eye... twisted tail. I turned the pages, looking for more. But there were none. I turned back to look again at the snake, but couldn't find it. It was as if it had fallen from the page or crawled into some nest in the spine. Suddenly I felt tired, feverish. I closed the Bible, and slept.

I'm not sure exactly how long I was asleep. Two nights and days at least. I remember footsteps, voices on the wharf. Trying but failing to get up. On maybe the third day, I woke, dripping with sweat. I stumbled to the bathroom, looked in the mirror. My mouth felt horrific, as if bursting with splinters, nettles and wasps. I peeled back my cracked lips.

Then I found it: the first letter.

The *i* was tucked teasingly on my lower right incisor, but quite definitely there. Identifiably black and Gothic. I drank some water, brushed my teeth, pulled down my lip again. The dot and stalk seemed fainter. My weakness returned. I took hold of the sink, steadied myself, put out the light, crawled back to bed.

Within moments (though it may actually have been hours) my mind and body, it seemed, were spinning. I saw the roulette wheels on the gaming tables at my father's clubs. Him – cock of the walk – all winks and smiles, swaggering past. The roulette wheels gave way to the toy windmills at The Word. They roared on their wire fence like a line of power saws, threatening any second to fly off. At the same time, a wooden spinning wheel – the ornament I took from the cabinet in the farmhouse but now life-sized – danced a jig while turning furiously on the kitchen's flagstone floor. Beside it was the woman in Welsh dress – black hat and shawl – moving weirdly, like a marionette, as if she were made of pieces of china joined together with string. Above all of this, Cat's voice, calling out.

Fleecing hillbillies! Fleecing hillbillies!

Llewellyn and his wife now stepped into sight. Not in boiler suit and pinafore but each of them shoulder to shin in freshly-shorn wool. Running around the kitchen table, chasing a child. Woolly white hoods part-covering their heads. Their strange sheep's clothing flapping from their bony, grey limbs. The boy showed his face, and I saw that it was me.

'Everything!' Llewellyn was saying, licking ice-cream from his lips.

'Everything!' echoed Ma Llewellyn, at his shoulder, toy windmills-turned-saws whining horribly in her claw hands.

Llewellyn's tongue shot from his mouth. Not a pink, human tongue but the thin, rust-brown fork of the snake in their Bible.

Vanilla foam sprayed from it as it uncoiled.

I came-to. The sheet on my bunk was soaked. I dragged myself to the bathroom, cleaned up. I threw on some clothes and went on deck. The light hit me like a camera flash. I felt incredibly weak, but steadied myself and walked to a café on the lock. I ate some flummeried version of fish and chips followed by a ton of ice-cream.

Later, back on *Bella*, I stuck on some flip-flops and shorts. I spread out on the little platform at the stern that Cat called my sundeck, where – when not in Bali – she liked to read. I tried ringing her. Her mobile went straight to answerphone. I wondered if she'd left me for ever. I lay back. The sun warmed me. I fell asleep.

I was woken by a skirmish between two swans beside the boat. I got to my feet. As I did so I stubbed my toes against one of Cat's flowerpots. I cursed and hobbled indoors, vowing to throw her stuff overboard in the same way she'd dumped me. I was looking for some mules or pumps to put on when I saw it: the second letter. To be accurate, what I actually saw was a coal-coloured speck – like the tail of something – peeping out from between the toes of my right foot. I bent over and pushed them apart. There it lay, in the interior, curled like an earwig: the letter *a*. I rubbed a finger over it in disbelief. The skin reddened, the letter remained. I went to the bathroom, dragged down my lip in the mirror. The *i* on my incisor looked back at me. I brushed at it madly. A sea of foam and blood surrounded the tooth. But the *i* stood there – defiant – like a lighthouse in a storm.

In the days that followed – try as I did to tell myself that it wasn't happening – more letters appeared. Sometimes singly and secretively – a *b* in the hair above my groin, a *c* under my eyelid, a *d* and *e* in the lobes of my ears. At other times, they sprang across me, surprising me with their sheer numbers, taking root on my chest, my buttocks and my thighs, like toadstools in the dark.

Soon the letters began to link up in ladders, streams and whole rivers of text. Examining myself in my wardrobe mirror one evening I finally started to make sense of their chains. Like a history or legend written on medieval vellum, my skin – my entire body – was telling the story of my life. My flesh was a journal, a log, a herd book, if you like, of all of the farms, houses and cottages where I had ever been.

A ledger forensically documenting my business, my plunder, my sins.

On parts of me – my back, my neck – you could barely see my skin for ink. *Marsh Farm, Lincolnshire – dresser, settles, silver salver, paintings x four. Highfield House, north Herefordshire – sword, flintlock pistol, Wedgwood sundries, harpsichord. Cairn Cottage, Exmoor – pocket watch, snuff boxes, carriage clock, letters from the Peninsular War.* And so, like the lines of the Llewellyns' Bible, the names and inventories went on. They ran like serpents, from my head to my toes. The longest, by far, was for The Word. The sloped, copperplate hand climbed both sides of me, from my ankles to my ears, penetrated my head and poured from my nostrils in black, purple and sea-green flumes. These cascaded from my jaw to my chest and circled my nipples with a maze of dizzying whorls – *organ, medal, spinning wheel, bellows, brasses, fishing reel* – that had the arresting appearance of Maori tattoos.

I was no longer a man. I was a manuscript.

It was as if an entire abbey of monks had held me down in some vaulted library and set about me by candlelight with their sharp quill pens. I had no idea what to do. I stayed on the boat, curtains tight shut, went without food for days. I sipped water from the bottles I stored on board, crept around like a recluse. I was on my final bottle, its very last drops, when I remembered the article about the Llewellyns, the appeal from the police. Weak as I was I made up my mind to go to them, regardless of whether it incriminated me. I caught the bus to Kentish Town. I wore gloves, sat upstairs, shrouded my features with a scarf and a cap, as if a leper or a beast.

The desk clerk was a woman whose face was not unkind. But she could not... *would* not... understand, no matter how I tried to explain myself. I took my scarf from my face. When this drew no reaction I began to undress. I threw my jacket to the floor, started to unbutton my shirt, abandoned the buttons, tore it open instead. 'Look at me!' I screamed through the glass. 'Just look at me!' Two officers appeared, took hold of my arms. They told me to calm down, which I did. They said I needed to see my doctor, to leave quietly, to get home, to mind how I went.

I went to my surgery next morning, refused to leave until I was seen, till every inch of me was seen. The doctor said he could find nothing wrong. 'Some time in the country. Out of London. That's what you need.'

'But the letters,' I said. 'My letters.'

'Don't worry,' he said, without looking up. 'There's time enough for that. They'll be here when you get back. Get away somewhere. Rest – that's what you need.'

There was only one place I knew for that.

And so I am here... under the stars... waiting my turn.

We come and go... all of us... don't we?

You, me, the Llewellyns in their ashes.

No matter how big our bundle, how sleek our cattle, the vastness of our flock.

But *not* The Word: *Y Gair*, call it what you will. *It* endures.

Even if you never find it, it shall be there, believe me... in its place, up on the hill – counting, knowing, reckoning, judging – as it always has, as it always will.

I *don't* blame the Llewellyns. Really I don't. Despite what I said. Because I – and surely you – have come to see that it's written, isn't it? It's written.

The moon watches us. Frost fills this cold field.

And now it... *scours* me, the frozen grass wire-brushing my skin.

Summoned songbirds and shivering hares stand witness as I kneel.

And all of my words, all of my testimony, peels to the taut pasture, falls from me in scrolls, on this hard, white hill.

The Cheese

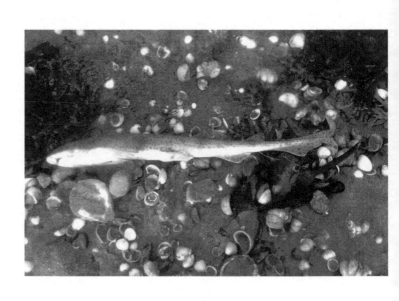

It was afterwards that it began. My performance at the inaugural Llanymaen Literary Festival had itself passed off reasonably well: an audience of eight in the marquee at one point. And a pigeon. This had flapped about somewhat noisily during both the first *and* second of my readings, defecating at one stage on the pages of my opened book. But I soldiered on, ever the trouper.

True, an elderly lady did, in spite of my self-evident female form, mistake me and my work... persistently... for that of the Anglo-Irish author Connor Sewell, requiring me to field several questions on the plot and characters of what she called my... *his* 'wonderful' novel *Treago Road*. Mercifully, during maybe her fourth or fifth lengthy inquisition, a minister of religion, in a cream jacket and dog collar, rose and (despite some resistance on the biddy's part) cut her off.

Still, I did manage to sell her a copy of my own, latest offering, *Year of the Camomile Turtle* (the only one, I confess, of the afternoon) which I signed in Sewell's name, her violet eyes sparkling as she looked on.

My bed for the night was at *The Castle Inn* – the only 'hostelry' in the village. After attempting, and failing, to get online in my room, I went down to the lounge.

He was, in appearance, a modest little man. He entered the room quietly and stood at the bar, waiting to be served. The way his huge and unseasonal tweed overcoat swaddled him made me imagine him first as a mole and, later, as a mouse.

Furnished with his beer, he turned and surveyed the assembly, as if looking for a place to sit. With this, the other customers seemed to quieten. After asking if the empty chairs at my table belonged to anyone (which they did not), he joined me.

He was difficult to age: his coat concealing so much of him in a manner that was monkish. But it was clear that he was not young. A few drab hairs reached from his forehead over his otherwise bald crown. These represented what at first seemed to be the sum of his significant distinguishing features. However, I noticed that he seemed to be not very clean: his fingernails, in particular, were black. He also smelled: the kind of whiff encountered in grubby corners, or in a fridge where something has gone off. That apart, he was inoffensive enough.

'You're a writer,' he said after our conversation about the weather had petered.

After the sparse attendance at my event at the festival I was heartened by this moment of recognition. Wine and fatigue playing their part, my tongue loosened and I was soon running – rather foolishly, I confess – through a résumé of the thinly-scattered high points of my career. Throughout he nodded, smiled and raised his eyebrows in all of those places where I gave him his cue, especially when it came to my longlisting – more years ago than I cared to remember – for the Fennelhume Prize.

'Ah, the Fenney... yes, of course,' he said, appreciatively.

To my gentle disquiet, he also cleaned his teeth. This he did with a grimy matchstick that he produced from a pocket in his coat: not picking his teeth exactly but working at them as if with the bow of some tiny violin. I couldn't help but notice how those in his lower gum rose in a gruesomely ugly reef.

'I also write,' he said, when I had finished talking and he'd finished his make-over of his molars.

His small black eyes shone bright. Mine dulled no doubt at this

utterance of the refrain that writers – *real* writers... let's not beat
about bushes – loathe to hear.

He put away the matchstick.

'I am the cheese correspondent of the *Llanymaen Evening Mail*.'

I decided to humour him: he was original, at least.

'An important position,' I said, knowing full well that, in all
probability, little Llanymaen boasted no more than a monthly
newsletter with accounts of flower festivals, lawn bowls and the
passing of its parishioners, never mind an evening newspaper (and
correspondent for cheese).

'It is indeed important,' he said, animated by my response.

'Home or... foreign correspondent?' I asked.

'What do you mean?' he said.

I sipped my wine (*milking*, as it were, the moment): I saw how our
conversation was being followed by the clientele of the bar.

'These cheeses on which you correspond. Are they domestic, or
continental? English,' I asked '... or Welsh?'

'Oh Welsh,' he said, in an instant. 'There are no finer cheeses than
those to be found in the land of Wales.' A murmur (of agreement, it
seemed) ran through the room.

My odd little associate drank from his glass, set it down with great
solemnity, and then he began.

There followed from his lips what I can only describe as an epic
oration, which took me back to my uni days and the lectures at our
plate glass by 'Dodgy Dave' Docherty who, never mind his wife and
his brown polyester flares, fancied himself as a rebellious lothario,
but spoke – it has to be said – with a strange spellbinding passion (or
so it seemed at the time, at least, to young girls like me). Beowulf,
Chaucer, Cervantes, Karl Marx – Karl Marx? – and Proust (not to
mention those long and dense accounts of *begatting* in the more
impenetrable passages of the Old Testament)... for a moment as my
companion listed and described every cheese he claimed might be
found in the clefts and valleys and peaks of Wales.

'Flintshire Fancy... Pembrokeshire Blue... Wye Witch... Radnor Goat... Dee Devil... Gower Gorse...'

And not only their names, but – at times very lyrically – their tastes, textures and bouquets.

'Crumblier than a spinster from the Siege of Ladysmith... a rind firm as the behind of a six-month-old baby... silkier than a sewin taken on a misted morning from the mouth of the Teifi... an aroma sweeter than all the fresh-baked breads of heaven... a tang to it equal to the spraint of any boar badger worth his salt... fiery as, apart from itself, only a flame-haired woman of the Rhondda Fawr can be...'

And not only that, but he told (gesturing with his hands to demonstrate cutting, stirring, sprinkling and other culinary actions) how these cheeses might best be served and consumed – acclaiming those of special excellence with kissed salutes, pressing his grubby fingers to his amusingly puckered lips.

'... unadorned, with nothing more than a glass of still, farmhouse cider on a scorching summer day... equally at home grilled as a rarebit or served on a sliver of toast in Welsh onion soup... highly suitable for sandwiches as *snap* on an excursion to Forest Coal Pit, the Black Mountain, Arthur's Stone or Devil's Bridge... handily stuck on a stick and conjured as a canapé...' (this pronounced with a camp snootiness worthy of Noel Coward) '... for the *cruchach*, or Taffia, as they now also are known, and various other... *swanks*' (this last word escaping him like some particularly irksome piece of phlegm).

I noticed how he glanced at me after its ejaculation: his look lasting only an instant, but long enough for me to feel that I had been singled out among otherwise blameless congregants in a hushed and sainted place. Within seconds, though, he was smiling, as if nothing had been said.

Finally, he described a Cheddar-like confection he called *Capel Anodd* ('Chapel Tough' he translated in an aside). '... somewhat hard to swallow and certainly not to my personal taste, but each, shall we say, to their lot... or maybe that ought to be Lot?... with a capital *l*.'

He stopped and drew breath, the pondered '*I*' hanging over the bar's onlooking occupants – hypnotically, it seemed – in the manner of a note that his dirty fingers had plucked from some golden harp or lyre.

At this point I would have made my excuses and left but for the fact that during this hymn-to-cheese of his he had drawn himself so close to me that bodily – and possibly also mentally – I found myself trapped.

'And you,' he said to me after refreshing himself with some of his beer, 'what is it that *you* write?'

'Fiction,' I replied, 'mostly.'

'Please go on,' he said, with the utmost civility.

'Well,' I said, 'I suppose I like to bring in the animal kingdom, when I can, as a metaphor for the human condition. In my new book, *Year of the Camomile Tur*—'

'Like Jack London,' he interrupted keenly. '*White Fang.*'

'To a point,' I said.

He then looked around the bar as if quietly demanding the ears of all who were there (albeit that, to a woman and a man, they were listening anyway).

'Of course, the thing about Jack London,' he said, 'was that *that* wasn't his name. Do you know what his *real* name was?'

Every eye and ear in the bar was upon us, he knew. The landlord, who'd been drying the same glass for at least ten minutes, laid his towel on his shoulder, cocked his head.

'No,' I said. 'I can't think that I do.'

'Edinburgh!' he said. 'Jack Edinburgh! *That* was his name!'

Another murmur rippled around the room.

'I'm surprised you didn't know that,' said the man, '... as a writer... at *our* festival.'

'Fascinating,' I said. I made to rise from my seat. 'I'm sorry, but I really must—'

'Take a look at this,' he said, moving from his chair and seating himself next to me on my settle. He reached into a side pocket of his coat.

He placed on the table something wrapped in a red handkerchief which, after a moment, he began to tug at, teasingly – his gaze switching in quick darts from the object to me and then back to the object. A narrow, grey tongue emerged *eelishly* from his mouth and touched the tip of his nose.

Eventually, a cheese, about the size of a shop-bought brie or camembert, sat revealed on the table between us. It was perfectly formed, like those samples of work produced by apprentice carpenters to demonstrate their skills; yellow in colour, but with what seemed to be a tinge of pink.

'Isn't she beautiful?' he said.

He bent so that his eyes were level with it: gazing at its circumference, as if inspecting some intricate detail on a model railway, or even a glass-cased tiara encrusted with exquisite jewels.

'The Llanymaen Coch,' he announced, reverently. And then, looking up, '*Coch* means red – in case you are unfamiliar with the tongue.' His own tongue – whose tip had been moving excitedly between the left and right corners of his mouth – he drew back, thankfully, into its none too sweet-smelling recesses. '*Not*,' he continued, 'that she is a scarlet woman, by any means. More that she is the possessor of a virginal *blush*. Albeit,' he said, his voice trailing away somewhat, 'that she can, when angered, be given to the falling of a certain red... mist.'

He lowered his eyes once more and stared at the cheese.

'What,' I ventured, 'with all respect, is so special about the... Llanymaen Coch?'

The man looked up.

'Special?' he said. 'Oh, my good lady, there is nothing... *special* about the Llanymaen Coch.'

'Then why—' I began.

'Sacred? Yes! Mystical? Most definitely! Unique? Unquestionably!'

'Because of what?' I said, looking at the cheese (very probably with insufficient awe).

He ran a hand over his head, clamped the ends of his few strands of hair to the nape of his neck in the high, upturned collar of his coat.

'What,' he began, 'you must understand about the Llanymaen Coch is that she has always been with us and that she will always be with us. Always!' he said.

'When Glyndwr slew the Saxon at Pilleth on what did our Welsh warriors feast before and after that mighty battle?' he asked, his eyes – black as mineshafts yet strangely fiery – fixed on mine.

'I suspect you're going to—'

He cut me down faster than any flying arrow.

'The Llanymaen Coch! And what,' he went on without pausing, 'was with them in nineteen hundred and five when we put to the sword that other enemy, this time of the sporting field, the invincible All Blacks?'

'Could it have been—' I began.

'Yes!' he said. 'You learn quickly, madam.'

We enunciated it together, each watching the other's lips: 'The Llanymaen Coch.'

Slowly but surely every person in the bar took up the incantation, whispered at first but soon full-throated.

'David Lloyd George?' the man called out.

'Llanymaen Coch!' they chorused.

'Rebecca Riots?'

'Llanymaen Coch!'

'Archers at Agincourt?'

'Llanymaen Coch!'

Those present did this, I noticed, not with any great physical fervour, but almost robotically, as if mesmerised. Even the mouth of a sheepdog lying on the flagstone floor rose and fell with the chant.

I felt sure that at that moment every person, beast and bird in the village was proclaiming the words: ministers placing hymnals in chapels, cows in their fields on the cud, cockatiels in front of small mirrors in their cages, the old lady to whom I had sold my book, tracing with a white, bloodless finger my signature, *Connor Sewell*...

All of them, together: 'Llanymaen Coch!'

The man, not so mousy now, rapped the table with his knuckles in an ever-quickening beat.

'At our first drop of rain?'

'Llanymaen Coch!'

'And our first shooting leaf?'

'Llanymaen Coch!

'The Coch! Coch! Coch! Coch!' all of the people in the pub chanted (though otherwise passive in the way that I have described).

His questions flew from him – crisply coherent – in machine-gun bursts. Their response merged into one deafening roar.

And then, staring at me, he clicked his fingers. And they stopped. And everything was as it had been.

I cannot deny that I was shaken, but I did my best not to show it, judging this the most sensible course. 'What,' I asked after a few moments in which I composed myself, 'are you going to do with... her?' I nodded to the cheese.

'Well I'm going to write, of course,' he said, '... to write. Stories, novels, sequels, scripts... *The Adventures* – and *Further Adventures – of the Llanymaen Coch.* Maybe I shall win a prize.'

He grinned (and I saw, again, those hideous teeth).

I rose, this time determined to leave.

He hemmed me in.

'Come on,' I said. 'It's time I called it a night. We've had our fun. You and I both know there's no – what was it? – *Llanymaen Evening Mail.*'

He drank his beer, set down his empty glass.

'Oh but there is,' he said. '*I* am the Llanymaen... Evening... Male.'

The bar fell silent; all those who were in it turned still as the dead.

'Let me get you another,' I said, picking up his glass.

He gave way at last.

At the bar, the landlord flicked his eyes in a signal that it was best that I went.

I set the pint glass down on the table and bade my companion goodnight.

'Nice to have met you, Connor Sewell,' he said.

His reference to the earlier events of the day threw me for a moment.

'Oh but that's not my name,' I said.

'I know,' he said. 'I know.' Then, slowly, he added, 'Ten pounds, wasn't it? The book that you sold to the elderly lady?'

'Yes,' I said, 'but only to—'

'*Humour* her? Yes...'

He took hold of the glass. 'Buy *this* with it, did you?' He lifted it and, with one tilt of his chin, drained every last drop. 'Anyway, I shall be on your heels. I also am spending the night here.'

I climbed the stairs towards my accommodation.

'Sleep well!' he called from the settle through the doorway of the bar. 'I do hope the cheese shan't disturb you! An old wives' tale, if ever there was!'

In my attic room I lay uncomfortably awake.

The moon, with all of its childish, cheesy connotations, dripped a whey-like light through a roof window onto the clothes of my bed.

When I did briefly sleep my mind was seized by horrible visions. In these, berg-like lumps of cheese impaled themselves on that ghastly reef in my erstwhile companion's mouth. Next, even more horrifically, the tails of rats swung from his jaws, like vines, as they feasted thickly on those same mired gobbets (while he winked at me and grinned).

Noise from the room next door brought me to my senses.

First I heard something akin to scratching... at, so it seemed, the skirting on the other side of the wall. Then came voices. A high-pitched falsetto, in ridiculous mimicry of a woman, was first.

'Oh please, Mr Sewell, do you have a moment for the *Llanymaen*

Mail?'

The mock 'educated' voice of a man replied, 'Why, yes. How do you want me? Who shall I be?'

The horrible falsetto returned. 'Oh just sign your name here, Mr Sewell... and here... and here... and... oh... yes... *there*... right *there*. Put it... *t-h-e-r-e*.'

'My *p-l-e-a-s-u-r-e*,' the male voice drawled back. (From the tone alone I could picture the speaker's leer.) And then, smartly, 'That will be ten pounds, for services, if you please.'

I threw off my bedclothes, rifled the pamphlets on the small dressing-table in my room. A card showed a taxi firm: *24 Hours* it proclaimed in yellow and red.

Whispering into my phone I asked the controller to dispatch a car as quickly as she could. Next I dressed, stowed my wash things in my case with my unsold copies of *Camomile Turtle*, and sat and waited on my bed.

To my great relief, lights appeared at my thinly-curtained window: the taxi's engine rattled outside.

I moved down the stairs swiftly. After pinning a cheque to the noticeboard in the hall, I began slipping the numerous heavy bolts on the pub's front door, quietly as I could. The last of these screeched as I drew it, like the muffled shriek of an owl. Nothing in the place seemed to stir, however... and I stepped out, into the dark.

I closed the cab door gently and, for what seemed like the first time since leaving my room, I breathed.

The dim, cocooned world of the cab was strangely redolent of a nightclub. An old-time crooner – Dean Martin, it must have been – was singing on the radio... about the moon... and pizza.

I was about to tell the driver to take me to a station where a train might be running – any train – when he... my companion from the bar... climbed in beside me, and shut the door.

'Mind if I join you?' he said (it seemed scarcely a question). 'For the ride?'

He leaned past me in his huge coat and placed a hand on the driver's shoulder. He smelled... ripe.

'Up to the castle, if you would, driver... please,' he said.

'I really need to catch a train,' I said.

'Oh but you can't leave yet,' he responded. 'You haven't seen the sights. Goodness knows when you'll next get the chance.'

'Well... quickly,' I said. 'The castle, then I'll have to drop you off.'

'Beautiful, it is, at dawn... our castle,' he said, paying me no heed. 'The light dwells upon it. Some think it like a corona or even a halo. I myself feel it has that *streak* of something that recalls the Llanymaen Coch.'

The cab reached the top of a rough track. Beyond it rose the dark form of the castle.

The man, somehow bigger now than he'd been in the pub, bundled me out into the chill air. 'Come back in an hour,' he told the driver. 'We'll be done by then.'

The castle, I confess, was a magnificent sight. Orange light the colour of fire pierced and crested its black ramparts as the sun slowly rose.

We circled its walls and climbed its towers. Through arrow slits and ancient windows I saw cottages and farms rising from grey mists that rolled in strange suspension to the castle's rugged cliffs. As we scaled its stones and wandered its courtyards, in the beautifully breaking dawn, those horrors that I had felt such a short while previously faded from me, like dreams. It was as if the events of the night and evening had happened not to me, but to someone else. Finally, he took me to the keep, where, in a chamber, we stopped.

'This,' he told me, 'is my favourite spot.'

I peered through an arrow slit, shielding my eyes against the gloriously burgeoning sun. A warm stripe of light fell on me through the aperture, bringing to life (so it seemed) my blood. When I turned back to him it was clear that his interest was not in what lay *without*, but in something that lay *within*.

'Do you know what that is?' he asked.

He pointed to a recess in the floor over which lay a grille.

'An oubliette,' he continued before I could answer. 'A French word in origin, I think. In this case a kind of dungeon-for-one. Too small for two. No good for you *and* Connor Sewell.'

He smirked in a way that irritated me.

'Its *guests* used to be left there for months... years – without so much as a piece of cheese. Can you imagine?'

I stepped towards the ironwork.

He stooped and (the exertion showing on his face) lifted a large stone that lay at one end of the grille. Then he stepped and, after a similar struggle, did the same at the other side. He pulled the grille aside. A black hole, something like a sewer or well, but narrower, was exposed.

'You know who this makes me think of?' he said, regaining his breath. 'A certain *literary* figure. Can you think who that might be?'

At that moment, I admit, I could not, all manner of nonsense suddenly colliding in my mind: the pigeon in the marquee crapping on my book, the clergyman rising to stop the woman who thought I was Connor Sewell, the biddy doggedly refusing to back down.

My guide's tongue touched the tip of his nose (as it had over the cheese in the bar) then coiled itself back, like some ghastly party horn.

'Ben Jonson!' he answered. 'Poets' Corner, Westminster Abbey. Buried vertically, he was. Standing Room Only. That's all the space he could afford. Perpetrated in the perpendicular. But you knew all that already, of course... as a *writerly* type.'

It was then that I noticed how horrific his eyes, so hypnotic the night before, now were: their whites a malarial yellow, crossed and re-crossed with hideous, red veins, like nets that might have been sewn by a sightless fishwife in the very darkest sea shanty.

'Try it!' he urged. 'Try it!' He was not mousy at all now, but like some booming fairground barker. 'Can you imagine?' he called out as if mocking my powers. 'Can you imagine? Your doom without a view!'

What filled my mind then was not the awfulness of the hole, but the same thing that had been occupying what had seemed like my every waking minute for weeks: the total failure of my novel *Camomile Turtle*. It had sunk without trace – 'an (empty) shell of a book' withered one review, 'this turtle has no tale' taunted another. The latest in my line of tiny sellers, never mind three years' hard work. What I needed, I told myself, was an *edge*... something that would help me swim with the likes of Connor Sewell and his infuriatingly successful Irish sagas. Sewell... my persecutor. His insufferably smug features flashed before me: cuddling a puppy on Twitter... crowded by puppy-eyed fans in a sick-making picture somewhere else on his (massively followed) social media.

My grinning guide began again. 'Think about the great lines you'll be able to write about *this*!' he declared, as if holding back the curtain on some astonishing invention. 'Drama! History! *Ee-rot-ic-ahhh*. Can you imagine?'

Yes! I told myself insanely. He was right! One minute down there and I would unquestionably have a story. Sixty seconds in that tiny cellar – and no more tiny sellers. What had Hemingway said? Something or other.

I lowered myself into the oubliette.

'Now let's try it with the grille,' he said. 'Let's just *t-r-y* it.'

Before I could answer he was lowering the ironwork and resting back into place the heavy stones at its sides. Most of this I could only hear – and not see – in the close confinement of the cavity.

Within moments I began to call for my release. What I felt, though, were pieces, lumps of something... *soft*... falling on my head.

I wriggled sufficiently against the wet stones to raise my eyes to the light. The shower that I have described now fell on my forehead and cheeks. I shut my eyes instinctively. When the tumble of debris momentarily eased I reopened them. Through the lattice of metal above me I saw him: standing in the now blazing light.

The cheese that he had unveiled to me in the pub in its red handkerchief hovered before him. Only now it was ten, twenty, one hundred times its previous size. The handkerchief, which also had extended enormously, spread itself liturgically beneath it in the manner of a high altar cloth. The man – if that's what he was – meanwhile recommenced digging into the cheese with his hands, flinging it down on me through the gaps in the grille.

The most incredible aspect of all of this madness was that no matter how he ripped and clawed at it, the cheese remained whole... pristine. Great clods clung to his fingers, smothered the cuffs of his coat. Yet *still* the walls of the cheese remained like those of the castle: unbroken and intact.

Finally, he stopped.

He and the cheese disappeared from my sight.

A golden glow now filled the round chamber. Within its aurora swirled – in the manner of paint that has been confected or that has collided on an artist's palette – fine, ribboning rivers of red. All this, of course, was written a million times larger, so that the light and its movement approximated something that I could only comprehend in those moments as being close to the mesmeric snaking, dancing and rising of a great Chinese dragon, cloaked in the most stunning and sumptuous silk.

I came to my senses.

I heard his shoes scud over some stones and then their tramp... fading... on a damp, gravelled path.

'Where are you going?' I screamed.

The idling engine of the taxi rattled in the near-distance.

'London! Or Edinburgh!' his voice called back. 'Cannes sounds nice, though; I quite fancy the beach! Fair play to the French: they know their cheese!'

Suddenly the scrunch of gravel under his shoes stopped.

'And then there's... Hollywood... Beverly... *H-i-l-l-s...*'

The words came from him in a slow rapture, as if he had been struck by the greatest revelation.

'... or even Bollywood! Why not?' he chirped.

His step re-started.

'What are you doing?' I screamed. 'Come back!'

'Don't worry...'

His voice was echoing now: doubtless he was on the lawn that we had crossed earlier, close to the gate.

'... I'll write!'

The door of the cab thunked shut.

Versions of the stories 'I've Got You' and 'Bait Pump' were published by *Heater* and *The Gull* respectively. 'The Word' has been published in a limited edition format by Three Impostors as part of the Wentwood Tales series. The photographs were taken by Matthew G. Rees in Wales and the Marches.

For more books from Three Impostors please visit:
www.threeimpostors.co.uk